"An author who has never let me down. [*Hero for the Holidays*], a second-chance, lovers-to-enemies-to-lovers story with deep emotional underpinnings just may be my all-time Yates favorite."

—*The Romance Dish*

"[A] surefire winner not to be missed."
—*Publishers Weekly* on *Slow Burn Cowboy* (starred review)

"Multidimensional and genuine characters are the highlight of this alluring novel, and sensual love scenes complete it. Yates's fans . . . will savor this delectable story."
—*Publishers Weekly* on *Unbroken Cowboy* (starred review)

"Fast-paced and intensely emotional . . . This is one of the most heartfelt installments in this series, and Yates's fans will love it."
—*Publishers Weekly* on *Cowboy to the Core* (starred review)

"Yates's outstanding eighth Gold Valley contemporary . . . will delight newcomers and fans alike . . . This charming and very sensual contemporary is a must for fans of passion."
—*Publishers Weekly* on *Cowboy Christmas Redemption* (starred review)

"Yates weaves surprises and vivid descriptions into this moving tale about strong and nurturing female family bonds."
—*Booklist* on *Confessions from the Quilting Circle*

"Fans of Robyn Carr and RaeAnne Thayne will enjoy [Yates's] small-town romance."
—*Booklist* on *Secrets from a Happy Marriage*

Cowboy, It's Cold Outside

Also by Maisey Yates

Secrets from a Happy Marriage
Confessions from the Quilting Circle
The Lost and Found Girl
Cruel Summer

Four Corners Ranch
Unbridled Cowboy
Merry Christmas Cowboy
Cowboy Wild
The Rough Rider
The Holiday Heartbreaker
The Troublemaker
The Rival
Hero for the Holidays
The Outsider
The Rogue

Gold Valley
Good Time Cowboy
A Tall, Dark Cowboy Christmas
Unbroken Cowboy
Cowboy to the Core
Lone Wolf Cowboy
Cowboy Christmas Redemption
The Bad Boy of Redemption Ranch
The Hero of Hope Springs
The Last Christmas Cowboy
The Heartbreaker of Echo Pass
Rodeo Christmas at Evergreen Ranch
The True Cowboy of Sunset Ridge

For more books by Maisey Yates, visit maiseyyates.com.

Cowboy, It's Cold Outside

MAISEY YATES

CANARY STREET PRESS

**CANARY
STREET
PRESS™**

Recycling programs
for this product may
not exist in your area.

ISBN-13: 978-1-335-65291-1

Cowboy, It's Cold Outside

Canary Street Press
22 Adelaide St. West, 41st Floor
Toronto, Ontario M5H 4E3, Canada
CanaryStPress.com

Printed in U.S.A.

To Sheena, this is for you, just like I promised.
Stay strong, stay healthy, throw some axes.

Cowboy,
It's Cold Outside

Chapter One

DENVER KING KNEW that it was a lofty goal for a man like him to avoid hellfire altogether. Given his lineage, it was easy to see why many people assumed that in the afterlife, he would be down south passing beers over a righteous flame with some questionable characters for company. But in truth, he had done his part to try and balance his moral scales a little bit.

But for his sins, hellfire was currently headed his way.

He was standing out in the brand-new, public area of King's Crest, where they had just opened their new event venue, and several places that were equipped for overnight stays.

That was when she appeared.

Dark hair flowing behind her, the twining ink vines visible from her shoulder down to her wrist thanks to the rather brief tank top she had on.

And it was *freezing*. But sure. A tank top. That seemed about right for Sheena Patrick.

But it wasn't the tank top, the fierce look in her eye, her absolute smoke show of a body or the tattoos that caught his attention.

Tattoos he had often wondered about the intricacies of. The vine on her right arm disappeared beneath her tank top, and he felt it was human to wonder where it went from there.

But that wasn't it. It was the bright red chip she held in her hand.

Lord almighty.

As she got closer, he could see she had a full face of makeup on at 8:00 a.m. He didn't know if it was because she was coming off the bar shift the night before and hadn't taken it off, or if she was ready for tonight. But the black liner made her green eyes glow, and the deep color on her lips was enough to make a saint consider what it might look like left behind on his skin.

And he was not a saint.

There was no denying that she was hot.

She was also 100 percent completely off-limits.

And Denver King did not push limits.

He had no *interest* in hellfire. Whatever form it took.

That was the thing.

She stopped right in front of him, lifting one dark brow, and holding the chip up just so it covered his view of her face. "I've come to cash in," she said.

Her voice was smoky. Like a late night and a shot of whiskey.

He looked at the chip. He didn't take it. "Have you?"

The truth was, he'd given out poker chips to any number of his father's victims.

In the years since, many of them had come asking for money. And that was the point of it. An acknowledgment that he owed them. That they had the right to come to him and cash in. Nobody had actually brought the physical chip with them.

Nobody else had waited this long.

Any chip that hadn't been cashed in so far belonged to dead men who had continued on in the rough life his father had been part of.

Sheena was the last holdout.

But then, he had been sending money to Sheena and her family ever since that botched job that had cost her dad his life all those years ago.

He held his father, Elias King, personally responsible for that. And it was up to him to make restitution for it. He had always seen it that way. It didn't matter whether or not he had done it himself.

The sins of the father would be visited on the son. And God knew he meant to try and wipe that slate clean. He surely did.

"And what is it exactly that you want to collect?"

She lowered the chip. "I have a proposition for you."

"Name a dollar amount."

She shook her head. "I'm not after a dollar amount, King. It's not that simple."

He frowned. "Go on."

"I have a business proposition." There was something sharp and clear in her eyes and he had a feeling this was going to be a long talk.

"All right. It's awfully cold. You want to go inside?"

She snorted. "Do I look like I'm shivering?"

No. She didn't. But he had always thought that Sheena might be powered by a hidden fire in her belly. God knew she'd been fighting a hell of a lot harder than most for a hell of a lot longer. He respected her. That was the thing. When her dad had died she'd been left with three younger siblings to raise. And she had done a hell of a job.

She hadn't allowed his family to fully take her in. But that didn't surprise him. Not that he and Sheena knew each other. They didn't. In fact, other than him ordering a beer from her on the occasional night out at Smokey's, he didn't have anything to do with her. Not directly.

He would go up, lay eyes on the place, make sure nothing had burned to the ground. Put an envelope of cash in the mailbox and go on.

They saw each other from a distance, if that.

This was the longest conversation they'd had in thirteen years.

"All right then. Tell me."

"It doesn't sit right with me," she said. "Being in your debt. But I have an idea that's going to help us both."

"You're *not* in my debt. Your father is dead because of mine. There's no amount of money on earth that can make up for that."

She snorted. "Your opinion, King, not mine. My dad was a worthless son of a bitch. Yeah. It was hard, being left without somebody bringing in money, but my dad himself wasn't worth the carcass of a moth-eaten buzzard. I'm not sorry he's gone. He did nothing but bring bullshit down on us. So no. It is not like you robbed us of our loving patriarch. And hell, you didn't even have anything to do with it. Not directly."

"Close enough," he said.

He'd been drawn in by his dad. By his proclamations about how what he did, he did for the family. The truth was, Elias King didn't care about his family. His wife had left him, and he'd painted it as a betrayal to their clan. He'd said he had to work even harder to make things right for the kids.

Denver had bought into it. But then their father's facade had started to crumble. The treatment of his sister after her accident was a red flag he couldn't ignore. And after that . . . the last job. The one where he'd really seen his dad. The violent man he could be.

And Denver had learned one thing that day for sure. Violence beget violence.

"All right," she said. "That's your opinion. But I'm not putting that on you. I want to pay you back. To that end, I want in on the expansion here at King's Crest."

He owed Sheena; that much was true. But the control freak inside him balked immediately at the thought of allowing anyone *in*.

"Is that so?"

"Yes. I have a business plan. You know I work over at Smokey's."

She knew full well he knew it. He had a feeling she'd said that to highlight the total separation in their lives. They knew each other. They kept it brusque and bare minimum like they didn't.

"Yes," he confirmed.

"And before that I was tending bar down in Mapleton. People need more to do. More nightlife. Smokey's is fine, but it's a very particular thing."

"A meat market," he commented.

She shrugged. "Sure. Everybody loves a little beef."

He couldn't tell if she was smirking or smiling. Or some combination of the two.

"All right. Go on."

"Axe throwing."

"Excuse me?"

"Axe throwing bars have begun to be a big deal. I hear you're making beer down here. Add a little bit of food, and you've got Pyrite Falls' newest hotspot."

"Axe throwing."

"Yeah. It's fun. You let off steam, you hang out with friends. You fling deadly weapons around."

"Sounds like a liability."

"I didn't take you for a bitch, King."

"I didn't think you took me for anything."

"Nothing but an envelope in a mailbox. And this chip," she said, brandishing it again. "Anyway. The point is, people do this all the time. It's perfectly safe. I had the opportunity to go check one out when I went down to Medford recently. It's a good time, and more importantly it's packed. I've got a lot of data about it as a growing pastime. Also, I'm great at it. You know, not so much in bars, but I do it for fun at home."

"They sound like hipster bullshit."

"Do I look like hipster bullshit to you?" She put her hands on her hips, her dark hair sliding over her shoulder, shiny even in the overcast light.

"A little bit," he said, looking over the tattoos. Really, it was like one continuous tattoo. Vines and flowers twined up her arm, down into the tank top, so where else it went, he didn't know. He wondered, though.

"That just goes to show that you don't know me."

It was deliberate. The not knowing her. He had wanted to help her while leaving her as untouched by all of this as possible. It was different with Penny. Penny had been alone in the world. No one was coming to save her or take care of her. Sheena had her sisters.

She squared up with him, the determination on her face something no sane man would dismiss.

"I have a whole business plan," she said. "This isn't coming from nothing. Believe me when I tell you, my survival instinct is strong. I'm not a dreamer. I'm a planner. I think this is really something."

"All right. Explain it to me."

"That's what I've *been* doing."

She reached into a bag she had slung over her shoulder and pulled out a binder. It was black and plain, with no adornment. His sister-in-law Rue was fond of binders. But hers were always floral. With decorative stickers for whimsy. The only thing ornate about Sheena was the tattoo.

"This is quite a bit," he said, opening up the binder and finding inside photos of different axe throwing facilities. A proposed menu, projected expenses.

"I thought it best to be thorough. You told me that you owed me. That was why you gave me the poker chip. You said that all I had to do was cash in. That's what I aim to do. But further to that, I think it can be something that benefits both of us."

"Why don't you show me what you've got."

"Excuse me?"

"I'll tell you what. Let's go throw some hatchets. And I'll see what I think."

Sheena hadn't expected this to be *easy*. Denver King set himself up as being some kind of savior, but she had never seen it in that way. To her mind, letting Denver King near her property was a lot like letting a wolf offer protection.

They *could* protect you. But they could also decide to turn around and eat you. She wasn't a fool. She didn't buy into this whole idea that the Kings were so reformed. That Denver was entirely different from his dad. He earned his money gambling. She knew that. It was a fairly covert thing, but she kept her ear to the ground. Paid attention.

He had made big bucks in the professional poker circuit.

He might not have a bunch of illegal gambling happening on the property, but it was still an indicator that he was part of that world.

And she knew that she was playing it a little bit dangerous, wanting to join up with him to do business. But her options were limited. There were very few people out there who felt that they owed her. But he was one of them. And that meant she was going to take advantage of it as and when she could.

She was a thirty-one-year-old empty nester—for all intents and purposes—with her youngest sister off at college and moving on with her life. Sheena was still tending bar, and she was beginning to feel . . .

Left behind. Which was dumb, and she didn't like it. So she'd taken a good look at that poker chip, and she'd decided asking for Denver's help was better than languishing in dumb, useless feelings.

But she wasn't asking for a handout—the only money she'd ever taken from him was for her sisters' benefit, not hers—but using him to get a real business up and running? She'd made a bargain in her soul so she could handle that.

She was tough. She was happy to use people as they used her. That was life, and she'd accepted it.

As long as she went in eyes wide open with Denver, she could do it with him too.

She could admit she'd expected him to just agree. Which was strange because she'd say she didn't trust Denver or anyone to do what they said, but he'd always indicated that he felt responsible for what happened to her father.

She also didn't want to owe him. But needed him to feel he owed her.

She also didn't want to rely on him or anyone, but had to.

She could appreciate the tightrope walk she was engaged in.

The red poker chip burned into her palm, and she squeezed her hand around it before putting it in her pocket.

"All right. You've got yourself a deal. What do I have to do? Outthrow you?" she asked.

"No. I think I just need to see the appeal. I'm the kind of man who needs to see something to really get a feel for it. To visualize it. I want to understand what it is you're offering to people."

"Well. That's kind of lame. I was hoping this was some kind of Paul Bunyan thing. As long as I could out hatchet your man-made machine you would let me and my big blue ox have our way with the place."

"Do you have a big blue ox?"

"The big blue ox is metaphorical. Do you have a place where we can throw an axe?"

"Sure."

He moved in front of her, and she did her best not to pay too close attention to the fine masculine figure that he cut. He was tall. Very tall. And she noticed because she was a pretty tall woman. A lot of men made her feel large and unfeminine, she didn't really mind that, actually. But Denver King made her feel dainty, which was as disorienting as it was unique.

He was at least six inches taller than her. His shoulders were broad, his chest well muscled, his arms massive. Men like that always thought they would be great at axe throwing. In her experience they tended to overdo it. Throw it so hard it bounced right out of the target. And it made them angry. She always enjoyed watching that.

He led her out to a space behind the shed, where a large axe was stuck into a round of wood. "I'll take you over to where we shoot," he said. "There's a couple of targets that are still set up."

"All right. Sounds good."

She did her best to not notice the way that his forearm shifted as he picked up the large axe and slung it over his shoulder.

He was a fine specimen of a man; that much was true. But she didn't have any use for men like him.

Sheena was in charge of her own life. In charge of her own destiny. *And that's why you're here asking him for a favor?*

Well. That little internal voice could shut its trap.

When it came to relationships, she didn't do them. When it came to sex, she liked to be in charge.

She got what she wanted; the guy got what he wanted. No harm no foul.

She preferred men who didn't have ties to the area. Tending bar in Mapleton had been more convenient from that standpoint.

It made scratching an itch feel a little bit less risky.

Denver King might as well have been wrapped in caution tape.

The first time she'd noticed he was hot, the cops had just loaded her father's body into a coroner's van.

To say the noticing of Denver King's physical attributes was problematic was putting it lightly.

But also, it meant she was used to it.

He opened up the passenger door of an old blue truck, and she stared at it, and him.

"Get in," he said.

"I was unaware this was a whole field trip."

"We don't shoot near the buildings."

"Responsible," she said.

She waited until he moved away from the door, and climbed up inside the truck.

Then he rounded to the driver's side and got in.

He started up the engine, and she looked out the window. All the better to not look at him.

"How are the girls?"

Abigail, Whitney and Sarah were all off on their own now. Far away from this place. And good thing.

And if Sheena ached with loneliness sometimes, she dismissed it.

She could leave. She could start over somewhere else. When Whitney had moved out six months ago she'd fully had that realization. But the problem was, nobody else owed her a favor. And then there was a tangle of the fact that she also owed Denver. And that didn't sit right with her. He might not feel like she needed to pay them back. But she wanted her personal ledger to be balanced up. It was important to her.

Because if she couldn't ultimately be free of that past, then nothing she had done since then mattered. And yes, she was aware that made it somewhat ironic that she was looking to actually get into business with Denver.

But she had a plan. Eventually, she wouldn't be here running the bar. She would open a second location elsewhere. Eventually, she would make her own way. Maybe somewhere closer to her sisters.

But after she got started. If there was one thing she was an expert at, it was surviving. But she wanted to be an expert at more than just that. She wanted to figure out how to thrive.

They didn't speak while he drove them up to wherever that shooting range was. Somewhere out on the top of the ridge. It was beautiful.

But this whole place was beautiful. But she knew that even with all of the magnificent surroundings, it was all only as serene as the life that you were growing up in.

The Kings had this place. She didn't deny it was possible that it might be a nice place that was shit to live in, given what she knew about their dad.

But she knew without a doubt her own growing-up years were worse.

Not only had she had her dad . . .

The house had been small and ramshackle. Instead of kitchen cabinets and counters they'd had tables lining a room, with a freestanding sink that leaked. She'd done her best to make that place a home after her dad's death.

Hung fabric from the tables to sort of mimic a cabinet-and-counter look. Something to make it seem normal. With sisters ranging in age from four to fourteen it had been a struggle. And she'd only been eighteen herself. But they'd managed. For thirteen years, they'd managed.

And now it was her turn. To try and do something more

than manage. To start the steps that she needed to build a life . . . somewhere else. A life that she had chosen. A life that was more than this.

It wasn't that it was a bad life. She liked to think that she had taken something really awful and turned it into something pretty decent for the sake of her sisters. But it had left her . . . hard. She didn't know another way to be. She was thankful for the resilience. She couldn't resent it. It had kept her safe. But she wanted to find a way to live where she didn't have to be this all the time.

An axe throwing bar was admittedly a little bit of a funny way to go about that. But she knew bar work. This had a slightly different focus. It wasn't about getting drunk; it was about having a drink with friends, having a good time. A little bit of friendly competition.

She had been working the rough dive bars for years. She was ready for a change of scenery.

She had been waitressing early on, when the girls had been really little. But the money was just much better in bartending. So when she felt all right to leave them at night, tucked up into bed with the oldest well aware of how to use a shotgun if she needed it, and their trusty guard dog Hank on hand to create a ruckus if anyone should approach, she had started taking that night work. Down in Mapleton the amount of work she had been able to get, the size of the tips thanks to the size of her . . . Well.

Her mama hadn't given her much of anything except her figure to hear tell of it. She was happy to make use of it. Consider it a gift from the woman who hadn't stuck around to raise her. It was the only one she'd gotten.

There were two ways to handle men. She could put them under her spell using her looks, and she could scare the hell out of them using her strength. She was familiar with how to do both.

She would like it if she didn't need to do it quite so often.

Being a business owner would be different than being a server.

Denver stopped the truck at the end of the dirt road. There was a view, spectacular, just behind a raised ridge of gravel with targets affixed to the front of it.

"Safety first," he said.

"Sure," she said. "Though, I don't want to be flinging the axe over the top of the target and losing it down below in the draw."

"I thought you were an expert."

"Well, I am. I actually meant I don't want *you* to lose your axe."

"I'm good," he said.

"All right. I'm going to demonstrate. And then I'll let you have a couple of practice throws. We can do best out of five after that."

He looked at her, and she could tell that she had greatly offended his delicate masculine pride by suggesting that he needed to warm up. And offer instruction of any kind.

"I think I can handle it," he said.

"Just . . . based on your feelings?"

"Yeah."

"Your feelings aren't facts, chief. No matter how much you might want them to be," she said.

"Based on my feelings and what I know about myself, I think I'm good."

She affected a very innocent expression on her face, grabbed hold of the axe and slipped out of the truck.

Then she went to stand in front of the target. She squared up, and decided to go with a classic two-handed overhead throw. She lifted the axe over her head and drew it back.

"Don't do anything foolish like hopping in front of me," she said.

"Yeah, I think I can figure that one out, thank you."

Then without overthinking it, she let the axe fly. She did her best to gauge the distance between herself and the unfamiliar target, and it flew end over end, landing with a satisfying thunk at the upper left of the target.

"That's my favorite throw stance," she said. "And it's how I recommend you start."

"It wasn't a bull's-eye," he said.

She rolled her eyes and walked down the slight incline toward the target. She grabbed the axe and wrenched it out of the wood. "The next one will be."

She walked back up, lifted the axe over her head and let fly again. This time, she was able to correct and get it right at the center of the target.

She pumped her fist, unable to stop herself from celebrating.

"There you go," she said. She regarded the implement, and then looked at him. "This is a pretty big axe. You might need a smaller one."

He lifted a brow. "I think I can figure out how to handle a big one."

She bit the inside of her cheek, uncertain of whether or not the double entendre had been intentional. That was the problem. She really didn't know him.

"The size of the axe doesn't really matter, Denver."

"That sounds like something people with small axes say."

He took the axe from her easily and stood a couple of paces back from where she had been. Smart. He was going to naturally throw with a lot more strength so he needed to put distance between himself and the target. She decided to focus on that rather than the comment on big axes.

He was a big man. She assumed he was . . . proportional. Though, sometimes men could be a surprising disappointment. Sort of a theme in her life, she had found.

But that was why she didn't depend on them for anything.

He pulled the axe back over his head, and his shirtsleeves came up, revealing the definition of his bicep, and she couldn't help but look.

Instantly, for some reason, she took a moment to imagine Denver King throwing axes shirtless. Okay. She was done with that.

There was really no point mooning after a specific, nice-looking man. Because again, it was no guarantee they wouldn't be disappointing.

He let the axe fly, with way too much force. It bounced off the wooden target and landed in the gravel below, the head sinking deep into the ground. "Deep stroke," she said, her lips twitching.

He looked up at her, his face completely void of expression. "I'm known for that."

She ignored the buzzy feeling between her legs.

"Go fetch your axe."

"Got any tips for me?" he asked as he walked over to where the axe was buried in the dirt.

He pulled it out one-handed, with ease.

"Well," she said dryly. "You don't have to go so hard. It's not a jackhammer."

"Noted."

Everything she said felt tainted by double entendre and she had no idea what to do about it.

"You could also do it one-handed."

His lips went into a flat line. "Could I?"

"You could," she returned, not taking her gaze off his. "Of course, using two hands gives you a little bit more control. And you know, it's not the size of the axe, it's the—" she lifted a brow "—motion of the ocean, so to speak."

"You're mixing your metaphors."

"Am I? Whoops."

She shouldn't be indulging in this. It made her blood feel a little bit fizzy. She was going to enter into a business partnership with him, and they didn't need to go teasing each other like this.

If he was teasing. She genuinely couldn't tell with him. He was inscrutable. Unknowable.

"Okay," he said. "I'll try again with your top tips in mind."

He stood back on the line, lifting the axe up over his head again. This time, he let it fly with a lot more control, and it hit the target with a satisfying thud. Her aim was still better. But he landed the shot.

"There you go. Now that you've found the sweet spot, you just have to keep throwing it at the same angle so that you can hit the same spot over and over again."

This time, she saw a glimmer in his dark eyes. "Is that how you do it?"

"For optimum satisfaction, yes. If you find a good spot, you keep going."

"I'll keep that in mind."

He went to the target and yanked the axe out again. Then she took it from him, and went to stand in the ready position. "Best out of five, Denver King. And when we're done, you can tell me if you want to continue."

"Okay. In the meantime, though, tell me a little about yourself. Like a job interview."

"Well, that wasn't part of the deal."

"You aren't setting all the terms, are you?"

"Okay," she said, her teeth mildly set on edge. She drew the axe back and threw it, letting it fly true until it hit the edge of the target. She was distracted by him. Which was unacceptable.

"What is it you want to know?" she asked, turning to face him.

"I want to know where your sisters are."

"Sarah is in college, so is Whitney. Abigail graduated. She got a job in Fresno."

"Fresno. Wow. Sounds like hell."

She felt defensive of her sister's life choices, but he wasn't wrong. "Yeah. It does to me too. But she's happy. And she isn't here."

"Right. But you want to start a business here?"

"Not my end goal."

She went and took the axe out of the wood. She handed it to him, and let him walk up to the line.

"Does this mean it's my turn to ask you a question?"

He let the axe fly, and hit the outer edge of the target. Just barely in.

He didn't tell her not to ask the question. He didn't invite her to, but he didn't tell her not to either. So.

"What's your ultimate vision for King's Crest?"

"I want it to be a little bit of a destination. I want to bring more tourism into the area. I want to benefit myself and my family. But I also want to . . . to do something worthwhile. My dad did nothing but break shit, as you well know."

"I do."

"I want to do better than that. That's it. End of story."

"My turn then?"

She put herself in the ready position, and let the axe fly. It went true, right in the center.

"Go for it," she said.

"So you don't want to stay here."

"No. Not long-term. Wherever my sisters end up, I'd like to be a little bit closer to them. It's possible that they'll be far-flung. Maybe I won't quite be able to pull that off. But I'm going to try. I don't have a legacy here. Not one to fix. Not one to give even a single shit about. I lived here because this was where my dad decided to hunker down and get in bed with a criminal—that's your dad. We didn't have roots here."

"But you want to start your business on my land."

"I want to start a business, I want it to become profitable, I want to pay you back. And then I want to take some of what I made and open another location. I'll leave you the place when I leave. And keep collecting some of the profits."

"I see."

"I don't have happy memories here, Denver. I don't have a reason to stay. It was . . ."

It was tangled. Complicated.

For many years, Denver had been the reason she'd stayed.

Oh, not him personally. Because she didn't even know him personally. But that check he left in the mailbox.

And . . . in spite of herself she had to admit, that feeling that there was a wolf watching over them. Maybe even keeping them safe. Plus, things had been hard enough. Trying to figure out, as a teenager, how to put a house on the market, how to take her sisters and move them to a different school, all of it . . . It was just a little bit too much. Where she had lived, where she still lived, sat between Mapleton and Pyrite Falls. She split the difference between the two. Working in either one had always been about the same. And it might be kind of a pain sometimes, but it was familiar. And they could afford the cost of living.

In a city that wouldn't be the case. And another small town would be just as difficult to navigate as this one.

So for years, it just hadn't made any sense.

He went and got the axe. His turn again.

"You want me to help you get a grip on that big axe of yours?"

He snorted, but when he threw the axe, it went wide.

That made her stomach twist a little bit.

Well. It was a good thing to know. That he wasn't immune.

He was just a dude, after all. Not really a wolf, or any of the other strange, fanciful things she had convinced herself he might be.

They didn't ask each other any more questions, and she was the hands-down winner of the round.

"All right," he said, plunking the axe head down on the dirt with a thud, his large hand wrapped around the base of the handle. "You got yourself a business proposition, Sheena Patrick."

"Good. I look forward to doing business with you."

She reached into her pocket, and took out the poker chip. Then she pressed it into his palm, and ignored the heat the transfer left behind on her fingertips. "Just let me know when you want to meet next."

"Depends. Are you going to quit your job down at the bar?"

"I have to put in my two weeks' notice a while ago, I don't have much time left."

"Fair. How about we talk after that."

"I guess we will."

"I guess we will."

Chapter Two

"WHAT DO YOU know about axe throwing bars?"

When they had their barbecue dinner set out on the table that night, Denver decided to pose the question to his brothers.

Technically, he didn't have to ask anybody's permission to do something like this. Yes, typically the money came out of the broader collective ranch pot for new endeavors, and they asked all four main families that made up Four Corners to vote.

Meeting with the whole collective at a town hall to make sure everyone was on board.

But in this case, he would be financing the whole thing from his own pocket. So he didn't figure it was up to him to consult anybody.

He realized, though, that his siblings might feel differently.

"Is this a trick question?" Landry asked, looking over at his wife and daughter, and then back to Denver. "Is someone in trouble?"

"I can't recall having done any raids on axe throwing bars recently," Daughtry said, still wearing his uniform from his shift earlier in the day. "Or *any* raids, for that matter. Since our dad leaving town functionally removed most of the crime."

"Well, I warned all my friends at the axe throwing bar that you were coming," Daughtry's wife, Bix, said. "Because I don't like cops."

"Which has made things very difficult for me," Daughtry said dryly as Bix grinned up at him.

Denver's siblings were disgustingly happy. He was thrilled for them. Honestly. It was all he had ever wanted for them. That was kind of the point of taking charge of everything. It was kind of the point of trying this to make a new life for them. A safer one. A happier one.

It was why he, who had never known anything about having a real family, who had never known anything about holidays or birthday parties and had never really had one thrown for him, had decided that they all needed these get-togethers.

It was why they had crowded table family dinners. It was why he had become a grill master. Not just because he liked beef. It was his life's work, after all. The gambling made a lot of money, because he was great at it. Because he was . . . He couldn't help it if his brain worked a certain way and he could count cards easily. At least, it wasn't his fault as far as he was concerned. He knew that other people, his competitors, might feel differently. He couldn't help them with that.

But the ranch, that was his passion. Doing honest work. He didn't gamble anymore. He'd made all he needed to. Between that and judicious investments, he netted himself quite a fortune. Enough to blot out some of the debt his father had left behind, enough to make sure that his family was taken care of.

Enough to support the ranch even when things weren't going well.

"I've been to one," his sister-in-law Rue said, down from her end of the table. "Back when I was with . . ." She slid a look over to Justice.

"I'm not threatened by Asher."

Justice and Rue had been best friends for years and years, and she had very nearly married another man a few months back. But fate had righted itself, and the two of them were together now.

"It was fun," Rue finished.

"Yeah. Well. We're going to open one up on the ranch."

"That's desperately random," Arizona said.

"Why is it random, Arizona?"

"It's random," Arizona's stepson said, chewing around a big mouthful of food.

"He says it's random. Therefore, it's random."

Denver looked to his brother-in-law, who simply shrugged. "I don't argue with either of them."

"Well, an opportunity came up. For me to go into business with Sheena Patrick."

"The bartender?" Justice asked, his brows lifting.

It was Rue's turn to shoot him a surreptitious side-eye. "The *hot* bartender?"

"I'm not blind," said Justice, who clearly felt convicted by his wife's characterization of Sheena.

"Yes," Rue said, sniffy. "But you've voiced your opinions on her very boldly in the past."

"In the past you were my friend, not my wife," Justice said.

"Yeah," Denver said. "The hot bartender."

"She's Dan Patrick's daughter," Daughtry pointed out.

As if Denver didn't know that.

Though, Daughtry was more connected to the fallout of that day than anyone other than Denver. They had both been enmeshed in their father's empire to a degree they were ashamed of. It was just that their hair shirts had taken different forms. Daughtry's was a badge and a uniform. Denver's was . . . the land, he supposed. The burden of trying to pay it all back. Ensuring that his family really was cared for this time. That it wasn't all a lie coming from a narcissist who was hell-bent on altering reality to suit his narrative.

"Yes. She is," he acknowledged. "I owe her a favor."

"You don't owe dad's victims," Arizona said. "Outside this house or inside this house. His actions were his own."

"But what people think of us comes down to him. And I can't just rest on the knowledge that I didn't do anything. It's not good enough. Not for me."

"I get it," Daughtry said.

Because of course he did.

Landry and Justice were younger; they had a different relationship to what their father had done. They had been abused. But they hadn't actively helped their father run his criminal operation. Not the way that Daughtry and Denver had.

They had their own personal feelings on what had to be done to make it all right. And nobody could convince either of them otherwise.

"Anyway, I think it's a good idea." He wasn't entirely sure that it was a good idea. But the truth was . . . he liked her. She was strong. She was scrappy. He understood what she had been through. In a sense. She was the youngest, and she had raised her siblings. Siblings who were now off enjoying a good life because of her. And maybe he had helped with that a little bit. Maybe it made him feel good.

That didn't really matter. The thing was, he understood her. And that made him feel like this whole thing was going to be good.

"So people are going to come here and have events and stay for the weekend and enjoy a little bit of axe throwing?" Landry asked.

"I think it sounds great," Fia said.

Landry's wife ran a farm at Sullivan's Point, her family's quadrant of Four Corners Ranch. Fia might have the last name

King now, but she was a Sullivan. And at Sullivan's Point, they had built a store a couple of years back that brought a lot of foot traffic to the ranch.

Pyrite Falls was a tiny town. It served as a rest stop for people headed to the coast, mainly. And of course the bar was popular with the locals who came down from the hills to go out after a day of hard work.

But it was beginning to change. In large part due to what they were offering at Four Corners. And while they had been met with some resistance from the town initially, now it was clear that them building the economy like this was only good.

"Something fun to do. And with the equine therapy happening at McCloud's, and the new place getting set up by Gideon Payne . . . Well, there's a lot going on here. Could be good to have something different. A lot of people are going to be interested in this. Locals and tourists alike."

He said that with a great deal of confidence. When just this morning he had never heard of such a thing, and hadn't been certain of it. But he had done a little bit of research since then. It seemed like places like this were popping up all over, and that they were often busy.

Why not do something different? Give people something else to do.

Hell, Mapleton didn't have an axe throwing place. Maybe people would drive from over there to here. Now that would be something.

"So you're opening a whole business on our property out of a misguided sense of guilt," Arizona said.

"We have tons of extra buildings. The old gaming hall can act as the host. Hell, we'll reinforce the historical part of it, put in some plaques and stuff. People will be interested in that. An axe throwing facility in an old den of sin. Sounds good to me."

They all avoided that place. It had been their dad's old head-quarters. Denver's blessing and curse was his photographic memory. He remembered everything. In detail. Just going near that place brought him back to sitting in that old building, stacking up bags of cocaine, or his dad threatening someone who owed him money.

A kingpin of a rural shithole, that had been him.

What a King.

The most ironic last name of all time, in Denver's opinion. He might have left all that behind, might have gone straight when his father never had, but the memories lingered all the same.

He'd deal with it, though. Sheena wanted the restitution he'd promised, and he'd give it.

That it would be right at the center of that old building seemed almost poetic.

"Yeah," Arizona said, looking reluctantly interested then. "I guess it does."

"And yes, there will be expenses associated with that, but let me worry about it."

"You're not going to take this to the collective?"

He felt a little bit like a dick not taking it to the collective. Because they were supposed to.

But this was his land, and it wasn't really going to affect anybody.

Well. The traffic that it brought in might.

But . . . he was just going to get the ball rolling on it before he brought it forward. That was all.

"We've done a lot of work to rehab our image within Four Corners too," Landry pointed out. "And not being quite so isolated is part of that. Nobody else goes off making all their own decisions, Denver."

"Well, I helped found the collective as it is."

Back when Gus McCloud had run his dad off, and the Sullivans had lost their parents, when the Garretts were trying to rebuild, and Denver's father had gone from the ranch, thanks to a hefty incentive from Denver himself, they had gotten together and decided how they were going to run things. That they were going to do them differently and better than their parents had.

And they had. They'd done a damned fine job of it. By helping each other, by banding together, they had brought the ranch out of its darkest era into something great.

He was proud of all of them. He might not show it, but he was.

They were in a different space now, though. And this was different.

"I can literally see it on your face," Arizona said. "You think it's different."

"What the hell?" he asked, unamused that his little sister was so adept at reading his thoughts.

"That's just who you are, Denver. You think if you want to do something it isn't the same. If you want to do it, then it's all fine. Justifiable. Your reasons are good reasons."

"My reasons *are* good reasons, squirt. And anyway, she has a whole business plan."

"You don't know her, though," Landry said.

"Are you worried about me getting taken advantage of?"

"Not exactly," said Landry, but his hesitation made Denver think that's exactly what his younger brother was worried about.

"Excuse me. I don't trust easily. And I certainly am not going to get fleeced. We all had the same dad. We all know to be suspicious."

"Sure. But you also have a savior complex that runs deep and wide, big brother. And a beautiful woman wanting you to do something for her . . ."

"Let's get one thing straight. Sheena Patrick is not a beautiful woman to me. She was a victim of our father. Her father is dead because of our father. She and her sisters experienced hardship because of our dad. The way she looks or doesn't look in a tank top has nothing to do with that."

"Well, no one said anything about a tank top except for you," said Justice.

Bix snickered.

"Regardless," he said. "It has nothing to do with anything. I'll treat her the way I would anybody. I might be more willing to get on board with this because of the circumstances but I'm not going to give her free rein. I am very much in control of what is happening on my ranch."

"What's the ranch called again?" Arizona asked.

"Shut up," said Denver.

"No, it's a question that I have, for real."

"King's Crest," he said.

"King's Crest. And I believe everybody in here is a King, by blood or marriage."

"But I'm the oldest," he said.

"I wasn't aware that made you the de facto leader."

"Don't be silly," he said. "I've always been the leader."

"Sure," said his sister, rolling her eyes.

Whatever Arizona thought, though, it was true.

But where his father had been the kind of man who demanded obedience from those he felt were less than him, from his wife to his children, to the underlings who did work with him, Denver believed that to be a leader meant more than just making the decisions. It meant taking accountability.

"The financial risk will be mine. If I get screwed over, then I get screwed over. Nobody else does."

Because he was in charge. And that meant that it all rested on his shoulders.

At least, that was how he saw it.

"Well, I for one can't wait," said Bix. "Throwing axes seems right up my alley."

"You're not supposed to throw them *at people*," said Daughtry.

Bix grinned. "Where's the fun in that?"

"I guess that's why you also serve beer."

All right. So maybe everybody was enthusiastically on board. But he didn't need their enthusiasm. This would work. Because it felt like the right thing to do. The right moment to make real amends to Sheena. Whatever she said. He was going to put all that money she was trying to give them back and put it in an account. And when she left, he was going to give it back to her. Because he didn't want a damned thing from her. No.

Denver was trying to buy his way out of hellfire. And if this would help him do it, then he was all on board.

Sheena moved quickly around the kitchen, stuffing food into her mouth as she went, checking herself in the mirror to see if her makeup looked good, and her boobs were looking perky. While she did her best to keep her phone held out, on speakerphone so that she could still hear her sister talking.

"Anyway, so there's this guy . . ."

"You're taking birth control, right?" Sheena asked.

"Sheena!" Abigail screamed so loud her voice warped over the speaker.

"Well, it's a valid question."

"I use condoms with new partners, thank you," Abigail said.

"Great. Double up."

"I take my birth control," she said through gritted teeth.

"Good. Because I know you're going to tell me how great this guy is, but in six months we may find out he's not so great and . . ."

"Your paranoia is deeply instilled in me, thanks. He really does seem nice."

"Good," said Sheena. She was happy for Abigail; she always was when Abby felt like she was in love. More power to her and all of that. Sheena didn't get what all the fuss was about, but she definitely didn't want to keep her sister as lonely and bitter as she was. Not that she was actually lonely. She just . . . did things differently than some people did.

"Are you on your way to work?" Abby asked.

"Yes."

"Are you ever going to quit working the bar?" her sister asked.

"Yeah, when I can no longer tie a cherry stem with my tongue and I can't get tips anymore."

"I'm serious, Sheena."

"So am I." But she wasn't. She grabbed her keys and headed out to the driveway, unlocking her car as she got in and jammed the key into the ignition. "Okay. I actually got something. I'm quitting the bar in two weeks. I'm giving my notice tonight."

"Really? Are you going to come down here?"

"Not right now. I'm not planning on staying in Pyrite Falls. I don't know if Fresno is meant to be my final destination. But I figure I'll wait and see where Sarah and Whitney land. Maybe I can figure out how to be close to all of you. As much as I can be."

She was reluctant to let her sister know everything. Let her know her dreams. In case she thought they were silly.

She wasn't sure why she thought of it that way. Only that she did.

It was just the whole thing felt like a big limb she was going way out on. And until it was somewhat established, she was just . . . Well, she was a little scared.

"What are you doing?"

"I'm helping with the expansion at King's Crest."

That was met with a resounding silence, and she set her phone down in her cup holder with it still on speakerphone, and through her car into Reverse as she headed down the dirt driveway.

"Go ahead. Judge me."

"I'm not judging you. Not really. I know that Denver gave us money. I know that he's the reason I got to go to college. That we all did."

"Well. It was his money, and your ability to get a good enough GPA to get scholarships."

"Still," Abby said.

"But you're surprised that I'm working with him."

"Yes. Because you definitely seemed to want more distance from the King family than not."

"Can you blame me?" Sheena asked.

"No. I mean, I can't blame you for that at all. Not given everything you saw. You . . . you protected us from a lot." That was an understatement. But she considered it a win that her sister could make such an understatement. If she was aware of everything, then that would've meant that Sheena hadn't done that good of a job. It would mean that absorbing all the impact wasn't worth it.

"So what made you decide to get involved now?" Abby asked.

"The potential for more. You might've gone to college, but I didn't."

She hadn't meant to say it like that. Because she didn't want her sister feeling guilty, or like Sheena had sacrificed things for her. She had. The truth was, if their father had never died, none of them would've had jack shit.

It was only his dying that had led to Denver paying the money. And it was only that money that had helped her sisters go to school. And without it, none of them would have. So Sheena hadn't been robbed of anything. Nothing had been available to her that she hadn't gotten.

When she told Denver she didn't really feel like he owed her, she had been honest. What she knew about her dad was simple. He didn't take care of anybody but himself. He didn't care about anybody but himself.

And now he was off spending his eternity as a presumably narcissistic ghost. Sheena hadn't wasted a tear on him. Never would. So she really didn't want to project some idea onto Abby that her not going to school was somehow related to Abby going.

"I just think that might be a path to something more for me. You just said you didn't want me at the bar forever."

"I didn't say exactly that," said Abby, sounding muted. "I'm not telling you what to do."

"Good," she said. "Because I can't be told. Flat out."

"Yes, yes. You're a total badass."

"I know."

She drove on, her sister silent for a second.

"Do you know what you'll be doing yet?"

"I . . . Not really. He and I are going to meet tomorrow to talk about some things."

She felt guilty lying to Abby. But hey, she had to lie to her sister sometimes to protect her. That was the way of things. And right now maybe she was lying a little bit to protect herself, but until she had all of this a little bit more settled, she just wanted to keep it to herself.

"Are *you* taking your birth control?" Abby asked, and the question made Sheena hoot with laughter.

"Never miss a dose, thank you."

"Just saying. If you're going to be around Denver King . . ."

Sheena felt like she'd been punched in the gut. "Bite your tongue. He's against the rules."

"Ah right. I forgot that you have a policy against exchanging more than two civil words with any man you sleep with."

"Damn straight. I don't have time for that shit. I have enough on my plate without having to take on the care and keeping of some guy's ego. I'm glad that you get joy out of relationships. I really am. It's not like we had an example of them working or being any good at all."

"No. But I just want to believe that since love and commitment seem to exist out there in the world maybe I can have it."

"And I admire that about you. I do. But as for me, I have spent way too much of my life dealing with men. Their fragility, their tempers, their expectations. It's like Hank. I loved Hank."

"You're really talking about our dog now?"

"Yes. I loved him. Sometimes I'm a little bit bummed out I don't have a dog anymore to make me feel secure at night. But I have a 12-gauge, some pioneer spirit and no desire to have my heart broken again."

"You're still talking about the dog?" Abby asked.

"I am. When he died it was sad. I don't want to have another dog, because that means losing another dog. As wonderful as the dog was, he was also work. I don't need to put that kind of work in. So I'm just saying thinking about having a relationship feels a lot like that."

"Like work."

"Yes. Work and potential heartbreak. I don't want either thing. If I want companionship I have no trouble finding it."

"Right. Companionship being sex."

"Yep. Don't cry for me, Abigail, I am free as a bird."

"Fine. Well. Have a good shift."

"Thanks. You too." And suddenly, her heart felt sore, and she felt just a little bit sad. "I really am happy for you. And I hope . . . I hope everything goes well with your guy."

"Thank you. I'll be okay if it doesn't. I'm always okay. But that's because you taught me how to be strong."

"Yes."

She got off the phone with her sister, and felt swallowed up by the silence it left behind.

She had helped her sister become strong. And she was glad of that. But there could be a loneliness and strength too, and as much as she had just spent all that last bit of the phone call assuring her sister she wasn't lonely, right now she felt it.

Not for a man. It was just that she had spent all those years caring for her sisters and they weren't here now, and sometimes the isolation, the emptiness in the house, did feel like a little bit much. Maybe she *should* get another dog.

But then she would have to bring him to the axe throwing bar every day . . . She didn't actually hate that idea.

Maybe she should get a dog.

Now that she wasn't working at the bar. She hadn't liked the idea of the poor pooch being at home by himself all night, while she slept half the day away. She was groggy, because she had gotten up ungodly early to go see Denver.

Nobody liked a groggy bartender, so she was going to have to get it together. Smokey's was usually okay, but every so often a fight broke out, and she did her best to make it clear that she didn't put up with that kind of nonsense.

You had to be tough in a position like that. Because you had to teach the men who went to the bar that you wouldn't put up with their bullshit.

That was why she didn't sleep with local guys. She didn't want all the sharks circling any given week, thinking they might have a chance with her. No, strictly out-of-towners for her. And never, absolutely never Denver King.

Chapter Three

"YOU GUYS WANT to go out tonight?" Denver asked.

He was painfully aware that he was the last man standing in his family. Everyone was paired up, and the times of going out to Smokey's to pick up women were definitely far in the past.

He didn't want to go to Smokey's to pick up women, though; he wanted to go to talk to Sheena. Though, why, he didn't know. Because they were going to meet tomorrow, so it seemed a little bit ridiculous to roll up to the bar. But if he was going to do business with her, on his property, he wanted to really get more context for her.

Daughtry and Justice looked up at him. Landry wasn't there anymore, having gone home with his wife and daughter an hour ago.

"I might head on home," said Justice, looking in the front room, where his wife was sitting.

"Me too," said Daughtry.

Because they wanted to have sex.

Assholes.

Well, or maybe it was true love; he wouldn't know. He could understand the sex thing. The companionship thing was a little bit beyond him.

"You don't need a wingman," said Justice, slapping him on the back.

"If anything," Daughtry said, "I bring the room down quite a bit given that I'm a cop."

"We know you're a cop," said Denver. "But thanks."

He realized that his brothers had lives that they wanted to be involved in. That they wanted to live. And he . . . Well, he had spent any number of years doing anything for his younger siblings. And they all had people in their lives that they would do anything for. But he wasn't the person. Because he was the caregiver. And it was a damn sorry thing, to get his underwear in a twist about it, but . . .

He was alone.

Dammit. He didn't need to go thinking about that. Didn't need to go thinking like that. It was ridiculous. His brothers were here. They were devoted to their wives. As they should be.

He would just go out by himself. It was fine.

"Okay. Well. Have a good evening then."

"Are you . . . moving us on?"

"Yes. Because I want to go out. And you don't."

"Yeah, but we could stay for a little while longer."

"No. Go home. Sleep with your wives. I have business to attend to."

"Are you that horny?" Justice asked.

"Do you want the answer to that question, Justice?"

Justice just looked back at him. "I thought we shared things, Denver."

"I'm glad you guys are married. Because I'm going to go out and pick up all the women that you would've picked up. It's a public service at this point."

He did relish that. The way his younger brothers looked at him just then. Like they weren't entirely sure if he was serious or not. And he wasn't going to tell them one way or the other.

"Okay then. We'll leave you to your foursome, I guess."

Denver snorted. If only.

What he really wanted to do was go talk to Sheena. He wasn't going to tell them that. He had had a moment of mystique, and he wasn't going to do anything to disrupt that.

When his brothers cleared out, he stripped his shirt off, and went into his bedroom. It was weird, living in the house now that it was just him. He didn't notice all that much, truth be told, because they were all out working together during the day, and then they often came for dinner. But it was different. Even Penny's—their surrogate sister's—soft presence was missed.

She was living in town, and she came out less and less frequently.

It was not like him to sit around being maudlin about his life. He didn't know what his problem was.

He put on some body spray, and a black T-shirt. Because it was nice when a man smelled good. And his brothers could talk shit all they wanted about stuff like that, but it was appreciated. He really could get laid if he felt like it. He didn't have to be lonely. That was the thing. Companionship for a night was always on the table for Denver.

And for a second, he considered it, because he felt like the odd one out. And there should be something good that he got out of that.

If they were going to go home to be with their wives, why couldn't he go be with a stranger?

He huffed about that all the way to his truck. He got in and turned the engine on, before heading out down the long dirt driveway that would carry him to the main road.

King's Crest was a little piece of paradise, a funny thing given that for a number of years his father had turned it into something toxic.

Yeah, there was a time when it hadn't been so great. But he could see it differently now. Surrounded by those purple mountains' majesty, with the fields that had his cows. His. Bought with his money.

He was a gambler; it was true. But his gambling had paid off.

He and Gus McCloud, Fia King—back when she'd been a Sullivan—and Sawyer Garrett had set this place up to be something like paradise, after the hill of their youth. A place where even he managed to play well with others. More or less. They helped each other. They exemplified the kind of humanity that he wanted to believe existed. Maybe it did or maybe it didn't in the broader world. But the important thing was, it existed for them.

They had made it.

He gripped the steering wheel, and continued on toward Smokey's. He felt a twisting sensation in his gut. Like he was stepping out of bounds, which was silly. He shouldn't feel that way.

Yeah, they had rules, but she had upended them by coming out to King's Crest today, and there was nothing wrong with him reciprocating by getting into her territory. The parking lot was already full of pickup trucks that ranged from envy inducing to pitiable. That was ranch life. And you couldn't really tell whose life you should actually envy based on their truck. Plenty of guys decided to stick with old reliable who never let them down, rather than getting saddled with a payment they couldn't handle. He whipped into the drive and pulled his truck up beside a faded blue Ford.

He got out and he could hear the music thumping inside. A line dancing beat, but he had a feeling nobody was line dancing.

No. On a Friday night, people were plastered against each other as tightly as possible as soon as they could be.

Ranch life was hard. That wasn't to say there weren't some real salt-of-the-earth guys out there who did the work and went home to a wife and family. But the truth was, a lot of them worked hard and relaxed harder.

It was just the way of things.

When he opened the door, it was as wall-to-wall packed as the parking lot suggested, guys in tight jeans, girls in short shorts. But then he zeroed in on her. Behind the bar, her movements were confident. She had on that same tank top she'd been wearing earlier, as she took orders, shook drinks, slung beer from the tap.

Her dark hair was up in a high ponytail, and her makeup was even more dramatic than it had been earlier.

The local men knew better than to hang out and drool on her at the bar. She had put paid to that pretty early on. But there were some out-of-towners there, leaning over and trying to chat her up. Right now, her expression was something like dismissive, but he knew that it could turn violent quickly if somebody got on her nerves.

He moved deeper into the bar, and he saw the moment that she sensed his presence. Her shoulders went tight, and the corner of her mouth twitched. He didn't know why he knew that was about him, but he did. She didn't turn to look at him. Yet he knew that she felt him all the same.

"Howdy," he said, sidling up to the bar and taking a seat on one of the shiny red stools. She turned then, slowly.

"What'll it be?"

She didn't acknowledge him personally, nor did she betray any shock at his presence.

"What do you recommend?"

"Pacific Northwest Lager," she said. "On tap."

"Great. I'll have that."

"Coming right up."

She turned and grabbed a pint, pouring some of the piney liquid into it.

She slid it down the bar. "Am I starting a tab for you?"

"Sure."

"All right."

He watched as she continued to interact with some of the other men sitting in the bar. A few women came up, sweaty with red cheeks from dancing, laughing while they ordered drinks. Sheena's demeanor softened with them, and she joked and laughed without some of that defensiveness in place.

He wished that he could experience that. It was a strange wish. A strange impulse.

He didn't quite know where it had come from.

He took a sip of his drink, and she turned, her eyes meeting his as he took a draw of the cold beverage. She watched him for just a moment too long for it to be casual. He didn't know what to make of that.

"Sitting at the bar tonight?"

"I came to talk to you," he said.

She arched a brow. "Why?"

"I thought we might have some things to discuss."

He felt a ripple of interest around him. Sheena looked to the left, where three men were clearly eavesdropping, and then looked back at Denver.

"I don't think we have anything to discuss."

"It's only that you left my place so fast this morning."

Only the color mounting in her cheeks betrayed her irritation. "I had somewhere to be."

He could tell that there was a lot of interest around them now, considering that it was probably easy for those men to imagine why she had been leaving his house early this morning. They would be wrong. But it was kind of funny.

"I thought you ranchers were busy."

"Damned busy," he said.

"Then I wouldn't think you had a bunch of extra time to sit around shooting the breeze."

"No, I guess not."

He shouldn't be enjoying this. Shouldn't enjoy sparring with her. Hell, if she were a different woman he would've said that it was flirting.

He looked away from her, and at the sea of people in the bar. There were plenty of attractive women out there on the dance floor.

"I just wanted to let you know that I'm feeling really positive about things," he said.

"Well, good," she said, her tone cool. "I hate to think that I was dealing with a wishy-washy cowboy."

"No, ma'am. My family is on board too."

That was an overstatement.

"Oh goody. I would tell you that you can come out to dinner and meet my parents but . . . sadly."

Their eavesdroppers were really confused now. Fine.

"Yeah. Same. Though, you're lucky. Your dad is actually dead."

That earned him a laugh. Husky and rich. And he liked it. It was too easy for him to play this game with her.

"Why don't you go out and mingle, Denver? I have work to do. And I haven't spoken to my boss yet."

Ah. Well, it was a good thing he had been playing vague then. He didn't need to go letting the cat out of the bag so that she wouldn't continue to work here before she was ready.

"All right. See you tomorrow."

He took another sip of beer and moved away from the bar. And as soon as he did, a soft-looking blonde approached him.

She was completely opposite to Sheena's looks. Where Sheena was sharp and bold, this one was soft. Big curls and round blue eyes. Pale pink lips. Makeup, definitely, but the kind expertly engineered to make it appear that she didn't have any on.

"Hi there," she said. "I couldn't help but notice when you walked in."

"What exactly did you notice?"

She smiled. "That you're sexy as hell."

All right. Not that soft. Well. If he wanted some, he was going to get it. He resisted the urge to look back at Sheena.

"My name is Denver King," he said.

"Delilah," she said.

"Exactly how many men have surrendered their strength for you?"

She pursed her lips. "Not as many as have used that line on me."

She'd called him out, but she seemed delighted that he'd used a line, and really, he couldn't have asked for better. He didn't have to be lonely tonight. Not if he didn't want to be.

Sheena felt out of sorts. She really didn't like it. What the hell did it matter to her if Denver King had moved on and started flirting with some cherubic-looking blonde? She didn't want him hanging out at the bar flirting with her.

Flirting?

Had he really been flirting with her?

It just was so off-brand for both of them.

Denver wasn't a flirt and neither was she. They were the type to get straight down to business, or at least that was her take on him. But there was . . . There was a *banter* thing. Every time they started talking, it turned into that. A kind of rhythmic patter that felt too easy between them. That made her feel warm.

She had watched Denver hook up with any number of women from this position behind the bar. She felt safe behind the bar. Men couldn't get to her unless she let them. And if they tried to cross the barrier, she had a knife. She also had a shotgun hanging on a hidden rack beneath the bar. Because if shit went down, she wasn't going to find herself lacking.

Yeah. She never wished she was on the other side of the bar. If there was a guy she liked, she went after him. And if not, she didn't. She wasn't used to this weird, forbidden sort of sensation. This feeling of desire that was completely impossible.

"Sheena," one of the guys down at the end, a regular, lifted his glass. "I need a refill."

"I'm not your mama, Edgar," she said. "So please and thank you will do."

He looked suitably abashed, and followed it up with both a please and then a thank-you when she took his glass.

The truth was, Smokey's was a pretty rough place but she managed it well. She was experienced.

She could deal with drunk, rowdy idiots; she could deal with guys who got overly friendly, or guys who were rude. She could pour beer while she kept one eye on the handsome cowboy and his beautiful target across the room. Yet. She was great at her job. She could do all those things.

Denver maneuvered the petite cutie out to the dance floor, and she watched the way his big hands settled on the woman's hips. Lord have mercy. Her thoughts went all to blissful hell. Because it was way too easy to imagine those hands on her own hips. Gripping her hard while he . . .

No.

Sexual fantasies about Denver King were a big no. Especially since now she was doing business with him. She had seen him do this before, but she had never really watched him. He had always been attractive. But she had tried to keep her distance, and there was something about breaking that barrier, something about coming to the ranch that morning, that made him feel too real. The axe throwing.

The easy conversation.

It made it too easy to imagine being a woman standing with him. Dancing with him.

She was never like this.

They finished the dance, and he pulled the blonde up the dance floor, touching her chin with his index finger and tilting her face up toward him. And Sheena found herself moving to the other side of the bar without even thinking. "Hey, King," she said. "I need to talk to you for a second."

He looked over at her, a flash of something in his gaze, but it wasn't irritation, even though it should've been.

"Hang on a minute," he said to his partner.

"Out the back," she said, pointing to the employees-only door that led into the kitchen.

"Are you serious?"

"Yes," she said.

She was jealous was what she was. Goddammit. It made her mouth taste sour. She wasn't one for self-loathing but this really put her there.

"Great."

She pushed through the door, past Dulce, one of the waitresses, who was making out with Tom, the cook. She didn't even pause to look twice, Denver, on the other hand, stumbled as he walked on by, and out the exit, into the little gravel strip behind the building. There was an embankment just past that, a grove of trees up toward the top. Deer often used it as a throughway. But luckily, there were no looming deer tonight.

"Dulce and *Tom*?" Denver asked.

"Oh yeah. And then he goes right back to cooking your food. Just so you know."

"Wow."

"I know. She doesn't want any of the guys to know that she's hooked up, because she likes how big you tip when you think she might bang you. That's how simple you assholes are."

"I'm not that simple," he said.

"Aren't you? You're telling me you don't intend to go home with that little wisp of nothing you're chatting up?"

"I don't see what business it is of yours."

"Oh, it isn't. Though, you did make those yahoos sitting at my bar think that I was at your house this morning because we hooked up. And I don't really give a shit about that. I like to be an enigma. But what I won't be is humiliated. I don't especially want them thinking that I hooked up with you, and then you went and hooked up with somebody else right in front of me."

"You grabbing me like a jealous lover probably isn't helping your cause."

"Oh, it is. Again. I do like to be unknowable," she said.

"What do you actually want?"

"I figured you came here for a reason."

"Yeah. Delilah."

She arched her brow. "Is that her name?"

"I believe so." He suddenly didn't look quite so certain.

"I see you're ready to pick out china patterns."

"I've never really understood what that meant."

She shrugged. "Hell if I know. I've never lived in a house with china."

"So, what is it you wanted to talk about?"

"Just . . . So, you did talk to your siblings?"

Yes," he said. "And they're on board."

She felt like there was something he wasn't telling her. But she really didn't need to know all his hopes and dreams. She was being a little bit of an idiot right now. And she couldn't rightly say why. Then it made sense. Because how long had it been since she had hitched her wagon to anything or anyone? She wasn't especially trusting. Never had been. And that's why this felt strange. She was hitching her resolutely solo wagon to a King of all people.

But then, she supposed their wagon had been hitched for a long time. Whether she especially wanted it to be or not.

"I don't have a lot of practice with this. Having business partners. Or partners of any kind," she said.

"Well, I do. You know all of Four Corners is run as a collective. And there's a reason for that. It's how you get by when times are tough. It's how you keep going, even when it seems like things aren't going your way. I'm a big fan of having people around to back you up."

He had always seemed like a lone wolf to her. It was weird to hear him talk about it like that.

"Well, I'm glad one of us has some experience with it. Because I don't."

"I'm happy to teach you all about teamwork," he said.

He really was such a compelling man. And she saw a lot of men. More than that, a lot of men were into her. Well, they were into what they thought she represented. They thought she was a wild girl, based on her looks. In reality, it was a bit more complicated than that. But she didn't care whether or not their impression of her was correct.

Not wanting an attachment definitely seemed to make men think she was something like wild.

Being confident made them think that too. Wanting control only made them think it even more. That was fine.

Men didn't usually *intrigue* her.

There were a lot of handsome men in the world.

Denver King happened to be both tall and handsome, which was a potent combination. Though, not one that had ever especially appealed to her. She preferred men around her height. Really, she just preferred things to feel a little bit more equal. She thought that was fair enough.

But that didn't mean she couldn't enjoy looking at him. For a minute.

Just a minute.

His jaw was square, his manner forthright and confident. He was the kind of man who didn't seem to be afraid to look anybody in the eye. That meant that he was either honest, or he was a very good liar. She had been around a lot of liars, though, and Denver didn't have the manner of a liar. Not really.

"Okay," she said.

She wasn't sure exactly why she didn't have a sharp rejoinder for that. She should. He was being a bit heavy-handed. She was allowing it. Which was not her MO. It didn't matter how attractive a man was; he didn't get to run roughshod over her. Not that Denver was running roughshod. He was just suggesting a little bit more joint work than she had been fully anticipating, and . . .

Well, why argue? Really. It was his place. And he knew it. She would bring her team and they would check the place out. It would be good.

Tonight she would give her notice . . . She was well on her way.

"All right. Well. You go get back to your other . . . team-work, I guess."

"Sure," he responded.

She watched him walk back into the bar, and she hung out in the back for a moment, realizing that what she'd done was stake some kind of claim on him, make it public that they had a connection, which they had both been careful to never do.

Not that people didn't know. It was a small town. Everyone knew that her dad used to work with Elias King. Everyone knew that he had died trying to collect money from some poor guy who felt threatened, backed into a corner.

She'd been glad the day that the judge had found that the man had acted in reasonable self-defense.

More people didn't need to have their lives ruined by her dad. He was dead; he couldn't hurt anyone anymore.

In fact, his death had only made her life clearer. Better.

She had always known that she couldn't rely on anyone to take care of her. And still, when you had a father in the house with you, you hoped. She had hoped. That one day, that man would show up and show out. That he would protect her. That when she told him that she was in danger he might . . .

No. Losing that for real, it had been a gift in a way. And this would be too.

She wasn't going to get all tangled up about it.

It was just change.

That was one thing she couldn't say she was a major fan of.

And there had been a lot of change over the last few years, because what was raising children but enduring change?

Getting them out of the nest was essential. It was how you knew you had done your job. But it also made everything different. And each time one of her sisters had flown the nest, it had been difficult.

But now she was left with a new path. A new way forward.

She went back inside, and was there just in time to watch Denver walk out of the bar.

She looked around, trying to see whether or not the blonde was still there.

Delilah.

Lord almighty, what an obvious name. It was probably a fake name. One she used when she wanted to let the men know she was a woman of ill repute, since she looked like a baby doll with a wig.

Well. Whatever. Fake siren was gone too.

Good for him. A body like his would be wasted if it wasn't getting sex regularly.

Good for him.

She turned back toward her regulars. "Anyone need a refill?"

Chapter Four

DENVER GOT UP bright and early to have a look around the old gaming hall.

It was in disrepair, to say the least. He sure as hell hadn't been in it since back when his dad stashed his liquor, his drugs, his weapons and all that other shit in there. He hadn't been in it since that chapter of their lives had been closed.

So it was dusty, with the impression of scandal, ill repute and liquor-soaked evenings stamped into every corner.

There were bedrooms upstairs, and he had considered turning those into guest rooms. Maybe people would enjoy staying above an axe throwing bar. Especially one that used to house prostitutes and gold-panners.

Maybe. He had dismissed the idea initially, but now this new venture seemed to be about embracing the slightly rougher edge of King's Crest.

He really would need to talk to the collective about that.

He wished it wasn't so damned early in the morning, because honestly, he could use a little bit of alcohol to fortify himself against Sheena Patrick. He had not gone home with Delilah last night, and it had been a pretty damned foolish decision.

He should've gone and blown off some steam. But local women were never really his thing, preferring to keep everything no strings to the best of his ability.

And . . . most of all, he had never in his life slept with one woman while thinking about another. Mostly because he couldn't recall ever wanting a specific woman with intensity.

He liked women. All women. All shapes, all sizes, hair color, skin tone, those that laughed loudly, those that giggled softly. He had a deep appreciation for the female form and function. All that was feminine turned him on. So when it came right down to it, he just wasn't picky. Some people called him a man whore. And by *some people*, he meant his brothers, who, with the exception of Landry, could hardly claim to be any better. Especially Justice, who had spent years giving himself away like he was a damn sample platter at Costco.

He had never found it to be a negative thing.

But last night, Sheena had been in his mind, and in good conscience he simply couldn't take one woman to bed when he thought the possibility existed that he might fantasize about another.

Even contemplating that made him feel dirty.

And not in a fun way.

He walked back out of the gaming hall, and got in his truck, driving it back toward the main landing of King's Crest, where their big event space was, and their overnight lodging. They were planning a big Christmas party this year, one for the whole town. Something different to the usual festivities that happened in the meeting hall. It had taken quite a bit of convincing to get the collective to allow it. Because everybody liked tradition, but thankfully, Fia King was his sister-in-law now, and that meant deciding to shift the venue from Sullivan's to King's had been an easier proposition than it might've been, considering he had an inside agent.

Years ago, when Landry and Fia still hated each other, it definitely would've been different.

Harder.

But now . . . Well. They were one big happy family.

So that would be great. A good chance to let everyone in the area see what they had going. He wondered . . . Maybe they could incorporate a little axe throwing. It would be cutting things tight, but considering they were just renovating the gaming hall, he thought it could be done. At least have it all in order in time for the big event.

Sort of like a speakeasy, all things considered. He had been trying to outrun the more unsavory aspects of the King family history, but maybe embracing it could be its own sort of reward.

He saw Sheena Patrick's car pulling up a moment later, but there were more trucks behind her. And he had no idea what in the hell that was about.

One by one, five big trucks pulled into King's Crest. Sheena got out of her car and made her way over to him. A guy he recognized as Manny Jiminez got out of one of the trucks. Manny was a contractor in the area. Though, Denver couldn't say he knew him well, since he was pretty sure the guy did most of his jobs up in Mapleton. As anyone looking to do more lucrative construction work would.

"Hey. I brought my crew."

"Your crew?" he asked, his eyes going laser-focused on Sheena. Today, she had long sleeves on. But the top still had a scoop neck, which gave him a clear view of her pretty spectacular cleavage. Damn. It was 7:00 a.m. He really needed to calm down.

"I didn't approve any crew."

"I have plans. I talked to Manny about it a couple of weeks ago."

"Did you? So before you talked to me."

"You made it pretty clear that you owed me a favor, Denver."

"My favor did not extend you being able to do whatever you wanted on my property. I have a plan. I have a venue."

"You didn't say that yesterday."

"I was unaware that you were going to show up with a crew."

"Why wouldn't I? I gave you the binder. Did you not read the entire binder?"

"No. I didn't read your dumbass binder from cover to cover, Sheena, because nobody does that. Literally fucking nobody. That is like reading the entire terms and conditions."

"I always read the terms and conditions, Denver."

"Liar."

She took a step toward him, her green eyes glowing. "No. I do. Do you know why? Because sometimes buried in that fine print is a promise that you'll sell your soul. Ask my dad. I wonder where I get my paranoia from."

"Your dad jumped at the chance to sell his soul. Anyway, I actually think his soul might still be a free agent, unless Satan claimed it. His body is the only thing my dad had a claim on."

"Just . . ."

She looked behind her shoulder, at Manny, who looked questioning, like he was wondering if he ought to jump in, or if he should leave well enough alone.

Denver made direct eye contact with the other man.

"I didn't realize that you hadn't been . . . I mean, I didn't know that you weren't informed," he said.

"Well, I wasn't," said Denver. "We've got our own crew here. We've done the majority of our own construction work."

"Sheena is a friend. I was willing to do the work at cost and labor, nothing more."

"Really," said Denver.

Manny shifted. "Really."

Well. They'd clearly slept together. Not that he was judging; it was just there was no earthly reason that a man would come with a crew to do work at cost for a woman he didn't have a vested interest in. And typically, that vested interest happened on a mattress.

Again. Not that he was judging. Not that it mattered. Though the whole thing was annoying. Really damned annoying.

"I want to do the axe throwing bar in our old gaming hall."

"Gaming hall?"

"Yes. It's rustic, and it has a lot of history."

"Why don't I even know that it exists?"

"Because my ancestors were involved in all kinds of illegal shit. Interesting, but not exactly the image that we've been trying to project. Still, I think it could be a little bit of a tourist draw. And I'm thinking that I might want to renovate all of it, and make it just a little bit more lawless around here. You know, in a tourist way."

"Well . . ." She sputtered. "I don't hate it. I don't. But . . ." He could feel the power struggle between them. The push-pull. She wanted to bean him over the head, fair enough. He had half a mind a frog-march her off the property.

So they were even.

"Just saying, you should've run all this past me," he said.

"Manny," said Sheena. "I'm sorry. You and the guys can take off. Clearly, my business partner and I have some things we need to discuss."

"Whatever you say," he said.

And Denver could only marvel at the way she had rallied the troops, and then dispersed them.

"You get every guy to do your bidding like that?"

He thought about the way the men in the bar had looked at

her. Like she was something magic and terrifying all at once. He imagined that she did.

"He's a friend."

"Oh. A friend."

"Yes," she said. "I knew him in high school. Geez."

"I'm just saying . . ."

"You're just implying that I'm trading sex for work."

"Hell no," he said. "I assumed the sex was in the past."

"For the record, I haven't had sex with Manny."

"Oh, then he's definitely hoping that you will."

"What makes you say that?" she asked.

"Because men don't do nice things for women if they don't want to get laid."

"You did *not* just say that. What kind of relic from a bygone era are you?"

"I'm just realistic. Maybe that's a gross generalization."

"Well. It is pretty gross."

He snorted. "Are you going to tell me that you have such a high opinion of humanity that you don't think that could possibly be a factor?"

She paused for a moment. "I don't have a high opinion of anyone or anything. If that's what he thinks is going to happen, that's fine. I'll give them a set-down. I don't care. I guess what I really don't understand is why you think that you have to warn me about anything. Or worry. I've been taking care of myself for a long damned time. Do you think I've never had to give a man a firm no? Do you think that I have never had to give more than a no? I'll put my boot up the guy's ass. I don't give a shit."

Her husky voice went sharp then. Like a blade.

She wasn't kidding.

"You can't go doing things like that without consulting me. We don't need to come to a consensus on humanity."

"You and I think pretty much the same things about humanity. You just think that it's your responsibility to protect me because you think I'm a woman and I need it."

"First of all, is there anything wrong with that? Second of all, I take it upon myself to try and extend protection to everybody that my dad messed around with. Regardless of gender."

"Yes, it is a bad thing," she said, her chin stubborn. "Because you're underestimating me. You're acting like the way that I've navigated my life these past thirteen years, hell, maybe even all thirty-one years of my life, somehow only worked miraculously. And your involvement is the only thing keeping me safe. That's ridiculous. I am totally and completely capable of handling shit. Okay?"

He thought of the way that she had rallied all those people. And he had asked himself what actually made him mad about it. Well. The lack of control. That was the issue. Because he really didn't like that. But also . . . maybe it was just something he didn't understand. Because he sure as hell didn't command that level of loyalty from anybody he wasn't related to.

He knew that people would look at him, at the situation in Four Corners, and they wouldn't believe that. They would think that all the Four Corners people were joined at the hip. But they all had each other's backs all the time. And while they practically did look out for each other, the Kings were separate, and they always had been. It wasn't because Arizona had gotten prickly after her accident.

It wasn't because Landry and Fia had splintered apart.

It wasn't because the only person Justice had ever really been loyal to was Rue.

It wasn't because Daughtry had work off the ranch.

It was because the way their father had spun his web of abuse was a particular kind of insidious. A particular kind of danger.

And it had done damage to them all in specific and terrible ways.

And it made it difficult for them to figure out how to relate to anybody. Made it feel dangerous.

At least, that was how he looked at it.

He couldn't trust anyone else, and he couldn't trust himself. That was the lesson he learned from his dad.

Because the truly terrifying thing about his dad was that Denver would never really know if his dad believed the stories that he spun. A narcissist who cast himself as the hero, he manipulated everyone around him.

He'd driven his wife away, had been openly cruel to his only daughter.

And he'd appealed to the weaknesses in all of his sons, and had used those weaknesses against them. Had he believed that he was doing what was best? Or had he just done it without conscience? He had taken Denver's desire to protect, to care for the ranch, to care for his siblings, and he'd corrupted it. The same as he had taken Daughtry's sense of authority, and turned it into something twisted up and dangerous.

They knew exactly what it was like to have those pieces of themselves corrupted.

And it was scary.

And he really believed that only a foolish man would be outright convinced that he would never fall for something like that again. It wasn't so much that he was worried about being tricked by somebody else. He was worried about his own ability to lie to himself.

"Come with me," he said.

"All right," she said. "How do I know you're not just looking to bury me in a back field somewhere?"

"Remember," he said. "The red poker chip is hardly a legally binding agreement. I wouldn't need to do anything half so dramatic as that to be rid of you. We don't have an agreement yet. So you need to not piss me off."

"I thought you owed me."

"And I didn't think you wanted to own me."

"This is my dream," she said.

"Yes. Your dream that you're planning on leaving for greener pastures as and when you can. So why do you assume that you're going to be completely in charge of it? This is my land."

He gestured for her to get in the truck, and she took her sweet-ass time doing it like putting a little bit of space between his gesture and her action would mean that she hadn't actually done what he'd said.

She got inside, and he started to drive them both out toward the gaming hall.

In some ways, King's Crest itself had been a little bit like a town.

His grandpa had made money through illegal enterprises, and there had been no real law enforcement out there to oversee it.

He had never really considered that an asset, until now. And he supposed that he had Sheena to thank for that indirectly.

"I really thought you were going to teach me about teamwork," she said.

"Here's your first lesson," he said shortly. "You let your partner in on all the different plans that you have."

"You too. You never said anything about this."

"My siblings brought it up last night."

"Well, we talked last night. And you didn't say anything about this."

"I had no idea what you were actually doing dragging me out of the bar last night. You didn't make yourself clear."

She looked angry about that. "Well, some of it was about controlling the conversation in front of the patrons. Obviously."

"Not obvious to me."

"Well, it isn't really my problem. But I put in my notice, so this needs to work. Because my boss was mad."

"It'll work," he said, his tone short.

When they pulled up front of the old building, she whistled. "Lord. Why didn't you say you had a damned palace out here?"

"Because it's a palace of sin. And I didn't really consider it something to be proud of. You of all people should understand that."

She nodded. "I do. But this is damned cool no matter what it was originally intended for."

"Yeah. I guess so." He killed the engine, and they both got out, and he looked critically at the place. It used to be white, but the paint had faded with time and age. Two floors, the roof hanging flat out over the front to create a porch. It looked like an old saloon. It looked, basically, like what it was.

It was something that faded into the mountains to him. Something he didn't pay all that much attention to.

A part of life here. As sure as breathing. Seeing it at the same time she did, he saw possibility.

"All right. I like this. And it isn't too far from the main road."

"No," he agreed. "What I'd really like is to get it completely renovated in time for Christmas. We're having a big Christmas party out at the ranch. I think this could be a great addition."

"Look who's taking the idea and running with it. Don't you think that we could use Manny's help if you're planning on getting it open that quickly?"

"Maybe," he conceded.

"Wow. That must have almost hurt you."

"Hush. Let's go in."

They pushed the door open, and his footprints in the dust were still there from this morning. She stepped inside one of them, her own foot much smaller than his print. She wasn't a tiny woman; she was tall, but he was much taller.

"This is very cool. We could put the throwing lanes over there."

"Yeah. I looked at that. I was thinking you could have four over here, three over here. Probably we won't need any more than that, not in a place this size. But I bet it could stay pretty busy. The bar can be at the center. Away from all the throwing action."

"Yeah. You definitely don't want to get hit with a stray axe."

"Why exactly made you take up axe throwing?"

"Oh, I throw all kinds of things," she said. "Knives. Hatchets. Dinner plates. Sometimes a motherfucker needs to get hit in the head."

She was funny, but there was trauma in that humor. He was familiar. He couldn't imagine what it had been like being a girl growing up in the environment they had been in. That was something else that made him angry about his father. Well. It was maybe the wrong thing to say. He was glad his sister Arizona had been protected from the kinds of unsavory characters his dad had associated with. But it just . . . It felt strange. They had been spared that immersion into the dark world their father had cultivated in Pyrite Falls. The drug running, the gambling, the debts. It was held for the people that had been treated so badly by his dad, and hell for the children of the ones who had worked with his father.

That was why even years after his father had left town, when he had found out that Penny Case's dad had gone to prison, he had gone to pick her up. Because what else could he do? That her dad was on that path was squarely down to his own father. He couldn't deny that.

"You ever stuck anyone with something?"

"Close," she said, smiling wide and pretty. "Anyway, how do you think I break up all those bar fights? It can be tough, being a woman who tends bar in places like this. Men can get the wrong idea. That they could take advantage of you, or that they can run the joint because hell, you're just a lady. I run my bar tighter than that. And I'll run this bar tighter than that."

"And you'll train up a manager for when you leave?"

She nodded. "I don't see it being right away. But I'm patient. It's been thirteen years since my father died. Thirteen years since I became responsible for raising my siblings when I was eighteen."

"I relate. Though, none of my siblings were kids. They were all a little older. It was tough, though. So I get it. You have to try to be an example when you have no idea what that actually looks like. At least, that was my experience."

She chuckled. "Yeah. I get that. It's not like we had a functioning family even before he died."

"I hope I was a help," said Denver.

He really did.

She didn't soften. But she did look just a tiny bit . . . friendlier, maybe.

"Why do you think we stayed? The help that you gave every month, that got me through."

"I'm glad."

"And I want to pay it back. Because you have to understand, it doesn't sit right with me. Being in any man's debt. I know you don't get it. I know you think it was your restitution. But you got us through. You got us through the damned worst, and I wouldn't say that I'm grateful like that. Because you know it's more complicated than that. But I can certainly acknowledge that without you we wouldn't have gotten by like we did. And without you, my dad might still be alive. And, I don't love the way that might've gone. So."

"Yeah. All right."

She was grateful, but she didn't want to be. That was fair, because he didn't really want her to be. He didn't do it for thanks. He had wanted to know that it mattered. But that was all for him, and maybe that was part of the problem with it. He was looking for a way to feel . . . redeemed, maybe, and it was possible that wasn't fair.

She paced around the room, and he could see that she was placing everything mentally where she wanted it to go.

"You're right," she said, turning to face him. "This is better than a new build. Lets us get open faster, has history to it. I like it."

"Well, you can see why I'm a little reluctant to have a whole construction team I don't know working on the place."

"Manny will listen to you. He's not macho like that."

"Macho like what?"

"Like *you*. You're that guy, right? You gotta be in charge."

"I don't gotta be in charge, Sheena, I *am* in charge. And that is a different thing."

She looked at him, her green eyes flashing, and something electric crackled between them.

"I'm not going to sleep with you," she said.

The words were so blunt, so direct, that they put him on his back foot.

"I don't believe I asked you to."

"You ask me to every time you look at me, Denver King. Even if you were all set on that cutie last night, if I had invited you home, you would've gone."

The words were like a gut punch, mostly because there was truth to them. Like the spark it took to make a flame. But he had more self-control than that, whatever she thought.

"You think so?" he asked.

"I do. I've seen the way you look at me. It's the way all men look at me."

"Well darlin', recognizing that a woman is beautiful is hardly an invitation for her to join me in bed."

Her eyebrows lifted. "Is that how you're going to play it?"

62MAISEY YATES

"I've seen the way you look at me too. I think you felt like you needed to say something because you're warning your own self off. I don't sleep with women I have an association with."

"Great. Because I don't sleep with men that I have an association with."

"Look at that. We both don't want to sleep with each other."

His body felt hot and prickly, and the heaviness in his groin called that a lie. Because he kind of did want to sleep with her. But not really her. If she was simple, uncomplicated, no strings attached. If she was a woman that he had come across in a bar, maybe. A stranger. Hell yeah. A stacked brunette with ink on her arm like that . . . Yeah. He would've been all over it. But she was Sheena. So he had never even thought about going there. Well. That was a lie. He had never indulged the vague thoughts he had about going there. How about that?

No. He was smarter than that; he was safer than that. He wasn't going there.

"Good, because just so you're clear, you're not my type." She moved over to the window and dragged her finger along the sill. "I don't like bossy men."

"I don't like mouthy brats. So guess the same goes."

"Because unlike you, Denver. I don't have to be in charge. I am in charge."

"Not here you're not."

She squared up toward him, her green eyes unreadable. "This is going to be my place. I'm going to manage it."

"And it's on my land."

This was why it was so much easier to just give people money. Because then he didn't have to actually deal with them. This was the problem. He actually didn't share his turf all that well. Not only that, but the way she looked at him got his blood pumping hot and fast and made a liar out of him.

She was stunning. And she was interesting. She made him think things he shouldn't.

She was a pain in the ass, and she was beautiful.

She was . . . she was derailing him. She could bring her crew out here, and they could renovate. With some oversight from him, but he didn't need to get involved. He had the whole Christmas thing to plan, the whole event space to get looking good, and he still had his damned ranch to run. They had the beer to keep producing; everything was busier than it had ever been.

The truth was, he couldn't afford to go micromanaging Sheena. He had jumped into this endeavor with both feet, partly out of guilt, and now she was sucking him in because . . . It was because she was challenging him. And he wasn't good at backing out from challenges. That was the beginning and end of it.

"All right. You can bring Manny out here, and y'all can get started tomorrow."

"Great. So what, we have . . . a month to get the place finished?"

"Pretty much."

"Well, I think it's doable."

And he was happy to let that verbal foreplay that had been going on a moment ago fade into the background. Happy to forget it had happened.

He wasn't going to sleep with her. Didn't mean he didn't want to. And he could see the way that she was appraising him now that she wasn't entirely neutral either.

They would . . . they would wreck the bed. He was confident in that. They were far too much alike, and the power struggle would be . . .

Lord. He had to stop thinking like that. Because he didn't want to sleep with her. Well. He didn't want to want to.

She was a complication. And that was one thing he didn't need.

"I'll be by to check on it every day. And if you have any big decisions to make, you need to run them by me."

"Sure thing, boss," she said, her voice waspy. "Guess we'll start when my time ends at the bar."

"You say that like I might be offended by it. Like I don't think it's my due."

"You really are a hardheaded asshole, aren't you?"

"Let me ask you something. Did you ever think that maybe there was a reason why I left the money without talking to you?"

"I assumed it was because you didn't have a need to make four tragic girls into your pet project."

"What I didn't have the need to do was taint four said girls with any more of the King family. I know who I am. I know where I come from. I've done an all-right job putting some of that behind me. I've done an all-right job of taking some of the family bullshit and scraping it off my boot. But at the end of the day, blood his blood."

"Do you think the same is true for me?"

"No. You're clearly not your father's daughter. Because you survived."

And then she did something he really didn't expect. She smiled. Big and bright. Then she laughed.

"That's funny as hell," she said, between great gulps of air. "Yeah. I'm not weak like my dad. One bullet wouldn't down me."

"All right. I guess I'll see you sometime tomorrow. We'll meet to discuss your progress."

"Sounds good."

Then he extended his hand, and she looked at it. The corner of her lips curved upward, and she stuck her hand out, shaking his.

The spark of their skin on skin was electric. They held each other's gaze, a dare. Because they both felt it. They were familiar with the spark of desire, both of them. But this . . . Well, he could say honestly that for him this was far and above anything he'd ever dealt with before. His whole body was alive with desire for her.

She was such a damned temptation. And he couldn't stop himself from looking her over. Slowly. That stubborn face, her well-curved body.

"Still not sleeping with you," she said, her voice going husky.

"Still not offering," he said back.

He moved his hand from hers slowly. The slide of her skin on his feeling like the flat of an expert tongue on the underside of his manhood.

He gritted his teeth. And in spite of her determination to look unbothered, he could see two slashes of red at the tops of her cheekbones.

"Partners," she said.

"Partners," he said in return.

Then he went back to the ranch house, took a cold shower and went on with his work for the day.

Chapter Five

SHEENA HAD A video call scheduled with all of her sisters that night. Whitney and Sarah were in their dorms at their respective colleges, and Abby was in the little house she was renting in a neighborhood in Fresno. It was cute. She had pictures on the wall, and vases with flowers in them on every available surface.

It was fun, seeing the way that her sister had made that new house into a home for herself.

Someday, she would do the same thing. Someday, she wouldn't be in this place anymore.

"I heard you're working with Denver King," Whitney said without preamble.

"I am." She might as well tell them. "I'm opening up an axe throwing bar."

"No way," said Sarah. "That's what you're doing with Denver King?"

She thought of the way his strong hand had enveloped hers earlier.

It wasn't the only thing she wanted to do with Denver King. But that was dumb. That was really dumb. Because sex was a momentary, fleeting pleasure, and this was a whole-ass entanglement.

There was no amount of attraction that would be worth pursuing. She had thought if she said something that it would dispel the tension. That he would suddenly turn into the kind of man that she could mold. Because she had seen that he wasn't immune to her. She had noticed it last night, and she had seen it during the axe throwing. So she had mistakenly assumed that if she went bold, he would shrink. That's what men often did. But no. He had just looked her dead in the eye and met her boldness.

He had said that he wasn't offering to sleep with her. And it was so apparent that he wanted to. She felt a restless ache between her legs. The problem was she wasn't unaffected by him. That was actually the biggest problem, because it was preventing her from escalating things with him so that she could figure out how to get the upper hand. Because it felt like a risky game. A deadly little competition to see which one of them had to swerve first. And for the first time, she was afraid that she might be the one that had to swerve.

It was ridiculous. He wasn't . . . He was gorgeous. Acknowledged. Long acknowledged. But he was not the kind of man she ever chose for her nights of fun. If she needed to blow off steam, it was always with a guy who let her take control. Because that was what she liked. And even more, it was what she needed. Denver King was not what she needed.

"Well, he owes me a favor. So, I went to cash it in."

"But why an axe throwing bar?" Abby asked. "And why didn't you tell me that when we talked yesterday?"

"I just had a few things to iron out. It felt tentative. And now it doesn't. So, I felt more comfortable sharing."

"But Four Corners . . . They're just such a weird whole thing. Isn't being there . . . ? Does that make you feel kind of like an outsider?"

Outsider was kind of her whole thing. "Why would that bother me? I'm not looking to make besties, I want to run a business. It's a good location, because they're adding so many features to the place. It's changed a lot, even just in the last couple of years."

"I mean it sounds fun. It actually makes me want to come back home and visit. And bring friends. There are things to do."

"And even places to stay," Sheena added. "Because Denver has been adding to the ranch already."

"It's just weird to hear you talk about him like that. Like you know him," said Sarah.

She knew that Sarah, as the youngest sibling, didn't fully understand what they had been spared when their dad had died. She knew that Sarah actually missed their dad. She tried not to disrupt that. Tried not to take it from her. But it was hard. Because she actually knew how little their dad had loved them, and that frankly, having a man around who didn't care enough to fight for you, but brought the wrong kind of people around, was worse than having no man around at all. Still, she wanted to respect that her sister was . . . grieving. In her own way. Though, she didn't want to take on board any judgment about it.

"It's just convenient. Finding another place would've been impossible right now. It isn't like I have any capital to invest."

She decided not to tell her sisters that she wanted to pay him back. Because she had never told them . . . She had never told them the extent of what she'd taken from Denver in the first place.

It was a point of pride.

She didn't want them to know that she hadn't been doing it all on her own. And maybe that wasn't fair. Maybe it was giving them unrealistic expectations about life. But . . . she just hadn't wanted to admit it. They knew about the college money.

COWBOY, IT'S COLD OUTSIDE

But not about the monthly funds. There was no way that her waitressing salary, and then her bartending salary, would have paid for the mortgage, paid for her car, paid for gas, clothes, all the things. And even though they had lived modestly, it had been much more comfortable than it would've been without Denver.

She had worked. She was proud of that. She was proud of what she had done to take care of them. But she couldn't have done it alone.

"New businesses often don't turn a profit for five years," Whitney said.

Little Miss Getting Her Business Degree.

Sheena had to fight not to roll her eyes.

"Sure. But I'm not actually paying for the property. That's the main thing. So my start-up is incredibly low overhead."

"I mean, good for you, I guess," said Whitney. "It's just weird."

"Well, may I remain a weird enigma to you."

They talked about Boston, where Whitney was, and Ohio, where Sarah was. They teased Abby about Fresno and her boyfriend, who was taking her out to a fancy dinner over the weekend.

"He sounds nice," said Whitney.

"He does," said Sarah, looking like she had hearts for eyes.

Sheena had never had hearts for eyes in her life. She had daggers for eyes, if anything.

"Yeah, well. Just remember that even serial killers sound nice until you go looking in their basements."

"You're so grim, Sheena," said Sarah.

"I don't have a lot of reasons not to be."

"You are the person that's trusting a King," said Whitney. "So it seems a little bit rich for you to try to warn Abby off a guy."

"I am not sleeping with Denver." She said that mostly for her own benefit. Mostly as a reminder. "Also, I have a weapon on my person at all times. Also, I don't trust him. I'm just using him."

"You're kind of scary," said Whitney.

"Scary is how you get through life sometimes."

Not for the first time recently, she wondered slightly if she had done them a disservice by hiding some of the truths about their upbringing. Except then what would be the point of protecting them? They were so much softer than she would ever have the chance to be. And that was a good thing.

The girls hadn't seen their dad's body. They hadn't experienced the conflicting feelings of loss and relief. Followed by a pull toward a man she had no business feeling a pull toward. That day. Everything had gone all to hell at the Potter ranch, and she had been called out by her dad . . . But then he was gone.

By the time she got there he was gone.

His eyes were vacant and hollow, and he had a hole in his shoulder. She had looked away after that. Because there was nothing she could do, so why keep staring at it? It was ghoulish.

They had covered him with a blanket before zipping him up into a bag. That was after they had put flags everywhere and made it a whole crime scene.

She had never been able to watch crime shows after that. Because she felt like she knew a little too much about how the real thing looked.

How a dead body looked, when there was no person left inside it. Just the organs and bones, not the soul. Yeah. She knew how bodies looked too. Denver had been there, younger than he was now, but no less serious, his pallor green. He was being questioned by police. But he wasn't in handcuffs. His dad was.

She remembered Daughtry being there too, but he didn't stand out to her in quite the same way that Denver did. His dad was in cuffs, hers was on a slab. And they were both the oldest. Right in that moment, she had more in common with him than she did just about anybody in the world. She wanted to go to him, even though he was a stranger. A man she knew only vaguely by name.

But she didn't. Still, they had looked at each other for a long time.

Like they were both sitting in their new reality.

She had gone home and tucked the girls in. She hadn't told them that Dad was dead yet. She waited until after school the next day, because it was a Friday, so at least they would have the weekend to try and get over it.

She didn't cry. It wasn't sad enough. He didn't deserve her tears.

"Whatever. I'm suspicious so you all don't have to be. And paranoid. But hey, no, you don't have to worry about me because I will no longer be working in a seedy bar where I have to break up fights."

Her sisters did let out a cheer over that. They cared about her. They worried about her. And sometimes their worry took the form of being concerned that she was a little bit too . . . hard. But they didn't realize how much she'd had to be. It made their concern grate a little bit.

That wasn't fair at all, of course. She knew that. But whatever, the shift of it all, the changing tide, it had her feeling a little bit out of sorts. She would get over it. She always did.

"Are you all coming back for Christmas?" she asked.

"Yes," Sarah and Whitney said.

"Undecided," Abby replied.

"Abigail," Sarah said, sounding scandalized. "You can't miss Christmas."

"Well, I might have to. I don't know that I get enough days off from my job. Plus . . . I dunno. I was talking to Alejandro about the possibility of meeting his parents."

A hush fell over the call.

"For Christmas."

"Yes," she said. "For Christmas."

Everything inside Sheena went tight. This was it. The real start of change. Where they wouldn't see each other again at the holidays. It just . . . It sucked. She didn't like it.

But also, it was good. Good for Abby, anyway. That she had found somebody that she really cared about. That she was happy enough in her life that she wasn't necessarily going to run back home all the time. It was good. It was what was supposed to happen.

It was just . . .

Are you jealous?

That question was so weird, so out of left field, and she felt absolutely got punched by it. She wasn't really jealous. She wasn't. But she couldn't show it. She just needed to look happy. Thrilled.

"Well, there's going to be a big Christmas party right before Christmas, at Four Corners. It'll be kind of the inaugural thing for the axe throwing. If you can bring Alejandro with you, maybe you guys can come up before Christmas. I can . . . I can get you a couple of plane tickets and you can fly into Medford."

"Oh. Well . . . You're not going to buy us tickets. We can buy our own. But maybe we will."

Right. Her sister could buy her own plane tickets because she was an adult. Because she was out there working a real job. An office job. Because she had a boyfriend who also had a real job, and could help pay for things.

A real grown-up.

In a way that Sheena maybe wasn't.

It was so odd. She'd had to grow up so fast. Be an adult in a lot of real ways. Worry about bills. Worry about holding down a job. About getting her sisters to school every day, having their hair brushed and their clothes clean. Helping them do homework.

Her own life looked exactly the same now as it had been, except she didn't have the responsibilities. So it was almost like reverting.

You're starting your own business. You are changing things.

She just felt so emotionally . . . stunted.

"Well, if you can make it, that would be great. I would love to have you all there. To see that . . . To see my new thing."

That got her a round of excited giggling and babbling.

And that, she supposed, was something a little bit like asking people to be there for you. What she wasn't great at. But she was glad that she had. Because the idea of not seeing Abigail made her feel stabbed, and she didn't like it. She thought about Denver. She wondered if he ever felt the same.

It was funny: All of his siblings were paired off now, and he wasn't. He had made it really clear that wasn't something he was interested in. She felt the same. The idea of depending on another person just seemed foreign. Weird and disorienting. She had to wonder if it was the same for him. Were they just that basic? Were they a predictable thing that happened when you had to be the parent at way too young of an age?

Were they the fallout of fathers who didn't care about their children as much as they cared about themselves?

Because Sheena had learned one thing from her dad. Not only did she have to take care of everyone else, but she would always have to take care of herself. She thought of how she and Denver had clashed earlier.

Yeah. They were . . . they really were the same.

She found it both comforting and jarring.

She could ask him.

But that felt dangerously close to getting to know him. And she wasn't sure she wanted to do that either.

Getting to know a deadly, handsome man? Maybe not the best move.

"I have to go," said Sarah. "I have studying to do."

"Me too," said Whitney, waving.

She and Abby said goodbye.

And the other two vanished.

"Are you okay?" Abby asked.

"I'm great."

"You didn't even ask me if I was at all worried if Alejandro's parents were cult leaders looking to initiate me and make me a sacrifice."

"Well, we both know you would be a pretty bad virgin sacrifice."

"Indeed. Failed at one of the basic bits of that."

Sheena scrunched her face up. It was the closest thing to conciliatory she could manage. "I'm happy for you. I don't actually want you to be as paranoid as I am."

"I'd kind of like it if you were less paranoid too, Sheena. I feel like maybe you'd be happier."

"I am happy."

But when she got off the phone with her sister, she sat with that statement for a long time.

She realized she wasn't entirely sure what happy was.

Chapter Six

NOW THAT HE was thinking of integrating the axe throwing into the Christmas party, Denver realized he could no longer avoid including the collective in the conversation. This was why he made a very unusual stop at Garrett's Watch midafternoon to see if he could catch Sawyer down at the barn.

When he pulled up, Sawyer was there, standing and talking to his brother Wolf. There were two toddlers running around the barn area, laughing and giggling. He knew that the older one belonged to Sawyer. He figured the younger one had to be Wolf's. He didn't do all that much keeping up with the Garretts and their young. There seemed to be more and more these days. But then, that was also true of the McClouds, and really, his family too. Kids everywhere.

A new era for sure.

"Garrett," he said.

He felt a moment of satisfaction when Sawyer Garrett's eyebrows shot up, and Wolf Garrett looked at his brother with confusion on his face.

"King," said Sawyer. "What is it that brings you by?"

"I have an order of business to enter into the next town hall."

"Well, that is short notice," said Sawyer.

"I know. That's why I came direct to the source. You're the one that conducts the meetings."

"Yeah. Surprise you didn't go through Fia."

"She would've just told me to come talk to you. She might be my sister-in-law, but she's not prone to giving me whatever I want."

"Fair. Guess it's not like she had a whole personality transplant."

"Indeed not."

"So what order of business are you looking to enter?"

"It's a matter of a new business proposition that I have for King's Crest. I'm self-financing."

"Okay."

"But I also want it to be integrated into this whole Christmas shindig that we're having."

"So it isn't anything that will financially benefit the collective."

"No, it will. I'm going to finance it, the money is going to go into the pot." He cleared his throat. "My share, anyway. Most of it's going to go to Sheena Patrick, who is proposing to run it. She wants to open up an axe throwing bar."

"What?" Sawyer asked.

"I know. But, it's what she wants. And I feel level to give it to her."

"I don't understand any of this. You're planning on paying, but you want to give your share of it into the collective pot."

"That sums it up."

"Why?"

"I have enough of my own money. I prefer to put money back into the ranch."

"Typically, when we do that, we've all invested."

"I know how the collective works, Sawyer. I was going to keep it to myself. But you know, now that I'm introducing it as part of a collective endeavor, I felt like it would be best to make it aboveboard."

"Well, you're more than welcome to propose it. I don't see any reason why I or anyone else would have opposition to it. You're using your own money."

"But you're allowed to have opposition," he said.

He didn't integrate himself much into the group. He knew that. And he also knew that people mostly thought of him as an asshole. But that was based largely on his lack of friendliness, and not anything he'd ever done. He didn't know how to be all about his family, all about his siblings and emotionally all about everybody else. He knew how to throw money at it. And that was what he did.

"I hope you invite Sheena to the meeting," Sawyer said. "Because I have a feeling everybody would like to hear about the business venture from her." Sawyer rocked back on his heels. "What if we want to invest?"

"The budget is done for the year," Denver said.

"We're headed into a new year, if you didn't notice."

"I did."

"Maybe we'll want to review that."

"It's up to you. I'm not asking anybody to do that." And he didn't like the idea of everybody having their hands in it. He liked the idea that he contributed to the ranch. That he helped. But he mostly liked to keep his own stuff . . . separate.

"Well, the floor is yours at the next meeting. I'll be sure to introduce it."

"Thanks."

He reached his hand out toward Sawyer. Sawyer shook it, a bemused expression on his face.

"See you at the town hall."

"See you then."

He had texted Sheena and asked her to make an appearance at the town hall, and after that it had been all about the usual work, plus preparation for the meeting. It involved a lot of grilling, because they tended to provide the meat; it was what they did.

He actually enjoyed it. Again, a little bit of a contradiction. But that was who he was.

He expected Sheena to meet him out of the barn at Sullivan's Point. He did not expect her to show up at the ranch house, knocking tentatively on the door while he was out in the back manning the grill.

He walked around the side of the house, and looked at her for a minute, as she stood there on the porch, toying with her dark hair.

He felt almost guilty, looking at her in an unguarded moment. But it was like seeing a whole new person.

She didn't look like she was suited up for war. Everything about her was slightly softer. Her posture, the expression on her face. She was wearing low-rise jeans and a studded belt, a short sweater that showed a bit of her skin at her stomach, and gave a good look at her rack. So, that was right on as usual.

"Can I help you?"

She turned, and it was like a switch flipped. There was Sheena the warrior. Sheena, who didn't take any shit from anybody, and in fact was ready to give a shit before it could be given to her.

"What the hell are you doing sneaking up on me like that?" she asked, hand to her chest like he'd just about scared her heart right up out of there.

"I didn't expect you."

"Well. I don't know what to expect with this whole town hall meeting. And you didn't give me enough information. Suddenly I have to make a whole case to the collective?"

"It just seemed like the right thing to do. But I'm willing to do all the talking."

"Hell no. It's my business venture."

"And it is my ranch. These are my people." The words felt dishonest on his tongue, because hadn't he just looked at Sawyer's shock and discomfort over seeing him do something that was really part of their whole thing?

He cleared his throat. "You don't have to speak."

"I want to. So we need to go over what we're going to say."

"There's not much to say. Just tell them what you told me."

"That I'm not going to sleep with them?"

"You *could* tell them that." She was being dry. He didn't find the topic funny.

"I haven't seen the hall yet. Maybe I do want to sleep with them."

"I thought you didn't do entanglements."

Her eyes went narrow. "I guess that's another question I have. How entangled are we with the rest of the collective?"

"We aren't. Because we aren't going to use their money to finance the venture. We're going to use mine."

"I have some money," she said.

"Save it. I'm happy to help get it launched the way that I want it launched."

"What about the way that I want to launch it?" she asked.

"Come back here," he said, gesturing toward her and turning, making his way back toward the grill.

"What is this?" she asked, making her way into the backyard where they had their smokers, flat-topped griddles and grills all set up.

"This is the barbecue pit. This is where the magic happens."

"I didn't know that you . . . that you did all this barbecue stuff. Can I serve this at my bar?"

He hadn't thought about it. Not really. They were all set up to basically have a whole barbecue restaurant if they wanted to, but it had never actually occurred to him.

"I mean . . . we could. I would have to train somebody. I can't do it all the time."

Fellow. He did grill almost every day. It was something that he loved to do. It was something that had helped him figure out how to take care of his family. They raised the food, and he knew how to make it. And he knew how to do it well. It mattered to him. It had been a form of therapy in a lot of ways.

But, the idea of sharing it more broadly . . . He wasn't sure. But he was also intrigued.

"I mean, people would pay a lot of money for this."

"We do big grilling like this once a month for all the town halls. Hell, I was planning on doing it for the Christmas party."

"That would be great. A good preview. I mean, you could just do a barbecue special. Whatever you want. You can have a big grilling day, and then we could serve whatever can be saved."

"Freezes pretty good, to be honest. Though I prefer everything to be fresh."

"Sure. But . . . I guess I just didn't really know that this was your thing."

"It's a hobby."

"So with these town hall meetings you . . . make a giant feast for everybody and talk about business?"

"Yep. Bonfire, music. Dancing. I don't dance."

"That's really shocking, Denver. I assume that you were proficient at the electric slide."

"No."

"You did dance at Smokey's."

He could pivot away from this. He didn't have to lean in.

He did anyway.

"That is dancing with a goal, Sheena. And I am a goal-oriented man."

She laughed. "So basically you only dance when you think it might end in sex?"

"Exactly. And nobody on this ranch . . . Not ever. I would never. I have never."

"Interesting," she said. "That is not the general methodology of Four Corners."

"My co-ranchers are happy to muddy the waters. I just prefer not to."

"I'm with you," she said. "It's self-preservation to my mind. I don't need a bunch of local men sniffing around me all the time thinking that I'm available."

Of course. He hadn't really thought about it from that perspective. That it would create a giant headache for her if any of the men she saw on a nightly basis thought they could get lucky.

"I just don't . . . I don't need anything that complicated," he said. "My life is complicated enough."

"Yeah, I guess it would be if you spent all the effort you do keeping connected to everybody that your bastard father ever wronged."

He hadn't thought about it that way either.

That he had a lot of connections, and maybe that was why he felt exhausted. Plus there had been his stint doing the poker circuits out of town. He had to navigate a whole different world then. Figuring out how to be in Las Vegas, when he felt deeply uncomfortable surrounded by neon and concrete.

"Yeah. I guess so."

"My sisters would love to come to the Christmas thing."

"Sure," he said. "The more the merrier. Because it makes me look like my idea was good."

"Walk me through your whole idea."

So he started to tell her about the point behind the Christmas thing, and how it was really a big unveiling of the event center at King's. How they were going to host weddings and corporate parties, birthday parties, vow renewals. All kinds of things.

"I think the barbecue is going to be a great addition. A great idea. It's definitely something you should push."

"I guess I'm going to add that to the docket tonight too."

He had a good team. That was the thing. So if he had to spend a little bit more time manning the grill, it was totally possible to do it. He wasn't necessarily a master at sides, but his sister-in-law baked bread, and made all kinds of other delicious things.

And it was sort of a business, so she knew how to charge for it, and had the necessary approved kitchen to do it.

The hour or so that Sheena had come early went by quickly, and he was surprised when it was time to load up for the meeting.

They got all the barbecue put in the back of his truck. "Can I drive you over?" he asked.

And he decided to ignore that it felt a little like asking her on a date. Because he had never actually asked a woman on a proper date.

His life was kind of fucked, actually.

It was a weird and inconvenient time to sit with that.

He asked women he met in public to go back to hotel rooms with him. He didn't ask them on dates.

Especially on the poker circuit. He had lost hold of himself there sometimes.

And if he felt that tug toward hellfire, it was only because as much as he was always walking a line in his life, he had perhaps fallen on the wrong side of it most often then.

But he had been away from Pyrite Falls. And in many ways, away from that need to perform that he was a decent human being.

Yeah. That had been . . . It had been a whole thing.

A lot of drinking. A lot of sex. Women he knew that he would never run into again. It had made him feel free. He didn't feel the weight of his reputation, and he didn't feel that nagging sense of responsibility that he had to the community back at home.

Two weekends a month and for major tournaments, he'd been in Vegas. And no one at the ranch had any idea what he'd really been up to. It had been his escape.

It had also been how he'd cared for that community. The money he'd taken in at the poker table had set him up for life.

What happened in Vegas really did feel like it might stay there.

Except he hadn't counted on carrying the shame back with him.

That he was able to write a story that turned him into a version of himself he wasn't entirely sure that he liked.

And in that sense, he had given himself a clear view that he might not be as different than his dad as he wished he was.

And maybe that was actually the real problem. The thing that kept him from getting too close to anyone here.

It was better. Better to hold himself back and hold himself accountable.

"Well, come on. Time for you to attend your first town hall."

Chapter Seven

SHE HAD NO idea what she had been expecting, but this wasn't it. When they pulled up to the quadrant of Four Corners that was known as Sullivan's Point, there was a surplus of food already set up on long tables out in front of the barn. There were big propane heaters with lively flames set up around the place, designed to keep everybody warm. There were also musicians carrying instruments over to an area that had been fashioned into a small stage.

There was a big bonfire roaring off to the side with chairs around it, and there was a table with solo cups full of beer.

"This is something," she said.

"Yeah. Typically, we try to get to the meeting as quickly as possible. All the families, and all the ranch hands, plus some members of the community, come to hear new orders of business, but mostly it's an excuse to party. To stay connected."

"Wow."

"Yeah."

It was strange, because she couldn't really imagine Denver being social on this level. It was interesting. Definitely a good way to keep everybody connected. She could see the point of it when you lived in a place this big. But she also had to wonder if it wasn't something that suited him entirely. It probably seemed like extra. Extra connections, extra work.

Maybe it was presumptuous of her to guess that. But she felt like she identified with him. Felt like she understood him.

Maybe.

"This isn't really your scene, is it?"

She didn't look at him when she asked. She could feel him look at her. "How did you guess?"

"It wouldn't be mine."

She could tell him that she wondered if perhaps their experiences as reluctant heads of the household had turned them into a similar type. But she had a feeling she didn't really need to say it. Because of all the people, Denver had actually seen some of it.

Even though they had never spoken during all that time.

He had seen the house. He had seen her the day that she lost her dad. Dry-eyed.

There were some deep things about her that Denver King might know better than anybody else.

So perhaps it was just self-defense that she wanted to believe there was maybe something equally real that she knew about him. When she couldn't be entirely certain that was true.

"I show up, though. I make food. I do the thing."

"Don't we all."

"This way." Denver touched a spot low on her back, and she jolted. She hadn't meant to react. But his touch was like an electric wire. Something she really was not used to. Having a reaction to a man that she couldn't control.

What was the point of that? She didn't see the point in any kind of association with a man that didn't simply . . . give her a nice evening, and let her go on her way without ever thinking about the guy again.

This was . . . She didn't like it. It was one thing to think he was good-looking. It was another to not be able to control a frazzled response to him just because he had put his hand lightly on her clothed skin.

"Sorry," he said, his tone mild, but a little bit too knowing.

She couldn't help but look at him. She saw low, banked fire in his eyes. Dammit. He had felt it too.

He had touched her and felt that exact same over-the-top jolt that she had.

That was inconvenient as hell.

That she knew it. He could feel whatever he wanted to. She just didn't want him sharing it with her.

She moved away from him, and when they walked into the room, it was already full. His siblings were there, and she suddenly felt a little bit awkward coming in with him. Like she was the one meeting the family. Like Abigail had just been talking about doing with Alejandro. Even though this was not that. Not even close.

Still, they found themselves having to squeeze close to each other in two folding chairs at the end of his family line.

Sawyer Garrett, who she knew by sight, though not really as a person, made his way up to the front of the room then.

"All right. We have a couple of items of business today. First we're going to have Fia King come up and give a report on the farm store, then we will have a discussion about the dividends for those who invested. And after that, Denver King has an item of business to introduce, with guest speaker Sheena Patrick."

Hearing her name in this context, connected to this place, made a zip of discomfort blossom in her midsection. Or maybe that was just stage fright. Not that she would have ever said she was the kind of person that got stage fright.

She did find herself more interested than she would've thought in the business overall. It was interesting to hear how they ran the place. Interesting to hear everybody speak their own piece. Sawyer, for his part, seemed to be the showrunner. And he disseminated information with neutral clarity, which made it easy to see why he was the mouthpiece for the place.

She found herself curious. Not just about the facts on how they formed this place but also the more personal aspect of it. Especially knowing what she did about Denver. That he found this kind of thing difficult.

Too soon, it was their turn to speak.

She followed him up to the raised platform at the front of the barn.

"Hi," she said, into the microphone they had set up there. "I'm Sheena Patrick. I live a few miles out of town. Most of you know me because until recently I was tending bar at Smokey's." She proceeded to present the business idea, and then Denver came in and talked about the logistics, that he was financing it and that his portion of the profits would be going back into the collective. That information surprised her.

"If there are any strong objections to the bar, speak now," said Denver.

There was a ripple in the room, and people talked to each other, but nobody spoke up in objection.

"Then we consider this a done deal," he said. "The bar is going to at least have a soft open around the time of the Christmas party."

"Do we get discounts?" one of the ranch hands asked.

"Definitely," said Sheena. "And I'll probably have a punch card system of some kind. Or maybe even a membership. It seems to me that the people who live on the ranch ought to be able to use all the facilities."

That earned her a pretty broad approval.

And then it was over. Just like that. Painless. She didn't know why she had thought it would be difficult. Maybe because she wasn't used to people just talking to her. She was more of an acquired taste than an instant delight. She knew that. But maybe it was just that the idea was good enough that it didn't matter it had come from her.

When the meeting was over a few people came up to talk to both of them, but not many. She had a feeling both she and Denver gave off vibes that suggested they didn't exactly want to spend the whole evening chatting it up with everybody.

It was almost funny.

He gestured with his head toward the door, and she went with him.

They slipped out into a darker corner of the outside area. The sun had gone down since the meeting had started. "Let's get some food."

"So I'm curious," she said. "How exactly did you guys get together to form this collective? When did it happen? How?"

"Oh. I never really had to tell the story before. You know a little bit about Gus McCloud, right?"

She shook her head. "Not really.

"His dad tried to burn them alive. True story. So, as much of an asshole as our dads were, it wasn't like that."

"Good God," she said.

"Yep. But fast forward, and Seamus McCloud went after one of Gus's younger brothers. Gus beat the hell out of him and the guy ran off. There were rumors for a lot of years that Gus actually killed him. I think Gus got some mileage out of that. But I always knew he hadn't done it. Because I know what it's like. To have that dad that's monster enough you know you have to make sure you aren't him. But anyway. Around that time, everything went down with my dad. When your dad got shot and killed, when he got arrested. Then it was easy to take control of the ranch, and once he got out of prison, I had made money in the poker circuit. And that was when I bought them out. But it was around that time when both of them were removed from the equation that we got together and decided that we needed to do something different with the place. That we needed to make a change. Back in the eighteen hundreds, Four Corners was founded as a collective. But over the years, it had splintered. And there were reasons for that. The Kings were always doing things their own way. They were always doing things under the radar. Making profits they weren't sharing, all of that."

"That's why you're doing it the way you're doing it now."

"Yeah. Part of me wanted to keep it from everybody to avoid the headache, but at the end of the day, it doesn't really feel right. Not given the history of everything. You know, the saloon and all of that."

"Your great-great-great, whatever, grandpa was out there with prostitutes and poker games?"

"He was indeed. I don't know. We were always the black sheep. And I guess in our own way we've all taken it upon ourselves to try and lessen the blight a little bit."

"You've done it quite a lot, I would say."

"But you still don't trust me."

"Listen. I trust you as much as I trust anybody. It's just that I don't trust anybody. No one but myself. That's life, as far as I can tell. Every man for himself."

"That's definitely how I've seen it. Always."

"It's unavoidable. At least, when you have the experiences we do."

"Fair."

"But still, you decided that the way forward, the way to redeem yourself was to do all of this. Even though you clearly don't love it."

"I do," he said.

And she could hear the fractured honesty in that statement. There was something that he did like about this, even if he didn't know how quite to be involved in it. That made her feel a little bit sad because it reminded her of how she felt earlier when talking to her sisters.

She hadn't asked to feel feelings for Denver King. It was annoying.

"My sisters got out. I'm glad of that. Honestly. I'm glad that they are not stuck here."

"You don't like Pyrite Falls, do you?"

"I don't have any reason to. I don't dislike it, I guess. It's more what it represents. Like you said, your siblings have spent a very long time trying to undo some of what your dad did. I didn't want my sisters to have to do that. And I'm not saying that you wanted your siblings to do it, or that it's somehow worse that they're trying. But I just . . . I wanted them to go live lives that had nothing to do with our dad. I wanted them to get to be themselves. Whatever that looks like. And honestly, if they are our father's daughters, then that's up to them. But I didn't want it to be a decision that was made for them."

"We've spent a lot of time living in decisions that other people made for us."

He said it low and slow. And there was deep truth to that. Just deep fucking truth.

"Yeah. But you know, there's no call wasting time being mad about it."

"I agree."

"You just have to keep moving."

"Also agree."

They looked at each other. She could honestly say that she had never known anybody who had the potential to understand her quite the way that Denver King did. Yes, he had been involved in some of the stuff that their dad had done, but if she had been older she probably would have been too. The truth was, if she had been older, not only would she have likely been

involved in helping out with drug running, but her dad probably would've pimped her out. That was just true. He hadn't
given a single shit when one of his friends had . . .

Men had tried it with her. Her dad didn't care. She had to
take care of herself. Bottom line.

If he could have made money selling her body, he would've
done it.

And she wouldn't have even really known it was wrong.
That was the really screwed up thing. The messed up part about
the lives that they lead. He knew that.

She knew it. It messed with your moral compass. And then
in the end, you couldn't really afford to have the same morality as the people around you that had grown up in safe, loving
homes. You had to have the kind of morality that sustained you.

Everybody didn't start at the same starting line in life.

That was why she felt kinship to Denver. Not resentment.

And sure, maybe that was tangled up in a lack of trust. But
she didn't especially trust anybody.

She took a bite of the food on her plate. "This really is
delicious."

And she pondered what it said about him. The way that he
had learned to barbecue. Because he hadn't just spent the last
few years serving up the bare minimum to sustain the people
around him. He had learned how to do it well.

He was reaching for something that they hadn't been given
inherently.

She understood that too.

"Thank you," she said. "For all the financial assistance that
you've given us. Because you know you're why my sisters got
out. They're at college, and it is because of you. My sister Abigail graduated. She has a house. She has a good boyfriend." She
winced.

"What?"

"I hesitate to say that any man is good. Based on the testimony of a woman who's sleeping with him."

He huffed a laugh. "That's probably a good call."

"Yeah. I'm known for those."

"I'm not comfortable taking thanks for all that. The world is just a big messed up tangle. People who deserve better get worse. People who deserve worse go off into the sunset and live whatever the hell lives they want. If I can do anything to balance the scales of all that bullshit, then I want to."

"Has anybody ever told you that you are a saint for what you do?" She looked at him, at his profile. He was so damned handsome.

"No. Nobody has ever said that I'm a saint, Sheena."

"People have said it to me. That I'm a saint for raising those girls. For taking care of them when my dad didn't. Which is pretty damned hilarious, the idea of anybody calling me a saint. I certainly haven't gone out of my way to live perfectly. Mostly, it just feels so wrong. The worst description ever. I have never felt like what I was doing for my sisters was some kind of higher calling. It's just sort of the mantle that settles over your shoulders, right? Like everybody has a burden to carry, and that one's mine. And it isn't that I don't want to do it, or that I feel put upon, or whatever. It's just . . ."

"There's not another choice," Denver said.

"Exactly. I had a couple teachers . . . My sisters' teachers say to me that I did a good job with them. But everybody does the job they do with their own lives, right? We had a shitty dad, but he didn't have the final say in who we were. And I did my best, but they're not great because of me. I just don't like . . . I don't like people acting like I'm somehow better than somebody else because I did what people ought to do in that situation. Right? That's what you want to do."

"Yeah," he said, and he looked at her, his eyes glittering. "Exactly that. I get why people don't understand the gambling. People think that it makes me a lot like my dad. But mostly, his money was dirty. It was dirty money, and it was dirty money that I used to play with. I could make something out of it. Something better. I've invested that money in King's Crest. In the future of Four Corners. I've invested in my father's victims. And it isn't because I'm good. Any more than gambling is something I do because I'm bad. It just is. If you have the ability to make things better and you don't, then you aren't any better than the shitheads that came before you."

She lifted up her solo cup. "To not being saints."

"I'll drink to that."

They both tipped their beer cups back. "I'm okay with being a sinner, to be honest," said Sheena.

"I heard somewhere that we all were anyway."

She laughed. "You've been to church, King?"

"Nope," he said.

"Me either. But I used to sign my own permission slip to go to the Bible story hour when those people came by the school."

"Really?"

"Yes. Two things—school was boring, and the second thing was that I figured I had to do something about my immortal soul. Since nobody else was going to."

"I can relate to that."

"So this whole thing is going to be great," she said.

"Yeah," he said, seeming grateful for the change in subject.

That was when a whole group of people came over to them. A gaggle of redheads, in fact. Redheads that she knew to be the Sullivan sisters, because as a bartender, she did tend to absorb basic information about everybody around her. There were also several tall, good-looking men with them. The most recognizable to her was Gideon Payne, because she had gone to high school with him in Mapleton, and he had been a legend and a half. A football star, who had then gone on into the military. You couldn't go to Mapleton High and not know who he was. Even though he had graduated when she had been a freshman, she had seen his trophies lining the halls.

It was Fia King who spoke first. "I think it's a great idea," she said. "Of course, Landry had filled me in on the details before the meeting today, but I think it's going to be really fun. In fact, I think I'm going to like to spend time there."

"Hey," said Landry. "I thought we were cool."

"Eh," said Fia.

"You had my baby," he said. "Twice."

"Yeah, yeah."

"Ignore them," said one of the younger Sullivan sisters . . . Quinn, maybe? She had trouble with the younger girls. She knew their names: Quinn, Rory and Alaina. But she had trouble remembering who was who.

"Yes," said Denver. "Definitely ignore them. Glad to know that I have all your support with what I do with my own money," said Denver.

"Get over it," Fia said. "It's a collective, whether you want it to be or not. But luckily, that means that there's extra help."

Extra help. Sheena really didn't know what to make of that.

"I have my own crew," she said. "I am contributing to the cost of some of this."

"I didn't dream otherwise," said Fia. "But you know, if you do something on Four Corners, you get all the worker bees."

"Well that's . . . nice."

"We are going to need all the worker bees' hands on deck for the big Christmas shindig. That's going to take a lot of manpower." Denver had an intense look about him. She understood. She didn't need it explained to her. He felt so responsible for all of these things. And it was unbearable.

It was why it was so obnoxious when people tried to tell you that you were good. She was going to make a note not to tell him that again. Because it didn't feel like you were being good. It didn't feel like you were being caring. It felt like you had been given a mission. To walk through swampland. To struggle through enemy territory. It was like being conscripted into a war. One you didn't choose, but one you had to engage in.

And she knew that he was still pushing, struggling toward victory. She knew it, because so was she.

"I'm willing to help with that," she said. "As much as possible. Between the two things. But I don't have another job right now, and my sisters aren't here, so honestly, I can work around the clock."

He gave her a hard, indecipherable look. "I don't need you working around the clock."

"But I can," she said.

"Appreciated. But as you can see, we've got plenty of manpower. And then some." He looked past her, and she turned. Where she saw all of the ranch hands, the Garretts, the McClouds. Yeah. All right. They had a robust team. But there was no reason that she couldn't help.

Because it was another one of those burdens. Another one of those things. She had gotten involved with what was happening here, and she really wanted to help. Wanted to be part of it.

Or maybe *want* was a strong word. There was a need to. To prove herself. To make herself useful. They chatted for a few more moments with the Sullivans, and then she and Denver mutually moved closer to the fire. Closer to blending in with the rest of the group. Even though she had a sense that Denver never quite folded in.

She took another sip of beer, and then the back of her boot heel hit a rock, and she stumbled. Denver reached forward, grabbing hold of her arm and steadying her. His touch was like fire. His hands were rough, big. And it was far too easy to imagine what it would be like to have them on her body.

"Careful," he said.

"Sure," she responded, trying not to sound all breathless. She didn't do breathless. It wasn't in her repertoire. She was the one that left men breathless.

Though, he seemed like he was breathing pretty hard.

"Hey."

The voice, unfamiliar and not from her or Denver, felt intrusive as it pierced the moment.

She turned to see a man near her height, wearing a white cowboy hat and pretty damned nice boots, standing there smiling at her. "You want to dance?"

She could. She could dance with him. Maybe she could even let him take her home. Maybe it would do something to rid her of all the strange, conflicting feelings that she felt for Denver. It would be safer. Safer than ruminating on the heat left behind by his touch. On the way his own breathing had grown more labored.

Yeah. It would be safer than all of that.

"Sorry. My dance card is full." She gave him her best, charming smile that also served as the punctuation at the end of the sentence. There was no opening for him to ask again. And thankfully, he took her at her word.

"Maybe next time," the cowboy said, looking between her and Denver.

"No need to turn them down on my account," said Denver.

"Oh Denver, I don't do anything on account of a man."

"I believe it."

"Actually, I best be heading home. I'm meeting Manny bright and early."

"All right. I'll drive you back to your truck."

"I don't want to make you leave early. I bet I can get a ride."

"I'll take you back."

They walked away from the bonfire, and it was interesting to her, the way the crowd parted slightly when he walked by, when it seemed to fold in slightly around other people who walked on through.

"You scare people," she said as they got into his truck.

When the door closed, and they were shrouded in the quiet of the cab, her own heartbeat began to go faster. Suggesting that she herself might be a little bit afraid. But it wasn't the same kind of fear that she had just witnessed.

Hell, she was afraid of herself.

She had to minimize the bad mistakes she made in her life. Because her dad had made so many on her behalf. So many that she was still paying for. And she knew that Denver understood that. Knew that he understood the importance of keeping her personal tab just a little bit lighter.

"My dad scared people. I inherited his face."

"And his reputation."

"Yep. I'm a gambler, you know. Just like my old man."

"Not at all like your old man. You're not gambling with other people's money. You're gambling for it."

"Yeah. And people do know that. In the sense that I think everybody trusts that if I was bad news Sawyer Garrett would've had me out on my ass. And if not Sawyer, then Daughtry."

"Yeah. How does that work for Daughtry? Being a cop here, with your dad's reputation?"

"Tell you the truth, I think him getting that badge was the easiest and quickest way for him to declare that he was one of the good guys to all the people here. And maybe the only thing they would believe."

"But that wasn't your path."

"No. It's admirable. But it certainly wasn't going to pay back all those debts."

"No. Of course not."

"Daughtry didn't do it to get rich. He was there too."

"I know."

"You were too young to see all that," Denver said, as he started the truck engine and began to drive them back toward King's Crest.

"Can we not do this? It's sort of the same as being called a saint. I was too young for a lot of the shit that my dad put me through. But he didn't care. Because he didn't care about anybody but himself. I don't need you expressing regret over my lost childhood. It just feels . . . pointless."

"Even so, I hate that you saw your old man dead."

"I don't. If I hadn't seen it, I wouldn't have believed it to be true. I would've thought, all those years, that he was going to come stumbling back up to the house. That we weren't really free. Free of him and all the lowlifes that he brought with him. When I tell you that I don't mourn my dad, believe me. And I don't regret seeing him that way. Cold to the touch. Lifeless. Because I knew. I saw the blood drain out of him. I knew."

She knew that it sounded fierce. That it sounded cold. She didn't care. Life had made her cold on that score. Warmth, softness, they were luxuries for other people. For different people. It was part and parcel of the burden that had been put on her back when she was born to Dan Patrick. Everybody had their different issues that their parents kicked onto them at birth. For some people, it was an issue with their body image. A need to overachieve.

For her, it was something else altogether. A little bit darker. A little bit more sinister. But everybody had their burden.

So she just got hard enough, strong enough to carry the one that she'd been given. What was the alternative? Lie down to feel sorry for yourself? That was hardly going to save you.

"I can understand that. I wish that it had been my dad that day. Instead, he went to prison for a while. And now he's a free man. I'm not afraid of him coming back though."

"You'd kill him if you had to," she said, as the truck rumbled and rolled over the rough dirt road. "I know you would."

"You're damned right about that. I absolutely would kill him if I had to."

Because Denver was all about balancing the scales. And if he thought that his dad had come back to continue to hurt people, if he heard that his dad was still out there hurting people, she had a feeling that he would take it upon himself to put a stop to it. Because he would feel like that was his burden to bear.

They pulled up to the house, and she was relieved. Felt like she could let out a breath that she'd been holding.

He killed the engine, and she tumbled out of the truck as quickly as possible, because she didn't want to be sitting in there with him when the silence descended. When they were left with nothing but the pop of the engine in the stillness that came at the end of a long night.

Because she didn't trust herself to make the right decision. Because if he touched her, or so much as looked at her with the intent to put his mouth on hers, she wasn't actually sure what she would do.

She didn't lose control. That wasn't who she was.

Everything she did was deliberate. Whether she chose to let off steam or not.

And here she was, feeling precariously close to an edge that she had never stood on before.

She didn't like it.

So she gulped in a big breath of the cold night air, and began to walk to her car before he said goodbye.

"Sheena," he said.

"Good night," she called back.

And she didn't stop. Didn't turn back to look at him. Instead, she got in her car and drove away. And she knew full well that what she'd done had been for the sanity of both of them. Even if he didn't realize it.

Chapter Eight

DENVER KING WAS experiencing a moment of pure joy. A rare moment. There had been so much construction going on, so many changes, on King's Crest over the past few months that it was a rare day indeed when he and his brothers were all together, riding their horses at a breakneck pace across the fields.

But that's what he was doing today. The air was cold, biting into his face, and the feeling of the horse's hooves pounding on the ground was like a sacred drumbeat that resonated in his soul.

Sheena hated this place, and he could understand why. But for him, he would always be here. Not just because he felt obligated to the people that his father had hurt. Because he genuinely loved this land.

Yes, his family had founded this place on lies. But that wasn't what he was building off of. He was building off of a love for the place. He was building a sense of family around it. Creating a new definition for it.

He was building something. Because he refused to spend his life carrying around all this weight without doing something good with it. Something worthwhile. Because it couldn't all be a long slog up the hill. At least, he hoped not.

He tugged back on the horse's reins, and turned them in a wide circle, and his brothers followed suit. They were laughing, grinning. And this, this was the legacy. As far as he was concerned.

This was the one thing he'd done that he was truly proud of. Family dinners, and his brothers smiling. His sister having a family of her own. All of his brothers were married now, or about to be. Some of them were fathers, some with babies on the way.

He was the patriarch. He had put himself in that position. That was maybe the one thing he disagreed on with Sheena.

The thing they'd done to show up for their family, it was active. He could understand the way she felt about it. He could understand why she didn't want to take any credit for it. It wasn't truly credit that he was after. He felt like it was good to remember that something like this was a choice. A choice you had to make every day. It was the only thing that kept his head above water sometimes. Because if this was a choice, that meant he had control. If this was a choice, then that meant he wouldn't accidentally find himself waking up one day in the image of his father.

"When you think you'll be done?" Justice asked.

He looked over at his brother from his position on the horse. "What?"

"With the changes here. The expansion. You've been head down and running flat out for a couple of years now. And now there's this thing with Sheena. And it's dovetailing with the big Christmas thing . . . I'm just wondering, when are you going to rest?"

He thought about the years spent playing poker. Traveling between here and Vegas. Putting in a rancher's day's work at King's Crest, and then putting in a gambler's weekend.

Hard drinking. Nights of anonymous sex.

Waking up in the morning stained with shame. Coming right on back. The hard work like a baptism. An absolution.

The evidence that his family was doing well, evidence that maybe he wasn't so bad after all.

"When I'm dead," he said to his brother.

Justice didn't laugh.

"Seriously. Life is for living. Not resting."

"Some would argue that rest is part of living."

"Listen to you," he said. "A bastion of mental health."

"I don't know. Maybe just enjoying life a little more than I used to."

"Well, some of us here don't have sex on tap." He looked around at his brothers. "Okay. Only me. Just me."

"Denver . . ."

"Hellfire," said Denver. "Is this an intervention?"

"It's not an intervention," said Daughtry. "Just an observation that you're working harder than usual. Which is really saying something."

Genuinely, though. What was the alternative? Sitting around with his thoughts? No, thanks.

"Actually, it's a good time to mention that I'm considering selling barbecue. Officially. Like at Sheena's bar."

"Another thing?" Landry asked.

"Hey. You had a baby. Why can't I have a barbecue?"

"Not the same," said Daughtry.

"Why not? This is the kind of thing that married people always do. You can't stand me not doing things the same way. The changes that I'm making don't seem valuable to you because you think that life begins and ends with . . . love. Whatever. I'm good. I'm thrilled you and Fia have your little boy, Landry. Love that you have your girl. Arizona's babies are great. I don't want kids. I don't want . . . all that. This place is my kid. *You* were all my kids."

"We are not that much younger than you."

"It's the responsibility. And I'm not saying that you all didn't feel it. I am just saying that . . . the buck stops with me. Let's be honest about that. Nothing wrong with it. It's just a roll of the dice. Birth order."

"We are all adults," Justice said. "If you hadn't noticed."

"Some of us are very new to adulthood," Daughtry said, looking at Justice.

Justice was in his thirties. But Daughtry meant philosophically, since until very recently Justice's idea of a good time had been getting drunk and having anonymous sex. He was newly reformed.

"I didn't ask to be insulted."

"And I didn't ask to be born," Denver said. "But here we are. Anyway. None of you need to worry about me. Maybe you just need to accept that my idea of being finished looks different than what you think. That we are here, on this land, after all the bullshit our dad pulled, to me, that's kind of being finished. Arriving. I feel fucking healed by it."

"You sound like it," Landry said.

"And here I was just thinking that today was one of those rare peaceful days."

It was still peaceful. Honestly, he didn't mind his brothers worrying about him. That felt like something in and of itself. A bit of a win.

He looked at the green mountains, all pine. At the blue of the sky, so bright even in November that you would be forgiven for thinking it was warm outside. But no. Yeah. This was one of those rare wins that hadn't been a gamble.

They finished their ride out on the mountains, and by the time they got back to King's Crest, it was dark. He wondered if Sheena would still be on-site. He had said that he was going to check out the work that had been done today, but it was a little bit later than he had anticipated.

While he and his brothers put the horses away, they were discussing dinner.

"There's plenty of stuff to reheat," he said. "If you guys want to come over tonight."

"Fia cooked," said Landry.

"Bix did not cook," said Daughtry. "So I'll text her and see if she wants to come by."

Justice grinned. "I think Rue had plans."

He would take one out of the three. He already knew that Arizona was busy. It was why she hadn't come out onto the ranch with them today; they had taken their kids down to the coast. Even though the youngest of the kids was just a tiny baby.

He figured that parents were entitled to do whatever ridiculousness they felt like doing. And if they wanted to make baby's first beach trip before the kid could hold its head up, that was up to them.

It was better than what their parents had done to them, anyway.

"Great. I have to go check in on the construction for the bar. But feel free to go rummaging through the fridge and heating some things up."

"Will do," said Daughtry.

He walked out of the barn, and down the path that led to the old gambling hall.

There were no vehicles out front, save Sheena's car. He could see a light on inside that he assumed was one of those work lights.

He walked straight on through the door without knocking or signaling his presence. To find her perched up on a ladder, holding paint chips up.

"There's no point doing that in the dark."

She screeched, and grabbed hold of the top of the ladder. And then when she looked down at him, her eyes were furious. "Dumbass," she said. "You could've killed me."

"I didn't mean to startle you. But obviously your reflexes are good enough that I could not have killed you."

"For God's sake," she said.

She started to climb down the ladder.

"Walk me through today," he said.

"Nice to see you too. Really missed you."

"Did you want to engage in small talk? Last night it didn't seem like you did."

And that was a dumbass thing to say. It really was, because she had probably done them both a favor by leaving quickly last night. No. No probably about it. She had.

Because electricity had been crackling between them, and while he was fond of electricity, he preferred it contained. In wires. In a wall. Not . . . whatever this was. The sparking, deadly overflow that seemed to want to get everywhere.

It was on another level. Something he had never experienced before, and he was not in a space to be experiencing heretofore unexperienced levels of attraction.

"What did you all do today?"

"We made plans," she said. "Basically, we went over everything with a fine-tooth comb and tried to figure out what all we needed. We are going to have to open the walls and completely rethink the whole electrical situation. It looks like somebody added the system, maybe forty years ago, but it's not in good shape."

"Doesn't surprise me. I imagine all of it was done without permits."

"Yes," she said. "Which is another issue. We are going to have to pull permits, and while Manny has pretty good relationships with the county, that can still take a long time."

"Don't worry about it. I'll make a call."

"You can just do that?"

"Yeah. I can." It was complicated. The son of the guy who ran the building permits department at the county had gotten involved with his dad at some point, and he had been part of Denver's restitution scheme. And while some might look at that and say that it was akin to paying someone off, Denver disagreed. Because he hadn't sought to make things right with the guy to try and get something in return. It was just that the end result was they had a fine relationship. And to his mind, if that made things slightly more functional for the whole ranch, for the whole family, then there was nothing wrong with that.

"We started taking down the molding over here."

He looked over and scowled. He liked that molding. And, no, he couldn't say that he had any thoughts about it before, but now that she had gone and taken it down without talking to him, he felt damned annoyed.

"You can't go doing demolition without running things by me."

"It was hardly demolition," she said.

He walked over to where the ornate molding had been pulled off of that corner between the wall and the ceiling.

"I didn't agree to let you compromise the historical structural integrity of the place."

"I didn't realize you were a historian. This is an old-ass building that hasn't been in use for years. Anything that I do to it is going to be better than what it was before."

"That's what you think," he said. And as comebacks went, it was kind of a lame one. But this felt kind of lame.

He grabbed the ladder that she had been on, and dragged it over to the far wall, past a fair amount of debris, not bothering to shove it out of his path, just sort of treading on top of it, and brought the ladder up against the other wall. He picked up a piece of the molding, and a hammer and nails, and climbed up to the top of the latter, where he positioned the molding, even though it was a rather long piece, and it was unwieldy, and started to hammer it back into place.

"Are you kidding me? We spent forever on that today. You'll note that none of it is damaged, and that's because we took such a long damned time with it because we didn't want to destroy your molding and . . . Are you for real?"

"You have to ask," he said.

"So what is this going to be? One step forward and two steps back every damned day."

"How is this two steps back?"

She flung her arms wide. "I don't know. But that's some bullshit."

"I'm letting you use a historical building."

"You told me that it had to be in a historical building. I wanted to do a new build."

"There's no point. It cost too much money."

"Restoring this place isn't exactly going to be cheap. It's not . . . Whatever you're thinking, this is going to be complicated. The place is basically a shell," she said.

"It has good bones. More than good bones. This is nice molding."

"Listen, I love the idea of it looking like an old saloon. I do. But some of the stuff is just old. And it's not cool old."

"There is no such thing as not-cool old," he said.

"That just isn't true."

"He swung the hammer, bringing it down hard as he tacked the molding back into place on that far wall.

"There. That's better."

"You are such a control freak. You can't control every minute thing happening on the ranch. The Sullivans had a good point when they were saying to you that you're going to need help. You gotta try to get the Christmas thing going, and now you're thinking of doing barbecue—"

"That isn't fair to use the barbecue thing against me when it was your idea."

She sighed. "It isn't using it against you. It's being honest about what all you have on your plate. And believe me, Denver, I am a champion martyr. So I am the last person on earth seeking to call anybody out on their rather toxic behavior on this score. But even I recognize you are biting off a fair amount more than you can chew."

"It's not up to you to decide what I can chew or not chew."

"All right, so you're just going to control this, and control the Christmas thing and make all the food, and and *and*. What aren't you in charge of?"

"Everything I'm in charge of turns out okay."

"Yeah, but you don't have to be in charge of everything. The other people around you are good at what they do too."

"How would you know?" That sounded petulant. He felt a little bit petulant. She didn't know him. All right, maybe they had had a fair, honest conversation last night at the town hall, but that didn't mean that they knew each other. He didn't know what she did when she was alone. What kind of TV shows she watched, what kinds of books she read—if she read. He didn't know what kind of man she preferred to date, didn't know what her favorite pasta was. What her favorite food was. There was a long list of things he didn't know about Sheena Patrick, and she didn't know a damned thing about him. So her standing there acting like she had some deep insight into his life was just insulting.

What they knew about each other was this big intense lore that surrounded both of their lives. The same things that every damned person in town knew. And maybe, maybe, they understood each other better than the average person. Because their similar circumstances had left them with some of the same responsibilities. "This is how I live my life. This is what I do. I don't need you to tell me suddenly that I'm doing it wrong," he said.

"The problem is, you're up in my business telling me that I'm doing it wrong, King. And that is creating some issues."

"This is my ranch," he said.

"And my business plan."

And unspoken was the fact that he felt like he owed her something. And also that she felt like she owed him something. And the whole thing was a big tangle of obligation and pride that he had a feeling would only get worse if he and Sheena really locked horns over it.

"For heaven's sake," she said. "I guess that I need to consult you on what we ought to do with all these weird things we found in the back."

"Those might be family heirlooms," he said.

"Somehow I don't think so," she said.

"Why do you think you know?"

"You are so stubborn," she said, turning and walking from the room. He climbed down from the ladder and went after her.

"I'm stubborn," he said.

"I am also stubborn," she shot back. "I don't mean it as an insult. But it sure makes you a bastard to deal with."

"Yeah. Well. I never claimed otherwise."

"Fine." They walked down the dusty hall, and she flung open the door to one of the back rooms. "Be careful. I wouldn't be surprised if there were nests of mice living in here."

"You think baby mice are going to bother me?" he asked.

"True story, one time my sister Whitney found a bunch of baby mice."

"Is this going to be a heartwarming tale about a young girl finding pets?"

"Gross. Well, she thought that they were in need of attention. Orphaned and alone. She bathed them."

"She bathed the baby mice?"

"She did."

"How did that go?"

"Not well, Denver. Not well. Anyway, I have a little bit of an aversion to the things now. I know that I hear them rustling around in here."

"Charming."

The room was dim, the glow of the work light in the living room barely making its way in there, so he pulled his cell phone out and turned on the flashlight. She took out her own and did the same, and they rummaged around. "Some of this is cool," he said, looking at an old wooden cabinet.

"Sure. But it's decrepit."

"That seems like a harsh take."

Sheena shrugged. "I'm harsh."

"All right. Well there's . . . Holy hell."

"What? Did you find the baby mice?"

"No."

He paused in front of what looked to be a whole line of taxidermic animals in clothes. "This is a horror show."

"What?" She came over to where he was. "Oh my gosh," she shouted. "No. It's a nightmare."

"I wonder who did this."

"One of your ancestors was a serial killer," she said.

He bent down and picked up what looked like it had been—in life—a woodchuck. It was wearing a three-piece suit. "No," he said.

"This is wrong. It's disgusting. Horrifying," she shrieked.

"I have so many questions. I will never get the answers to them, because no one in my family spoke to each other long enough to pass stories down."

"You cannot tell me that you want to keep these."

"Hell yes, I do. Can you imagine them up on shelves around an axe throwing bar? That would be really funny."

"Ugh," she said. "So morbid. And unfortunately so correct."

"I think that polecat is supposed to be a schoolmarm."

"Oh, whoever did this is in hell for sure," she said.

"But you didn't do it," he pointed out. "And it seems like it would be a misuse of the animals to just . . . throw them away."

"We can give them a Viking funeral," she said. "Burn them on a pyre."

"Come on now, you can see it," he said. "Jaunty, dressed-up animals. Like Disneyland."

"Those are animatronic," she said. "Not corpses."

"As far as you know. I did hear that there were actual human bones on a ride at Disneyland."

She looked over at him, her green eyes glittering in the light. "Are you a big Disney adult, Denver?"

"No. I've never been. But I do like to collect trivia."

"Really?"

It was true. He liked an odd fact. It was something that had helped him out at the poker tables. A distraction. For the people around them. Seemed like it worked with Sheena, too, who was being a little bit less confrontational now, for whatever it was worth.

"Is this just how it's going to be?" she asked.

"What?"

"You come in ridiculous, we fight and then . . . I dunno somehow we're not fighting anymore."

"I am never ridiculous," he said.

"Not true."

"You don't know me," he said.

"But I do," she returned.

"You don't," he said. "You know a few things about me. Frankly, the same things that everybody does."

"Now I know that you know a weird amount about Disney."

"I know a weird amount about a lot of things. I like to make chatter at the poker table."

"Uh-huh. And now I know a little bit more about you. A boon for me, I think."

"Right. A boon for you. What exactly do you think you're going to do with this information?"

"I don't know, good to have. I've been a bartender for years, Denver. Hoarding information is part of what I do."

She bent down and picked up one of the animals. She turned it over, frowning deeply. "This is so . . . I mean it's sadly awesome."

"You changed your tune."

"I'm changeable." She looked up at him, the critter—dressed in overalls—clutched tightly in her hand.

He leaned in—to get a better look at what the hell that abomination was—and caught the scent of her. Spice and bourbon. Warm and intoxicating.

All the breath rushed out of his body. He felt like he was being gripped by a feral thing.

She was beautiful, yes, but there was something more. Something that made him burn. He couldn't rightly explain.

What he wanted was to lean in and take her in his arms. Taste her. Touch her.

And then he'd have to see her tomorrow. And the next day. And the next.

Pretty sweet deal if the sex was good.

She was Sheena.

She'd been hurt by the King family already. And he'd be damned if he was going to cause any more harm.

So he moved away from her. Fast.

"Just run any more big decisions by me," he said.

"Like should I . . . text you?" she asked.

She didn't seem fazed by what had just happened. Not at all. Maybe it was all in his head.

"Yeah."

"I don't have your number."

He thankfully still had his flashlight phone out. He handed it to her, and she quickly texted herself from his phone. "There," he said. "Now we're both covered."

"I think I might take this guy home," she said, patting the overalls demon on the head.

Well. At least someone was going home with her. "Great. Lucky him. See you tomorrow."

"See you tomorrow."

Chapter Nine

IT WAS TEN o'clock and he couldn't sleep. And he was sick of this. It was her. She haunted him. And he didn't do haunted.

He thought back to his time playing poker in Vegas. Traveling around to different games, wherever they might be. There was a thrill to it. To being separated entirely from the world that he knew, from the people who cared about him. From the place he had a responsibility to.

He had been able to engage in anonymous sex easily. And he had liked it.

He liked that feeling, of not having any debt between him and the woman in question. Because his whole life was a debt. Inherited from a father who had been a monster. There had only been so much he could do in his life with that kind of legacy. And the truth was, he wasn't entirely innocent of it.

He had loved his father.

What boy didn't? More than that, he had admired him.

He and Daughtry were the oldest, and they had loved being their father's right-hand men. They had gone out and done whatever he wanted them to do. Their father had told them that they were protecting the ranch, that they were protecting their legacy and the other children by making sure to collect money that belonged to them. He had positioned everybody who owed them as gamblers. They were the ones that were drunks, that were irresponsible. That were in the wrong. They had borrowed money and they hadn't paid it back, and Denver had believed that.

Perhaps not even because it was a very good life, but because it was one that he had been ready to believe. Because it was one that painted them as the good guys.

Denver had never wanted to be a bad guy. But his morality had been flawed. His father had been able to manipulate it, and he had.

There was a weakness inside of him.

And when he carried all of these responsibilities, all of these burdens, then he couldn't indulge that weakness.

When he went out of town, it all fell away. And it felt something like this. Like a need that he couldn't quite get on top of.

Except then it was generic. The desire for anonymity, a night of oblivion.

It didn't matter who the woman was, just like it didn't matter what kind of whiskey it was.

Now, though, it was like that . . . like that undeniable, burning need had gathered in his gut and increased exponentially, but could only be satisfied by her.

He rejected it. He didn't like it.

Because he had a responsibility to her. He damned well did.

And that was why he decided to go out. That was why he decided to do something he so rarely did. Which was to go to Smokey's and find him a woman. He preferred to go to places with women who might not know who he was. Who might not know his reputation.

But hell, there were plenty of women who came from out of town, plenty of women he didn't know. Plenty of opportunity for anonymous sex, even in a town this size, because people liked to mix it up. They moved around between bars, because otherwise, things could just get too tangled up.

What he needed now was a quick fix. Something to get Sheena Patrick off of his mind.

Sex would be a great way to do that. Something to help him blow off steam. He wasn't a damned teenager; he wasn't going to huddle up in a shower and take himself in hand. Hell no. He wasn't going to jerk off while thinking of the woman who had been left vulnerable and alone in the world thanks to his father.

That was a bridge too far.

No. He would just go find somebody who was looking for the same thing he was. Who had their own demons to exorcise.

He didn't feel guilty about the thought at all. When it came to this kind of sex, everybody was using everybody. As long as both parties were left satisfied, he didn't figure it much mattered.

He put on a black T-shirt, dark jeans. And grabbed a black cowboy hat. He took some condoms out of his nightstand, put two in his wallet.

Because what Denver King set out to get, he got. And then some.

Sheena.

He couldn't stop thinking about her, when he should just be thinking about sex.

He didn't understand this feeling inside of him, and Denver didn't truck in things he didn't understand.

He'd had to be in control, and in charge from a very early age.

The night that Sheena's father died was the night that the scales had been ripped from his eyes. That was when he had understood there was no way that they were the good guys.

They were terrorizing people. There had been children in that house, terrified children. They were . . . they were the bad guys. Anyone who terrified children was a bad guy.

When they had approached the house, the homeowner had come out, and Dan Patrick had drawn his weapon, which had resulted in his death. Because the homeowner had taken his shotgun out from behind the door, and had decided to make sure he wasn't the victim.

Denver had no doubt that his father would have returned fire, that he would've felt absolutely no guilt killing that man, but it would've done them no good. The man owed him money. And he didn't want to be at the center of a mass death. He didn't care enough about Dan Patrick to defend him. To avenge him.

Because his father hadn't actually cared about anyone but himself.

It took years to untangle that kind of mental abuse. When you had been tricked into caring so very deeply about a man who loved nothing but himself, when your whole reality was shaped around the lies that he had told you . . .

Denver never wanted to be tangled up like that again.

He had found that his responsibilities made things a lot clearer.

He got into his truck, and started to pull away from the farm-house. And then saw headlights. He slowed down, and his brother Landry pulled up alongside him. "Hey. Where you off to?"

"I might ask you the same question," said Denver. He could see that Fia was sitting in the passenger seat. "You're headed in the opposite direction of home," he commented.

"True. We were headed up to the old cabin."

He knew a little bit from his brother about the old cabin. Basically, when they were teenagers, that was where he and

Fia had engaged in illicit activity. He had a feeling that he had caught his brother about to go have an assignation with his wife.

"Nostalgic," Fia said, grinning.

Lord. Not even having a new baby and a teenager could calm those two down. And having a built-in babysitter with Lila—who was extremely delighted by her little brother—gave them some freedom.

"Great. I'm just headed out to the bar."

"Really," said Landry.

"Yes, Landry. Really. Do I answer to you now?"

"No," said Landry. "How's the axe throwing project going?"

And just like that, Sheena was top of his mind again.

The woman was a menace.

"Going great. Everything is great."

"You seem tense," said Landry.

"And you seem nosy. I'll see you later, little brother."

He rolled his window up, and punched the gas, heading toward town. He needed to do something to exorcise this desire from his body. She was driving him crazy.

All he could think about were those tattoos. The way that she smelled. The way that he had wanted to take her mouth when they had been standing there in front of . . . decorative animal corpses. Honest to God.

He was acting like a kid with a crush. And he could never remember being a kid with a crush. He had been a helpless soldier in his father's army. A weapon. And then he had fashioned himself into a responsible, decent human being. And it had been an effort. It had been something he'd had to learn. It certainly didn't come natural when you were raised by Elias King.

But this desire, this desire felt like something that came from him. That he would want, more than anything, this woman who . . .

They were too tangled up in each other. Bottom line. And there was too much power that belonged to him, and he avoided that. He avoided the power trips, he avoided any hint of wielding his position, his money or anything else as a method of manipulating somebody. And he really did feel that it was almost impossible to know if you were manipulating somebody when you had that much more than they did.

And that was him and Sheena.

He replayed that script over and over in his mind until he pulled up to Smokey's. Until he got out of his truck and walked across the gravel drive, and up the rickety steps into the building.

He repeated it to himself until the thick crowd around the jukebox parted, and he saw her. Standing there in one of the shortest dresses he had ever seen, revealing a mystery that had been driving him crazy.

That tattoo he was able to see on her arm continued down her side. Vines and flowers twining down the side of her leg all the way to her knee. Which meant it must go along her hip, her side, her whole body.

He wanted to trace it. With his tongue.

And then, like a magnet drew her gaze to his, she looked up.

And that burning in his stomach ignited.

This was a cosmic joke. With everything that had gone wrong in Sheena's life, it would be easy to see why she was a person who didn't have much faith in there being a higher power. She could understand why many people in her position no longer believed in such things. But Sheena found life far too ironic, and deliberately irritating to believe that there wasn't some de-ity somewhere mixing things around and laughing at the chaos of it all.

Because she had come here tonight to forget Denver King. She had broken her own role. Put on the most obvious dress she owned, and taken her ass down to the local bar to find a man.

Because she needed something. She needed to feel in control was what she needed.

She was used to making men fall to their knees for her. What she was not used to was what Denver made her feel. What she was not used to was this out-of-control, burning desire that had overtaken her earlier at the build site.

She had been holding the desecrated body of a woodchuck. And still, what she had wanted to do was grab his face and kiss him. She had wanted to invite him to take her in that dustbowl that was likely filled with baby rodents.

That was insanity. He wasn't her type.

He was way too commanding. He was the kind of man who thought he was in charge. No. She liked a man who was rendered speechless by her body. A man she could push down onto the bed and ride at her own pace, her own tempo, finding pleasure for herself before letting him have any.

She imagined that Denver King was not the kind of man who would let her play that game. And the worst thing was, the very worst thing, was that what she normally avoided with men, she found endlessly fascinating with him. Because she had thought about those big hands gripping her hips. While he pounded into her. While he set the pace.

While he moved over her, behind her. While he gripped her hair and held her fast.

Those were dangerous flashes of insanity that had nothing to do with her actual life, or the way she did anything. She didn't let anyone have control over her. Not physically, not emotionally. And here he was. Looking so hot her knees went weak immediately.

And she didn't do weak knees. His eyes glittered, and she could see that he wasn't any happier than she was.

That bastard. He was here for the same reason. He wanted her, but he was here to fuck somebody else.

They could do that. They could do it at each other. Why not. Because they were not going to sleep together. She had said that. She had declared it from the beginning. Was that not manifesting, or something like that? She had manifested never banging him. She wasn't going to. But he began to move toward her, and it was like everyone in the bar could feel the intensity between them. The sea of people parted and let him move through.

Maybe it had nothing to do with the connection between them. Maybe it was just him. Just Denver. Damn him.

He was magnetic. He was unlike any man she had ever known. And if she was very honest with herself, that had always been true.

Yeah. The first time she had noticed he was beautiful was when they had loaded her father's body into the back of a coroner's van.

Maybe this was more inevitable than she had given it credit for.

She could turn away from him. She could grab hold of one of the men who had been holding court with her all evening. Buying her drinks and basically competing for a spot in her bed tonight. Not that she would actually take them back to her bed. She would drive to Mapleton before she invited some guys who lived here back to her actual house. Not happening.

So yes, she could turn back to them. She didn't need to do this. And yet she found herself angling toward him. Found herself taking steps in his direction.

"Denver," she said.

He looked at her, his gaze sweeping over her curves. And she felt like he might as well have struck a match against her skin. It burned. It felt electric. Dangerous. She wasn't used to that.

Sex was low stakes. She didn't do edgy. She didn't do *this*. The control always had to be hers. And right now, he had taken that control, and he was holding it in the palm of his very large hand.

"Fancy meeting you here," he said.

"Well, there aren't very many places to go in Pyrite Falls, are there?"

"Guess not," he said.

"Of course, if what you're really asking is why aren't I at home asleep given that there is an early workday tomorrow, I guess I can give you the answer to that question."

"Go right ahead."

"I came out to preach the gospel to these poor lost souls."

His face, hard like a rock, shifted. He almost smiled.

Her heart fluttered.

Good Lord.

"Well, that is very kind of you," he said.

"What else would I be doing?" she asked, innocent as could be.

He leaned in. "I have a theory."

"Do you?"

It was like everybody else disappeared. The only thing was him. Him, that close. Him right there. She could back off. But if she backed off, then that was making this bigger than it was. Bigger than it could possibly be. Because when had any . . . thing with a dude ever mattered? It hadn't. And this did neither.

"Yes," he said. "I think that you were laying in bed at home, and you couldn't sleep, because you kept thinking about what you wanted. You were restless, and edgy, and you decided to get up and go down to the bar to see if you could find some guy to help you forget about what you *actually* want."

That place between her legs throbbed. It was actually so close to what had happened, exactly, verbatim, that it made her want to turn and run from the room. It also made her want to lean in. Because he was intoxicating. Because he smelled like dirt, but in a sexy way. Like the land. Like pine and wood chips, and all the things he did all day.

"Maybe," she said. "But then, I think the only reason that you know that is because you aren't doing any better, are you?"

His lips curved into a smile. "Is that what you think?"

"Yes. I think you were home, and the only thing you could think about was me." She moved closer to him, and she knew that it was a gamble. She knew that she was taking a chance. A risk.

Worse, she knew that she was toying around with something and someone that she might not actually be able to control. Okay. Worst of all, she had a feeling that she was attempting a response in herself that she couldn't control. Because she had never felt anything like this before. Didn't want to. And yet, here she was. It was so powerful that her resistance was beginning to get very, very poor. Really, what was the point of resisting?

That was the knife's edge she found herself standing on.

The more she resisted the more the more this seemed like it was singular. Sex was *never* singular. It could be fun, but it wasn't . . . It had never once rearranged her life, or changed her as a person.

She didn't need to make this attraction into something more significant than it was.

Denver was like her. He wasn't going to get attached. In fact, imagining him being clingy was laughable. He was not the type. So yes, he might give her a different kind of experience than she was used to.

Just thinking that sent a zip down through her midsection.

She suddenly understood the feral cats that lived behind the bar. The way that they wanted attention, but also wanted to run away. The way they would rub up against you, and if you bent down to stroke them, would hiss.

She was that cat. She wanted to rub up against him, and she wanted to bite him.

But maybe not even to get rid of them. Maybe just for fun.

She was losing her mind.

"We have a problem, don't we?" he asked, his voice heavy. And that was when she realized. Truly. That they did have a problem. But only if they made it one.

"I don't know about that," she said, sidestepping the juke-box, and edging away from the people who were now gawking at her and Denver.

"What makes you say that?"

"What makes me say that, Denver, is that it's only a problem if we allow it to be. All right. We both have rules. But that's the thing, isn't it? We both have rules. And if we both have rules, then surely, we're both on the same page. We want the same things. We're hardly going to get caught up in . . . feelings."

He huffed a laugh. "No."

"So why make a bigger deal than it has to be? We both know the deal. Sex. No strings."

"One night," he said.

And it was like that match that he'd struck against her skin was added to gasoline.

"Sure," she said. "One night. But not one time."

And that was when she did something not even she saw coming. She grabbed a fistful of his shirt, and dragged him down the hallway toward the single-person bathroom, and pulled him inside.

She closed the door behind them, and locked it. He stood there for a moment, looking at her like a caged tiger, his eyes glowing.

And then, then, he closed the distance between them.

Chapter Ten

THIS WAS CRAZY. But she was feeling particularly un-hinged. And when his mouth met hers, it was like the world shifted. Good and bad didn't matter anymore. Proclamations of how she wasn't going to sleep with him didn't matter anymore. The fact that somehow, with him, her intentions folded like a house of cards didn't matter anymore.

Nothing mattered but this. But him. But the firm press of his hot mouth against hers.

But that hard, solid body that was unlike any she'd ever had pressed against her.

She had been right about him.

He growled, gripped her hips and backed her up against the wall. His hold was firm, bruising. His kiss was punishing. And she liked it.

But it was only one night, so it didn't matter if it was a trip into totally foreign territory. If she was walking into a deep dark wood, unsure of where she was going. Because she would only be lost for a night.

Because tomorrow they would go their separate ways.

Because they both knew how to have sex, and turn it into nothing. Nothing but a nice memory. So it wouldn't be any different between the two of them than it had been any other time.

There had been some good reasons to resist, but they weren't good enough. That was the thing.

Nothing was good enough for her to deny herself this.

Maybe, in the fullness of time, this was the real way he could pay her back. With that glorious body of his.

This kiss. Which was so far removed from any other kiss she'd ever had in her life that it was almost an entirely different activity. His movements were confident, controlled and feral all at the same time. His tongue went deep, sliding against hers, and she nearly melted. But thankfully, his hold was strong enough to keep her from collapsing.

He removed one hand from her hip, gripped her jaw, held her face steady as he licked deep into her mouth. She shivered, shuddered. The hand on her hip began to drift beneath the hem of her dress, and around between her thighs, where he found nothing but a pair of thin, wispy panties that she knew betrayed how wet she was. Immediately, instantly. For him.

He growled, his fingertips brushing beneath the edge of her underwear, the first time his rough hands made contact with her tender skin like an electric shock.

"Denver," she gasped, and she hadn't meant to say his name. She didn't call out a man's name during sex, because if anybody was responsible for her pleasure, it was her. And she was okay with that. But not now. He was making her mindless. He was ruining her.

And she liked it.

God help her, she liked it.

She began to pull off his T-shirt, pushing her hands beneath the fabric, touching his taut abdomen. He was so . . . everything.

She couldn't wait to see him naked.

And she realized that they were actually going to end up having sex in this bathroom, with fifty people on the other side of the door who had seen them go in.

Okay. She was feeling out of character, but not that out of character.

"We need to go," she said, panting.

"I'm good," he growled.

"I'm serious. I'm not doing it with you in the bathroom."

He lifted his head and looked around, his expression dazed. His cowboy hat was pushed back on his head. And she realized that he had actually lost track of where they were.

If she wasn't so out of sorts she might've been flattered. That she was desperately needed. So much so that he didn't want to pause even for a breath.

"Let's go," she said.

She gripped his hand and unlocked the door, pulling her dress into place as they walked out, and straight through the bar. She didn't stop to look. Didn't stop to see if they were being gaped at. She didn't work here anymore, so it wasn't her problem if the men in this bar thought that she was a slut for Denver King. Maybe she was.

That was just fine with her.

They stepped outside of the bar, the cold air hitting her straight in the chest, like a punch directly to the lungs. "My place," she said.

And yes, she had just thought that she was never going to bring one of those men back to her house. But it was Denver. He already knew where she lived. They were . . . enmeshed.

No, that wasn't ideal. No, it wasn't something she would've chosen. But she hadn't chosen this. She hadn't chosen the intensity of the attraction that she felt for him. She hadn't chosen to want him more than she had ever wanted anybody else.

Maybe this was a closure thing, in a very weird way.

Maybe it was part of drawing a line under the past and really moving forward.

Yes. Maybe it was.

Because she had thought that he was beautiful for the first time that day her daddy had died. And she had thought it so many days since. While he was out there being this dark, angelic figure that had never been quite the substance of heaven. When he had given the money, and made sure that they could survive. When he had been there without actually being there, because he had been determined to let them have their own life. He had actually been the best, truest man she had ever known without really knowing.

And in some ways, this entanglement with him was about getting untangled. But maybe this was part of it.

All these unresolved feelings looking for a place to go. Well, great. They would resolve them. Tonight. In her bed.

"You know where I live," she said.

"I do."

It was unspoken. They wouldn't go over together. They couldn't. Not just because somebody would see their cars parked in the parking lot. She didn't care about that. She had sex, big deal. That wasn't the problem.

It was . . . She didn't stay the whole night with men. She bet that Denver didn't stay a whole night with a woman. They would need their vehicles. They were hardly going to be driving back down to the bar together in the morning on their way to work.

No.

This was an isolated incident. What happened in her bedroom tonight was going to stay there.

Thank God they hadn't lost their minds and done it in the bathroom.

"Lead the way," he said.

She got into her car, her hands shaking, and drove up the road. She tried to stay focused on where the headlights bathed the asphalt. Tried to keep herself from vibrating into a thousand pieces. This was just sex. And it might be with Denver, but that didn't make it something completely foreign.

Just one night. Just one night. One night. That was all.

And that was her mantra. That she repeated the whole way. All the way out of town, and up to the more windy, mountainous stretch that led to where her little house was.

They drove past the trailer park, and the little houses, ramshackle and coming apart at the seams, up the side of the hill, to the place she called home.

She had done her best to keep it neat and tidy. But it was old.

It needed a new coat of paint and it wasn't going to get it.

The siding was split, and haggard. But it was dark out, so he wasn't getting the full experience. Not that he hadn't seen it before.

She pulled up to the front, and turned her car off, getting out and walking to the front door. She heard him get out of his truck. She didn't wait for him. This wasn't a date. They were going to hold hands and walk up to the threshold. She wasn't going to look up at him and beg for a kiss with her eyes.

No.

He didn't seem to need that either. He simply followed her inside, shut the door behind them and locked it as he had done in the bathroom.

She dropped her purse on the ground, and flicked on a couple of lights. She had very good curtains in this house. Because she didn't need anybody peering inside and seeing any of her business. Which was handy, because that meant she could easily, and without concern, look at all of Denver's business without starting rumors.

It was one thing to not care if the barflies knew that she had hooked up. It was another for her neighbors to know that she was hooking up with Denver King. Because Elias King had done a fair amount of damage to all the people here.

And that was a conversation she didn't need to get into.

This was her mistake. Her wreckage.

It didn't need to become a community consensus.

"I want you to strip for me," she said.

He looked at her, and there was a light in his eyes that made everything in her go still. "Is that where you think this is going to go? You think you get to tell me what to do?"

"I want to see you," she said, tossing her hair. "And we're in my house."

"I guess we are," he said. "I've got no problem giving you a show, Sheena. But what you need to understand is that I don't take orders."

"Well, tricky thing. Neither do I."

"Do you ever stop?" he asked.

"Stop what?"

"Opposing everything and everyone just for the sake of it. What's it all for? So that I know you're tough? So that you know you're tough? I already know you are. You forget. I was there. When your dad died. I know that you're tough. I know that you're strong. So why don't you let me take control tonight."

"I could say the same thing to you," she said. "You do all the work all the time."

"True," he said. "But I consider this a working vacation."

"Cute."

"Take your dress off." She froze. Because her first instinct had been to obey him. And that freaked her out a little bit. "Do it, Sheena. Do you have any idea how much time I've spent wondering how that whole tattoo looks? I want to see it."

And he looked at her with so much hunger. Not the general sexual hunger that men always looked at her with. But appointed, sharp need that felt like it had lodged itself right between her ribs, and flexed. It took her breath away. It made her feel like she was . . . like she was losing her mind. Like she was the one who was suddenly pinned to the spot, undone by sexual hunger.

She had met her match.

That thought was so shocking, and so *horrendous*, that she pushed it aside and vowed never to think it again.

"I want to see your skin. I want to see every inch of you. I want to lick you. Everywhere. Follow the whole line of that damned tattoo. And I want to sit you down on that couch over there and spread your legs, get on my knees and feast on you."

Okay. At this point, resisting was just being petulant. She was not going to deny herself everything that he had just promised, so she unzipped her dress without thinking, and let it fall away from her curves. She stepped out of it, and out of her shoes, and looked at him.

"Like this?"

"Bra next," he said.

She reached behind her back and unhooked it, stripping it away from her before pushing her panties down and wiggling them away. She wasn't going to wait for a command for that.

He growled. And then he made a circular gesture with his finger. Wordlessly commanding her to turn in a circle for him.

She took a breath, and she did. Even when she was facing away from him she could feel his gaze on her body.

"Damn," he said.

She looked down, following the line of his eyes. Her tattoo started at her wrist and twined up her shoulder, down her side, with vines spanning part of her midsection, just beneath her breasts. It also continued down her hip, all the way down her side.

It had been a huge project. A strange reclamation of her when she had turned twenty-one. She had felt compelled to do something, to leave her own mark on her skin.

And she had chosen the vines and flowers, which were actually based on vinca, which was a damned tough plant, impossible to kill. Popped up everywhere, and just couldn't be strangled out. It had felt symbolic. For her. For her life.

So she had inked it all over. A reminder that much like a stubborn, beautiful plant, she was going to thrive. Insistently, angrily. Defiantly.

And people would be mistaken thinking all she was, was pretty.

Denver, however, did not seem lost in the symbolism at the moment. She knew the tattoo was hot. It wasn't like she had chosen it thinking that it wouldn't be sexy. She had known that it would be.

She sauntered over to the couch, and sat down, never taking her gaze away from his as she spread her legs, and then as he made his way over to her, she knew a moment of panic.

Because this was not something that she normally . . . did really. She had been sort of halfheartedly tempted. But she'd never had a man look at her like Denver was at the moment.

That was the thing about casual hookups. Usually, both parties were in it for themselves.

But he had the look of a man starving. For her.

And when he got to his knees in front of her, he draped her legs over his shoulders and went in, hard and deep, his tongue zeroing in on the center of her pleasure without error.

She flexed her hips up off the couch, her hand automatically going to his hair. She couldn't breathe. She was mindless. And he was eating her like she was a delicacy.

She had never . . . None of her past experiences could even . . .

She tried to move her hips, tried to find her own rhythm, but he denied her, holding her hips still as he forced her to submit to his touch. To his movements. This was entirely foreign to her. Her pleasure being entirely in her partner's control.

When her first climax broke over her, it was like a wave. A horse cry exited her body, like an exorcism. Like something that was beyond her control.

And she found herself shattering, her release so intense she wasn't even sure what all she said, what all she did. Except that when she came to, her thighs were squeezing either side of his head and her fingers forked in his hair.

"Oh," she said.

He lifted his head and looked at her, and everything in her rippled. Like she could come again just from seeing that satisfied, smug look on his face.

She felt like she was standing in front of the door that led into a room of self-knowledge she had not especially ever wanted to walk into.

And she still didn't. But she was pretty sure the sign on the door said You Sleep with the Wrong Kind of Man.

Maybe.

But the kind of man she had slept with historically allowed her to keep control, and while the pleasure wasn't like this, it also wasn't . . . altering.

She had told herself she didn't like men like this. Men who were too big. Too tall. Too strong.

Men who wanted to take control.

All she wanted to do now was melt. Like she was girlish. Like she was inexperienced.

All she wanted to do was get on her knees and beg him to give her more. Whatever he wanted.

It terrified her.

But she was too aroused to stop.

Because he had given her a hit of something she had never experienced before, and she wanted it. More. Again.

So she let him scoop her up off the couch, his arm around her waist, let him carry her, like she weighed nothing, right out of the room, unerringly down the hall to find her bedroom.

"How did you know which one was my . . . ?"

"I know how houses work," he said. He deposited her down onto the center of the bed, and stood back. "I know how a lot of things work."

"Okay," she said. Which was maybe the dumbest thing she could have said. But she felt dumb. Exceptionally.

"Now I give you what you want," he said.

He reached out and wrenched his T-shirt up over his head, and her mouth went dry. Instantly, the pleasure that she had just experienced wasn't enough. It could never be enough. She wanted to throw herself at him. She wanted to lick him. Everywhere. Everything that he had promised to do to her, she wanted to do to him.

She got up onto her knees, and moved to the edge of the bed. Reached out and put her hands on his ab muscles. "Shit," she said.

She moved her fingertips over all those bronze, perfectly defined muscles. His dark chest hair. He was so hot. She had never seen a man that hot in person.

"I thought abs like this were a myth," she said, leaning in and running the flat of her tongue from his hipbone up to the divot just beneath his pec muscles.

"*Shit,*" he said, closing his eyes.

"Perfect," she said, grabbing his belt and undoing it. She felt more herself now. A little more in control right then as she freed him of his jeans, and gave herself a real, full look at his body.

Her internal muscles clenched tight as she took in the sight of him. His cock was big and thick. Bigger than she'd ever seen in person. That was for sure. His thighs were muscular and glorious. And yes, she wanted to lick him.

So she did. She leaned in and tasted him from base to tip before taking him deep in her mouth. He growled, pushing his fingers through her hair and gripping the back of her head. "Sheena," he said.

And she had a feeling that it was weird for him to say a woman's name in the throes of pleasure too. As weird as it was for her.

She had a feeling that there were more ways that they were alike than she had even identified.

She luxuriated in him. His strength. His size. The taste of him, his scent.

Until she found herself being propelled away from him, pushed back into the mattress. And he was with her like lightning, and when he had retrieved condoms, she didn't know, but there were two blue packets up by her head all of a sudden, and she grabbed hold of one of them eagerly. "Just a second," he said. He kissed her mouth, deep and long, and for the first time in her memory, she got lost in a kiss.

They were pressed, bare chest to bare chest. The hard column of his arousal burning into her hip.

She was desperate. Needy and greedy for him to be inside of her, but at the same time, she could happily live in this moment forever.

It was incredible. And so was he.

She never wanted it to end.

It was somehow the most raw, sexual experience of her life, and it was just kissing. Except it could never really be called just kissing, could it?

He moved his hands down to cup her breasts, teasing her nipples. And then he kissed down her collarbone, moved to take one nipple into his mouth and sucked deep. She gasped, arching up off the bed. And then he made good on his earlier promise. He started at her shoulder, and quite literally traced the leaves and blossoms of her tattoo all the way down her body. She was trembling as he moved his mouth beneath her breasts, staying clear of the sensitive flesh there. And then moving down her hips, her thigh. When he stopped, he moved between her legs again, gripped her and opened her to him, as he tasted her again.

"You already did—"

He growled, not listening to her, working her up into another frenzy, her orgasm crashing over her more like a rockslide than a wave.

Tumbling down over the top of her and leaving her feeling bruised.

"I'm going to . . . I need to be on . . ."

She was going to tell him she wanted to be on top. She was going to tear open the condom with her teeth and make a show of rolling it over his thick length. But he was too fast. He grabbed the condom; he took care of the protection. And then he was kissing her again, lifting her leg up over his hip and thrusting deep, hard, in one smooth stroke that left her gasping.

She was overly full, in the very best way.

And she might have said his name. Or she might have called out to God. At the moment, she wasn't sure if those two things were very different from each other.

She could feel him. Every inch, as he slid in and out, his thrusts hard, her body being pushed up against the headboard with each stroke.

She wrapped her arms around him, forced her fingers in his hair, kissed him, bit him, just like she had fantasized about doing earlier. He growled, his thrusts becoming harder, faster. Sweat beading on his back. She ran her fingertips down his slick skin, her nails digging into him. Wrapped her legs around his waist as he claimed her, over and over again.

She had never simply enjoyed this part before. What she usually liked was to be on top, to control the rhythm, to control the depth.

But this was just wild, and she had surrendered to it. To him.

She let him take her to the heights, let him shatter her completely as his own orgasm overtook him.

She cried out, and if the neighbors hadn't realized she'd brought a man home, they did now.

The windows were single-pane, and they certainly weren't soundproof. And if they had missed out, his own growl, deep, guttural and one of absolute masculine pleasure, would have left them in no doubt.

She let her head fall back on the pillow, trying to regulate her breathing.

He moved away from her and went silently into the bathroom, getting rid of the condom before joining her back on the bed.

Normally, she would say something saucy. Just a little pithy remark to take advantage of the fact that a man who had just experienced an orgasm was likely too undone to gain the upper hand. But she was too wrecked. Too rocked. Neither of them said anything, and as the silence stretched over them, she felt a strange sensation expanding in her chest. And she did not . . . care for it.

But she also couldn't do anything about it. As the pressure built in her chest, she felt pressure building behind her eyes, and she really did not care for that.

So she rolled over onto her back and didn't look at him.

But then his large hand was tracing the same tattoo that he had just licked, and the touch was so different, so tender in contrast, that her eyes began to sting.

"Tell me about this," he said.

"I got drunk and did it on a whim," she lied.

"Sheena," he said. "We get one night."

"Oh. Is this going to be an AMA? Or maybe it should be in an AITA."

"I don't know what either of those things means."

"*Ask me anything.* Also *am I the asshole?*"

"Why are those . . . acronyms?"

"It's a thing on the Internet. Wait a minute. You know trivia about Disneyland, but you don't know that."

"No. But maybe I'll collect it to use if I ever go back to playing poker. I can distract somebody by throwing around nonsense abbreviations."

"It's not nonsense. It's very popular."

"I can guess what an AMA is. But the other one . . ."

"People post situations and then ask strangers on the Internet if they are the asshole, or the other person."

"Well, that sounds like everything could go wrong."

"It kind of does."

"I am certain in this scenario, I am the asshole," he said. "So you should be the AMA."

"That's really not how it works."

"I don't actually care how it works. If I wanted to know, I would be on the Internet. Tell me about the tattoo."

No one had ever asked. That was the thing. Not any of the men she had slept with since she had gotten it. Not her sisters, even. Like people just assumed she had got it because it was decorative. Which was maybe fair, or maybe her sisters knew that she wouldn't want to tell them, because she was notoriously private about anything that could be classified as personal. Maybe the fact that she was that sort of distant from everybody was just her own fault.

But he was right. It was just one night. And he was asking. Why not tell him?

"You know what vinca is, right?"

"Yes. It's a pain in the ass."

She loved that he knew. "Yes," she said. "Exactly."

He traced the lines of it. "No matter what, you can't get rid of it."

"Nope."

"I like it."

"My turn. Tell me about the professional poker playing. You know that's the thing that made everybody assume that you were actually just like your dad deep down."

He shook his head slowly. "Yeah. But I never really understood why. My dad never gambled with his own money. He encouraged other people to gamble with theirs. And with their lives."

"That is true," she said.

She felt so secluded with him in this little bubble. In this moment in time.

"And it felt good sometimes. To get away from here, while I was still . . . doing something for the ranch. For everybody. But on my own terms. It's . . ." He looked at her, and his gaze felt like a collision. "I believed in my dad. I did everything that he told me to do. Your father being killed, that was a wake-up call. It was bullshit, Sheena. All of it. He said that we were the good guys. That other people made bad decisions with their money and that wasn't our fault. We were making sure the people held up their end of the deal."

Hearing him say that did something so strange to her heart. She had never really thought about why Denver had worked with his dad. Or why he had changed afterward. She just had never thought of him as a whole person.

He had been symbolic of something, and that had been fine. Good enough.

"I believed in him. That was the worst part. To have to face the fact that I had been so profoundly wrong about the whole world. It was like looking at something upside down for your whole life, and then finding out your perspective was all wrong. Backward. He painted us as the victim sometimes. We were the people that were being cheated. I believed it. I can never forgive myself for that." He looked up, his eyes focused on the ceiling. "I realized that I was good at gambling. I learned a lot from watching people play games that my dad put together. And it . . . I dunno, it felt like healing. Or maybe like revenge in a small way. I gambled with his money. I won a lot of it. I'm way richer than my dad ever was, or ever will be. And the only person risking anything is me. I'm not going to say that I'm proud of everything that I did, or that it makes me a good person. But I . . ."

"Life sets you up in a certain way," she said, yet again feeling that deep, undeniable kinship with him. "Sometimes I think you can only be so good given how you started out."

"Exactly."

She sighed. She turned over to her side and looked at him. She felt safer in here with him. In the quiet of this room, in this house where she had once been small and scared.

She had never brought a man back here before. What had she been thinking?

But it had happened. And there was nothing to be done about it now. It was like a moment out of time. A cone of silence and safety. He had told her that, about himself, about his dad. He understood the tattoo.

"My dad never tried to justify what he did. He just . . . He made good money working for your dad, and that was that. The end justified the means. He could give us things, and that was all that mattered. But he always said . . . he always said that protecting us was the most important thing. But he didn't. He left us alone, and he . . ."

She didn't want to talk about this. She really didn't. There was no point bringing it into this conversation. Into this moment.

"Do you want to know why I learned how to throw knives and axes?"

She had never told anyone this. Not anyone.

"Why?" he asked, his voice sounding dry.

"There was a guy. A *man*. He worked with your father, and with mine. He used to come around here all the time and drink. Hang out with my dad. He started coming by sometimes if my dad wasn't around. My dad . . . He always told me that . . . that we were important to him." Her chest felt pinched. Hurt. She hated this. She hated this memory. Because it was tied up in this vision of her dad that she had once had that she had never been able to have again after.

One that she liked to pretend she had never had.

Because it was one thing to acknowledge all of his failures. But it was quite another to remember what it had been like to love him.

What it had been like to believe him.

"I told him. I told him that I might be uncomfortable. I said I had a bad feeling about the way that Tim was when he was around, and my dad said I had to trust him. That he would never let anything happen to me."

Denver shifted, going up on his elbow, looking at her fiercely. But he didn't interrupt her; he didn't push her. Didn't ask her any questions. He simply let her talk.

"One time, he came up when my dad wasn't there. He tried to kiss me. I pushed him away. He grabbed hold of me and he told me that I was going to give him what he wanted. And that my dad wouldn't believe me, because they were best friends. And anyway, because he worked for Elias and so did my dad, he wouldn't do anything."

She gritted her teeth. "It right then I believed him. Not because I thought he was telling a deep truth. But because I had told my dad. I told him. I knew . . . he didn't do anything. He still let him come around. He didn't listen to me. He didn't . . . believe me, or something. I don't know. But he let him come up there, and he felt emboldened to try to . . .

"He pushed me into my bedroom, and . . . I had a knife in there. I had one under my pillow, because the thing is, there were always men coming and going, and things happening, and I didn't trust anything. I never did. It was a paring knife, I grabbed it and I stabbed him in the shoulder. I held onto it as hard as I could, because he tried to take it from me, and somehow . . . I don't remember all of it, we ended up outside. I was trying to stab him again, so he finally started to run. There was an axe buried in the top of a log out there. I grabbed it, and I threw it at him. It hit the tree right next to him. I told him that if he ever came back he was going to find it buried between his shoulder blades. Because I didn't need my dad to protect me. And I didn't give a shit about Elias King. I told him I protect myself, and my sisters. He ever came up there again . . . If he came up there again I'd use that knife to cut off his dick. And then I'd kill him."

She was breathing hard, her whole body trembling. It was just such a . . . The memory itself in some ways made her feel powerful. Because she had won. For herself. But it also made her feel weak and sad, because it had been the moment when she had truly understood that she was on her own. So when her dad died a couple of months later, she knew it didn't matter. Not really. Because everything he'd ever said about protecting her had been a lie. That was it. He didn't matter. Not at all. Without him there, men wouldn't come up anymore.

Thankfully, they had their dog after that. She had thought a good guard dog was necessary.

And right then she wanted to cry. Because the dog was gone. And not for any other reason really. She really missed that dog.

Denver sat up, covered his mouth with his hand. Then he looked down at her. "I'm sorry," he said.

It wasn't like the way people said it when they didn't know what else to say, and it was just a gesture. It wasn't like when somebody was apologizing for something they had nothing to do with.

Because she could feel the weight of how responsible he felt.

"Don't," she said. "It's not your fault."

"I know that. I do. But I was in that same . . . that same circle of bastards, and somebody should be sorry, and we all know that they never will be."

It was just the most perfect thing. Because he was right. The only thing any of them were ever sorry for was getting caught, having to be accountable.

Denver lived accountable. It was all he was.

She sat up too, and put her hand on his shoulder. "We have one night, Denver. It doesn't need to be all about all those skeletons we have buried in the backyard."

"Do you have a skeleton buried in the backyard? I would support it."

She smiled, and rested her forehead against his shoulder. "No. Because he never came back. Because I wasn't kidding. And he knew it."

"You're a hell of a woman, Sheena Patrick."

It was the nicest thing anyone had ever said to her.

Chapter Eleven

DENVER WAS A man of action. When words failed, doing the right thing served even better. His father had been a man who kept a store of pretty words designed to manipulate the people around him. Denver wasn't sad, usually, that words weren't his primary method of communicating.

Right now he wished he could give her vows. Like a knight in shining armor, which he'd never been. Not even close.

So instead he just kissed her. He wanted . . . he wanted for things to be different. He wanted to take the whole world and rearrange it. For her.

It was different than wanting to pay for things because he was responsible for it. This was a deep sort of grief he didn't fully understand.

Anger at the way life hurt people like her. Over and over again.

But she was right. She was that flowering vine. Stubborn and endless. She wouldn't be uprooted, just because some asshole tried it.

She kept growing. Beautiful and stubborn with it. A blooming middle finger to a world that had tried to suppress her.

He had known that she was strong. But he hadn't realized just how much she carried. No wonder she hadn't mourned the death of her father.

Denver wanted to dig up his body just so he could spit on it.

He kissed her, and he waited. For her to deepen the kiss. For her to show him that she wanted this.

She put her hand on his face, and kissed him back.

Need vibrated through him. This feeling of sorrow and connection, driving him now. Something different than anything he'd ever experienced. But then, it had been. From the beginning.

From the time they'd kissed at Smokey's to now.

And when he laid her down on the bed, put the condom on and buried himself inside of her, it was different than just chasing pleasure.

He looked into her eyes, and kissed her. And felt his whole world ignite.

Then she shattered beneath him, her own orgasm claiming her, her need the most beautiful thing he'd ever seen.

He could feel something, sinking down into the cracks inside of him. Those weak points.

And he knew that he'd let it go too far.

When she looked at him in the gray light of the bedroom, he knew she felt it too.

Suddenly there was distance where before there had been a driving closeness. He could feel a clawing in his chest, something like panic, except he never panicked. Not under gunfire or when his father had gone to prison. Not ever. But it told him he had to go home.

It was the strangest feeling. This desire to pull away and stay at the same time.

"I needed this," she whispered.

"Me too," he said.

They both knew that it was goodbye. Not to each other, because they would see each other tomorrow. But goodbye to this. To whatever had compelled both of them to strip themselves naked, past skin, and down deeper. To the deepest, darkest parts of themselves. But maybe that had been as inevitable as the rest of this.

Maybe they had needed to tell each other those things.

He would take what she'd told him and bury it down inside of him with all the rest of those secret horrors. And she would keep his own sad truth, she supposed.

He got out of bed and disposed of the second condom, before heading out to the living room and beginning to dress. She didn't follow him.

But once he was dressed he did go back into the bedroom, compelled toward her because he just was. "Are you okay?"

"Sure am," she said. "All that was news to you. It wasn't news to me."

His lips quirked upward. "Fair."

"Plus multiple orgasms are a surefire way to lift the mood."

Normally, yes. Why he didn't feel *lifted*, he couldn't say.

"I guess you better get a quality couple of hours," she said to him.

"Yeah," he said, rubbing his hand over his face. He found that he didn't actually want to leave, not really. There was discomfort clawing at his chest that had told him to get up, get ready and go. But now that it came right down to it, he didn't want to walk out the door.

Which was empirical evidence that he needed to.

He left, and he drove back to the ranch, but he didn't go to sleep. Instead, he went into the main event hall and started plotting and planning things for the Christmas event. Which was where he still was when Landry showed up.

"Hey there. You made it back."

"Yes, I did," said Denver.

"What's going on?"

"Not much," he said. "Just getting everything ready for the Christmas thing. Fia is on to take care of the baking, right?"

"Yes."

"I don't want to put her under too much stress. With the baby and all."

"Don't worry about it. The entire army of Sullivans is going to descend to handle the baking, plus I guarantee everyone is going to take turns holding Gray, given he's the newest addition. It's going to be awesome. But you know, Evelyn and Violet Garrett have offered to make some things too."

That struck him as . . . strange. Not that they didn't all help each other; they did. The Kings always contributed barbecue to every event. But usually, they weren't events happening at King's Crest.

"They really want to come out here and . . . help?"

"Yeah."

That just struck him as being strange. Something he didn't expect. And it was maybe the one thing that could get his mind off of Sheena, the intensity of last night and how exhausted he was today.

"I need some coffee," said Denver.

"Okay."

"I haven't had any."

"Are you sick?" Landry asked.

"No. Just . . . preoccupied with all of this."

He walked out of the event space, and out into the gravel drive, just in time to see the taillights on Sheena's car as she drove through to get to her the gaming hall.

He had the sudden, intense urge to run after the car. Which was . . . He needed coffee.

Denver shook his head, and began to walk toward the farmhouse. He could feel Landry watching him.

"Anything you want to talk about?"

"No. I really don't," Denver said.

Landry looked at him, all serious. His brother had always been hard to read. Hell, he'd had a whole secret baby in high school and no one had known about it. "I worry about you, you know. Because you took care of us for all those years, and nobody really took care of you."

"Oh please. This is all soft nonsense because you went and got yourself married. And I am really happy for you. Because God knows we've had enough . . . enough stuff."

"I just thought that maybe you might want the same thing."

He thought about it. He really did. Because maybe the truth was, all of this stuff, all of this planning, all of this shifting, was to try and do something about the fact that he felt like life was moving in a direction he couldn't go. That his family was moving at a pace he wasn't going to be able to match.

Maybe that was it. Maybe that was a problem that he was having.

"I don't know," he said. "But I'm not going to have it."

"Why?"

"There's too much to do," he said.

Maybe he was just still . . . reduced a little bit, from that night with Sheena, from sharing with her; maybe he was just tired. And he didn't have the normal defenses in place.

"That doesn't mean that you can't have a wife. Kids."

"It's a job well done that you do," Denver said as they reached the front porch. "Honestly. That's what I wanted. Was for you guys to be . . . able to have better than what we did. And don't you worry, I already have better. I can be proud of what we did here. What we are doing."

He could stay busy. He could keep working. But the problem was, he was his father's son.

And so he just had to keep going. He had to keep proving that he wasn't Elias King.

To himself more than anything else.

Everything that Sheena had told him . . . It left a sour feeling in his stomach.

Because his dad had called the kind of men who hurt her his friends. She'd had to take care of herself. Nobody else had.

He hated that. More than anything.

He didn't spend much time wishing he could go back in the past and change things, but he wished that he could go back and protect her. He wished that he could go back and take care of her.

When Penny had been left all alone, he had gone and taken her in. He'd been older than her, and things had been more stable on the ranch. He'd been in charge of things for several years, and he had felt equipped to actually do something good in her life.

He just wished that he'd . . . done the same for Sheena. And her sisters.

"Whatever you're thinking, stop," said Landry.

Denver pushed the door open and walked into the kitchen, pushing the button on the coffee maker, which was thankfully ready to go, because he didn't like to have to put together a whole pot of coffee before he'd had his coffee, so he always set it again after he emptied a pot.

"How do you know I'm thinking anything?"

"It's . . . it's you. I look around, I see you . . . already hard at work at seven in the morning. You've been out there God knows how long, without coffee, Denver, like a damned masochist. But you never think that you're doing enough. You never think that it's enough. It's always going to be the next thing, the next poker game, the next win, the next victim of

Dad's that you have to pay off. The next new venture at King's Crest. And all of that is stuff, and it's great, Denver. You've done some great stuff. But none of it is . . . None of it is yours, not really. You're doing all this for everybody else, and what are you doing for you?"

"I don't need to do anything for me," Denver said. "Because the truth is . . . The truth is, Landry," he said, grabbing a mug and slamming it down on the table as he stared at the coffee, which was making far too slowly, "I am just really grateful that I haven't . . . that I haven't transformed into our dad. And I don't want to upset the balance of everything. So yeah. Yeah, I look at what you guys have and . . . it's great. Who wouldn't want it? But I just can't. I can't for the life of me figure out how I would . . ."

Because love was such a powerful thing. It worked its way right into the cracks of a man's soul. And there were a lot of cracks in his.

He had done things in the name of love that had devastating consequences, and he just would never put himself in that situation again. He would never put anybody around him in that situation again.

"At a certain point, I start to question how much of a martyr you can possibly be."

"A pretty fucking big one, Landry."

His brother chuckled. Finally, there was enough coffee in the pot to make a mug, and he yanked it out from under the spout, and poured a measure of it, lifting it to his lips and giving thanks.

"Landry," he said. "I'm really proud of you. And how far you've come. But you know . . . You know it's not simple. Think of everything that you and Fia went through before you were actually able to . . . find each other."

"Our problem was that we fell in love when we were kids,"

said Landry. "We didn't handle what was happening between us well because we didn't know how to do anything yet. She was sixteen when she got pregnant with Lila." Landry paused for a long moment. "I have years of regret, Denver. You don't need to remind me."

Denver felt an unfamiliar twist in his gut. "I'm sorry. I didn't mean it that way."

"You don't have to feel bad about it. I'm just saying, I'm very aware of all of my shortcomings. But the point is that I got over them. The point is that I'm not the same kid that got his girlfriend pregnant, and handled it like an ass. The point is, you can change. You can move on from the dumb bullshit that you've done. You can have the life that you want."

And it was so complicated he didn't quite know how to articulate it. To him or to himself.

"This is the life that I want." That was the simplest way to say it. Because he had what he wanted. He wasn't doing any harm, and he wasn't . . . Yeah. He couldn't ask for more than that.

He pounded down the coffee. "Let's get to work," he said.

He worked until he was cross-eyed. He was ready to fall over where he stood. But he still needed to go check on Sheena and the work out at the axe throwing bar.

He had to wonder how that was going to look. If things were going to be exactly the same between them or if they were going to be different.

He had hooked up plenty of times, but he hadn't had to deal with the woman the next day in a totally different context.

He drove his truck over to the gaming hall, and saw that all the construction gear was gone, but her car was still there.

But when he walked inside, she wasn't anywhere to be seen.

For some reason, that caused his heart rate to pick up.

For God's sake, what had she done to him?

He looked all around, noticed that the place was clean, looking more put together.

There were some walls that were ripped out, too, but the progress was obvious.

Still, no Sheena.

He walked outside and listened. He didn't hear anything but the sound of birds.

It was getting cold. But then, it was nigh unto December, and cold was to be expected. So her being outside would be a strange thing, but Sheena was her own thing. So he couldn't discount it.

He found himself walking down a path behind the building, and he wasn't sure if he had a feeling that she was back there, or if he was just walking.

He didn't do it often enough.

The trees were thick here in this part of the property, the forest floor soft, covered in pine needles. The pale sun filtered through the trees, casting eerie shadows all around.

He came up over a rise, and that was where he saw her. Standing on a fallen log covered in moss. She was wearing a dress that the sunbeams rendered completely see-through, shafts of light pouring through the gaps in the trees in the shape of a star. Her head was tilted back, her dark hair streaming over her back.

She took his breath away. She was the most beautiful thing he'd ever seen.

He wasn't going to touch her again. He'd already decided that. Because like she'd said last night, they both knew the deal.

He didn't really want to touch her right now anyway. He just wanted to look at her. It made his chest ache. To see her like this. Free. Unencumbered.

Bathed in sunlight.

Her life had had enough of these moments. She deserved them all.

She turned sharply, like she had just suddenly realized that he was there.

She breathed out hard, her breath a cloud in the cold air.

Now the sun made a halo around her hair, and he was undone.

"Come to check on my work?"

"Yeah," he said.

He didn't believe in magic. He never had. But right now if someone had told him she'd put him under a spell, he'd agree with them, no question.

"No," he said. "I mean . . . I don't want to interrupt you. We don't need to go over everything today."

"Don't be nice to me just because we had sex," she said.

The words were like a punch to his gut. "I'm not."

"Liar."

"Have it your way, then, don't let me disturb your forest bathing."

She laughed. "I had no idea that you would even have heard the term *forest bathing*."

"I'm very learned," he said.

"About forest bathing and Disneyland. But not the Internet."

"Everybody else knows about the Internet. Why do I need to carry that information around? All I had to do was ask you, and you had the answer."

"I won't always be around," she said.

She was teasing, but the words hit him in a strange, low place. "Right. But there is one thing I know how to do on the Internet. And that is how to use a search engine. So, the Internet can just answer all my questions about it."

She shook her head. "Great."

"It's pretty out here," he said, looking past her.

"It is," she said. "How is everything going for the Christmas party?"

"Good," he said. "Trying to figure out exactly what to do with the food. And how I'm going to position everything in the barn."

"I'll tell you what," she said. "Feel free to check my work really quick. But . . . why don't we head back and take a look at your project."

He shouldn't say yes. She had enough on her plate. But he found he wanted to ask her opinion about his ideas. So he found himself saying yes.

Chapter Twelve

SEEING HIM LIKE THAT, totally unexpected, had been like a punch to the gut. And she'd been punched in the gut before, so she knew what she was talking about. She had done her very best to deal with the fallout of last night in the privacy of her own room, her own bed.

She had cried after he'd left. She felt weird and shaky, ashamed about it.

There was no reason to cry. And she couldn't figure out if it was because of talking about Tim and what he tried to do to her, or if it was because of the sheer volume of releases she'd experienced in a row. Sexual, and emotional.

Maybe it was even because of him.

Because of all the things that he shared about himself, that made her feel tender and sorry.

She was not used to this. She didn't like it. And she felt, somehow, like the scales were imbalanced again. She wanted to do something for him. Do something to ease the burden, because Lord knew he was carrying too much of it. There was no avoiding him; that was the thing. So exposure therapy was probably the only solution.

And that would be killing two birds with one stone. She could help him, and she could deal with the intensity of her emotion surrounding him. Because it was just . . . It was too much. She didn't need it.

So now she found herself following him down the dirt road, her car behind his truck, a strange echo of last night. They pulled up to the event space, and got out.

"Okay," she said, trying to stay brisk and certain sounding. "Let's see it."

She wasn't prepared for what she saw inside. The floors were beautiful, highly polished and beautifully restored recycled wood that gave it a rustic, but very expensive feel. A large light fixture hung down from the center, casting a beautiful golden glow around the place. The walls were whitewashed, and there were big heavy beams stretched across the ceiling.

She could see a thousand girls wanting to get married here. It was just so . . . perfect enough that it made her almost picture what it might be like to have a wedding.

Another gut punch, straight from her own brain.

She did not like that.

She shoved it down deep.

"It looks beautiful," she said.

"Right. Well. I think this is what we need to do."

He began walking her through the plans. Table placement. Space for dancing, food. There was still work that needed to be done on the loft area, and on the bathrooms.

She took a mental note of everything. Because by day she would be working on the bar, and by late evening she was going to be helping with this. And there wasn't going to be anything he could do to stop her.

The next day, she came by early. And wordlessly joined him in painting some trim.

But then that meant that he followed her out to the bar and started to work with the construction crew on that. Which was not the idea.

So in the evening, she followed him back and helped him drag tables and chairs out of the storage unit to the back of the building. They discussed the finer points of tablecloths, flower arrangements and other decorations.

The Sullivan sisters had a greenhouse, and they ended up going over there and looking at flowers, which she had some ideas about.

And they didn't talk about the fact that they had slept together. They didn't talk about the things that they had revealed to one another. It went on like that, for a week. And every time she went to bed she was thankful that she was exhausted, because that meant she couldn't think about how aroused she felt every time the sheets brushed against her bare skin. How her thoughts went directly to Denver, no matter how hard she tried to make it otherwise.

But after she'd been doing it for eight days, she noticed that she felt a little bit more run-down than normal. And by day nine, she was starting to feel body achy.

She was very, very worried that she was sick. But she wasn't going to acknowledge it. Especially not in front of Denver. Who chided and lectured her on the amount of work that she was doing like it was any of his business. So whether or not she felt slightly ill wasn't his business either.

But of course, Denver couldn't leave well enough alone, and maybe, just maybe, her cold was turning into something a lot more flu adjacent, and she felt a little bit weak while she was trying to move a ladder around the event space, and had to stop.

She leaned up against the wall, trying to hide the fact that she was doing anything other than taking a casual rest.

"Are you okay?" His eyes locked on to hers, and she genuinely didn't know how to interpret the expression there.

She hadn't seen it before.

But before she could muse on it too deeply, he was across the room, right in front of her. "You look terrible," he said.

"Well, Denver, you really know how to flatter a girl. If you want to sleep with me again, just say so."

She broke the unspoken rule. The one where they ignored that the sex had ever occurred by saying that. He ignored her.

"You're sick," he said.

"I'm not," she said.

"Yes, you are." He lifted his hand and pressed his palm to her forehead.

She froze. Because she really didn't know what this was, combined with that fierce expression in his eyes, that rough hand against her skin, but all gentle and tender like, and not even trying to take her clothes off.

"You have a fever," he said.

"I don't," she said. But she shivered as she said it. "I don't," she insisted. "I'm just warm, because you're touching me."

"Knock it off," he growled.

"I'm fine," she said. "I'm more than able to finish work."

"Bullshit."

"Fine. It's almost time to be done anyway. I'll just go home."

And then there was something a lot like . . . worry in his eyes. And she suddenly realized what all of this was. Concern. For her well-being.

No wonder it was so foreign to see.

"I'm not sending you back home by yourself. I'm taking you to the farmhouse."

"What?"

"Don't argue with me," he said.

Then he swept her up into his arms, like she weighed nothing, and for a woman who was five foot nine, that was something. She felt like she needed to do some sort of cursory resistance, so she kicked her feet a little bit, but she did feel dizzy, and it was a revelation to be carried like this.

He ignored the kicking. He carried her out of the barn and across the gravel lot. She was thankful that everybody else had gone home some time ago. Because she didn't want anyone to see this. Didn't want anyone to see her swooning in a man's arms like she was Scarlett O'Hara.

She didn't wrap her arms around his neck or do anything that would make it seem like she was complicit in being carried. She let her arms fall limp at her sides, and did nothing to help him whatsoever, but that didn't seem to bother him in the least.

"You're a menace," he growled as he stomped up the stairs and into the house.

She hadn't been inside his house. He set her down, and she looked around, at the braided rugs on the floor, the homey furniture.

It was not anything she had expected from a King family dwelling.

She didn't know what she'd expected.

A pile of rocks and maybe a dragon horde in the corner?

What she hadn't expected was homey, brass lamps and . . . There was a doily on one of those tables.

"All my mom's old stuff," he said. "Let's go into the kitchen. I'm going to take your temperature."

"Really, as pickup lines go, that's not a great one. Did you need me to bend over and cough?"

"I'm not taking it like *that*," he said, his eyes boring into hers. "I'm not wasting that sort of thing on illness."

She snorted. "Good to know."

She followed him into the kitchen where he opened up a cabinet and pulled a plastic bin down. It was filled with miscellaneous medicines, and there was a thermometer sticking out of the top.

She had something like that too. Everything in it was old, because it had been a long time since she had bandaged any wounds. Over-the-counter pain reliever was pretty much the only thing that got bought with regularity. It was funny to see how much her life mirrored his, even in this.

"Open," he said, holding the thermometer out to her.

"The last time we were in this position, it wasn't a thermometer you were putting in my mouth."

He let out a low growl, which was evidence that she was pushing it. Pushing him. Good. She was happy to do that.

She obeyed then, because there was no point arguing. He pushed the button on the thermometer, and waited for it to beep.

"Hundred and one point six," he said when he looked at it, scowling. "You're sick."

"Oh, that isn't so bad," she said, but then she shivered, because it did feel so bad.

Actually, she was suddenly exhausted, her eyelids heavy, her whole body sluggish.

"Sheena," he said. "I'm going to take you upstairs, and I'm going to put you to bed."

"And?"

He leaned in, his nose almost brushing hers. "No *and*," he said. "Unless the *and* is you're going to get hot tea and chicken soup."

She felt dizzy just then, and she must've swayed on her feet, because he reached out and caught her, holding her upright.

"Are you okay?" he asked.

She didn't know how to tell him that it wasn't so much the illness getting to her right at this moment, but the sheer strangeness of being taken care of on this level. It was just . . . completely unfamiliar, totally outside of her comfort zone. And . . . maybe even a little bit wonderful, and that made her want to hiss and spit and push him away.

Sadly, she was actually sick, so she couldn't do that.

She found herself being lifted up again, carried upstairs. He brought her into the room closest to the head of the staircase, a feminine-looking space with a patchwork quilt on a brass frame bed.

"Penny's old room," he said.

They had never talked about Penny. She knew Penny, because she was a little girl in that old community that she lived in. Because Penny had been left alone when her father had been sent to prison, a few years after Sheena's dad had died.

Penelope Case had stayed here. A girl from the exact same neighborhood as Sheena.

A strange sort of jealousy began to expand in her chest. She'd been taken care of by Denver. She had this soft, nice room for all those years, and Denver had sent her to college and . . .

He had done the same for her sisters.

Well. *She* had.

She had taken his money and that was what she had used it for. She had chosen not to use it on herself, because how could she choose to use it on herself?

But suddenly then she wished that she'd had him.

Because she wished that she could have been taken care of in that way. That she could have been the one who was swaddled up and given a handmade quilt.

"I'll be right back," he said.

He disappeared, then reappeared a moment later while she was still standing there lost in some kind of petulant grief that she couldn't quite parse. He handed her a white T-shirt. Soft and oversized. His, clearly.

"Change into this," he said. "Get under the covers, and I'll bring you some medicine, and some tea."

"Okay," she said.

He left, closing the door behind him, and she began to take her clothes off, and she was wondering why she was letting him do this.

You're hilarious. You were just standing here feeling violently angry about a quilt, and all the care you didn't get, and now you're mad at yourself for accepting a little bit of help.

The truth was, she didn't want to drive home. She felt gritty and exhausted, and that feeling that had descended upon her in his kitchen right when he'd taken her temperature had only gotten worse. The one that was something like getting hit by a freight train of fatigue.

So she put on that soft T-shirt, and climbed beneath the covers. And it felt so good.

To sleep in a bed that she hadn't made. In comfortable clothes she hadn't had to go and find for herself.

There was a light knock on the door. "Come in," she croaked.

He came inside with a tray. And on that tray was a steaming bowl, and a steaming mug. "Soup and hot tea. Eat what you can. He handed her a packet of orange pills. "Pain reliever and fever reducer. Might make you a little bit more comfortable."

"I'm going to get you sick too," she said.

"I'm pretty sturdy," he said. "You don't need to worry about me."

"But I do," she said. "Mostly because I'd feel guilty."

"Well, I would actually pay to see that. You feeling guilty."

"Oh, come on," she mumbled. "We're not so different, you and I." She laughed ruefully through her pain.

He shook his head. "I guess not."

She took the pills with the tea, and grimaced when the hot liquid hit the back of her throat. It was good, but intense.

She managed a couple bites of soup after Denver left the room, and then she fell into a weird, dreamless sleep that was a lot like being unconscious.

When she woke up, it was dark out, and her head was pounding. And like he had sensed it, Denver was suddenly coming into the room. "More medicine," he said.

He had a large glass of water, and when she swallowed the pills this time it felt like she was being stabbed directly in the back of the throat.

"Oh my . . . blehhhh," she groaned. "I feel like garbage."

"Don't try to talk," he said.

That was when she first realized just how gross she sounded.

"Oh no," she groaned.

"You're fine," he said.

"What time is it?"

"You're very bad at following instructions."

"Obviously."

"It's about two o'clock in the morning."

She put her forearm over her eyes, and felt that her forehead was scalding hot.

"You're all right," he said. "Just get some rest."

She went to sleep after that, and didn't wake again until morning. She felt like she'd been run over by the truck that had hit her yesterday.

But Denver brought her oatmeal and pancakes, and it was by far the nicest thing anyone had ever done for her. Well. Maybe the cold pills were the best part. Yeah. That felt pretty significant.

"I need to get up," she said.

"You don't," he insisted. "You're still a mess."

"People can go home and have colds."

"Sure. But then you're going to have to take care of yourself. And that seems silly, when I'm happy to do it."

"Why?"

He looked at her, a strange expression on his face. "You know why."

Obligation?

The fact that they'd slept together?

She didn't think it was the second one. Because he was like her. That stuff never mattered. Not especially.

So it just had to be because of all the guilt that he had about her dad, and then being alone.

"Denver," she said. "Why did you take Penny in?"

"Because she was alone," he said.

He sat down on the edge of the bed and looked at her, his expression far too earnest for her to handle. "She didn't have anybody. Her mom was long gone, and her dad was in prison. She was just . . . She was young and vulnerable, and I was in a position to take her in.

"You didn't take us in."

She felt so stupid, the minute that came out of her mouth. Because he had taken care of her. She'd been an adult, anyway. Penny had been something around fifteen when her dad died. Sheena had been grown.

Denver looked away from her, his jaw set into stone. "I know," he said. "Sheena, if I was in any kind of place to do that when your dad died, I would have. But honestly, right then it didn't even occur to me. I was a mess. I was climbing my way out of that same pit. I knew that I wanted to take care of you, I knew that I wanted to . . . make sure you didn't suffer because of him, but I was still lost in the programming, basically. Until that day, I had been working with my dad. Until that day, I was complicit in what he was doing, and that haunts me. It's really just a terrible thing to have to contend with. I'm not making excuses for myself. Not really. I feel guilty about being taken in by my dad in the first place. It's more to do with the fact that I did not know who I was yet." He let out a heavy breath. "I went off gambling after that. I was trying to make money, because I thought if I could pay for everybody's pain and suffering some things would be better. Fixed. I took my dad's money, and invested it in the poker games. But I was losing myself at the same time."

"What are you talking about?" She didn't know if he was being hard to follow or if it was all because she was illness-addled.

"I'm just not proud of who I was then. I was playing the part of stalwart older brother, helper. A man redeemed here. Then I would go to Las Vegas and get drunk. Have lots of sex."

"Sounds like a good Saturday night to me," she said.

"It's not so much what I did, it's how selfish it was. That's all self-indulgent stuff. I left my brothers behind and yes you're right, I took Penny in. I gave her a place to stay, but I wasn't . . . really engaged with anyone not here. And when I was there I was just in oblivion. Drunk and hooking up. Fleecing people out of their money because my brain works in a certain way, even if I do drink."

"You were a drunk, horny Robin Hood. What's wrong with that?" She shrugged beneath the covers. "Those men who sat down at those tables, they must have had the money to gamble."

"You and I both know that isn't true. My father built a whole empire off of the fact that men gamble when they don't have enough to play with. It was his extortionist interest rates that made him real money. He was able to get those people so desperate that they took loans from him. That was the real money. I hate that I was part of that. Even a little bit. It was climbing out of that hole, coming back here, seeing the effects that were still echoing through the community, that's why when I heard that Penny's dad had been taken to prison I thought to bring her in."

"I'm just sick and whiny," she said. "We had a fine life. I didn't really need you to bring us in and turn us into your passel of plucky orphans."

"I don't think I could've managed a passel of orphans. The truth is, I don't know that I've managed much of anything as well as even my siblings think that I did. They're so quick to talk about how I took care of everything, but for the first few years I had that outlet. Gambling, sex, drinking. I wasn't reformed. I was playing the part of a reformed man."

"Honestly," she said, feeling a little bit better after the pancakes. "Wouldn't it have been better if our fathers had *tried* to play the part of reformed? A little bit of playacting might have made our lives a lot better. But we didn't even get that. Don't you think . . . don't you think that there are points for doing the right thing even when you don't feel like it? It's like you were saying before, you don't like it when people say we are extra good. Because we don't feel like we are. Because we know that we are just . . . people. Dealing with all of this garbage that got dumped into our laps. But what really matters to the people who were depending on us was that we came through for them. Not that when you were in Vegas you blew off a little steam. Sometimes, I finished a shift and went to some guy's hotel room because I just . . . needed somebody to see me for a little bit. For an hour or so of somebody's life to be about me, because my life was all about my sisters."

"There's no harm in that," he said, gruffly.

"I know there isn't. Any more than there is harm in what you did. I mean, unless you were out in Vegas being a secret serial killer."

"No. Nothing like that."

"Then you didn't cause any harm. There's nothing wrong with having a little bit of something for yourself, is there?"

Even feeling as gross as she did, asking that question, looking at him while she said it, sent a lightning bolt of desire through her body.

"Maybe not," he said.

"Forget I said anything about . . . you taking us in. I'm tired, like I said."

She had only meant to reference being tired right that second because of her illness. But she felt like she was admitting to a much broader exhaustion. Which was truer than she wanted to acknowledge.

"Get some rest then."

He stood up from the bed, and walked out of the room. And left her lying there in all her state. She felt exhausted, and sorry for herself, and when she fell into a deep sleep, it wasn't dreamless this time.

She saw herself, young and standing in a field, staring down at her father's dead body. And when she looked up she saw Denver, reaching his hand out to her.

And all she wanted to do was take it, but for some reason, she couldn't make her feet move forward.

It went on like that, for three days. In and out of consciousness, barely out of bed. Sweating through sheets and T-shirts. Taking short showers and promising to keep her phone close by so she could text him if she fell, and acknowledging that if she was longer than fifteen minutes he was going to come in and make sure she was all right.

And something changed inside of her over those few days. Because nobody had ever done this for her. Not when she was a kid, and sure as hell not when she was an adult.

She could remember catching the same awful illness as all of her sisters, and still taking care of everything. Cooking, cleaning, bringing them food.

And if they ran out of soup, she would be the person who didn't get any.

She had never considered herself a martyr. She supposed she was.

She didn't know how else to be, though. Because everything she had done had made her sisters' lives better. So what was the answer? Because the self-sacrifice had been a reward. It had gotten them through. It had turned them into functional adults. Better adults than she was.

So it mattered. She couldn't regret it. But being taken care of like this, it made her feel a lot of things.

But more than that, it was the way his hands had touched her fevered brow, the way he had looked at her intensely.

She had felt too awful to be turned on by it at first. But as she had started to heal, the intensity of his attention had begun to stoke a different kind of fire in her. One that had nothing to do with a fever.

When she woke up on the evening of the fourth day, it was dark outside, and she finally felt good.

She listened for sounds in the house, anything to suggest that there were other people around.

She got up, her legs shaky, still dressed only in panties and one of Denver's white T-shirts. She looked at herself in the mirror. Her dark hair was a total disaster, the T-shirt just coming to the tops of her thighs. It was see-through, her nipples visible as she stood there staring at herself.

It was . . . perfect.

She opened up the bedroom door, and walked out into the hall, then slowly made her way down the stairs as muscles she hadn't engaged for days made themselves known.

The lights were off downstairs, so maybe he wasn't home. Disappointment hollowed out her gut. But then she saw one of those antique brass lamps on in the corner of the room, and then him, sitting in a chair beneath it, holding a glass of whiskey.

And right then, he looked up at her, his eyes connecting with hers. She padded the rest of the way down the stairs and crossed the room to him.

"Did you need something?" he asked, his voice rough.

"As a matter of fact," she said. "I can think of something."

She moved toward him, and climbed onto the chair, straddling his lap. He didn't move, his jaw clenched tight, his eyes glittering. Then she reached out and stole the whiskey cup from his hand. She put it up to her lips and knocked back the rest of the alcohol. She leaned forward, putting it on the table with a firm click. That brought their mouths close together. Almost touching.

"Just one more time," she whispered. "Please."

And then his strong hands went to her hips, and he pulled her down hard, so that she could feel the iron length of his erection. "This is not why I took care of you."

"I know. And I'm not paying you back."

"Good."

And then on a growl, he claimed her mouth with his.

Chapter Thirteen

THIS WASN'T WHAT he was supposed to be doing. He had lost track of exactly *what* he was supposed to be doing. The moment she had come down the stairs looking like that . . .

He'd lost himself.

The thing was, she had been sick the whole time she was here. He wasn't that big of a bastard that he was obsessing about her body while he was taking care of her. No. He had his limits. But he also wasn't blind to the fact that she was beautiful. And the memories of their night together had played havoc on him while he was sleeping, every night. So in fairness, it had been every night since they'd been together.

All the while they were working together, all the while he was supposed to be putting all that behind them. He was stuck on her in a way he had never been stuck on another woman. And then . . . when she'd gotten weak-looking in the barn he had . . . All he wanted to do was rescue her. Take care of her. All he had wanted to do was scoop her up into his arms and take her home where he could give her hot tea and feed her with soup.

So he had.

And it had been . . . the perfect torture having her in his house like that.

But this . . . this was exquisite. Having his hands on her again, her shapely hips, that small waist, her breasts . . .

She took her T-shirt off, revealing all that bare skin, all that glorious ink, for him to gaze at openly.

He loved how confident she was in her beauty. In his reaction to it.

She stripped his shirt off quickly, and he moved his hands down her bare back, pushing them down beneath the waistband of her panties.

"You're so beautiful," he growled.

It felt like not quite enough.

It felt like an inadequate description of her.

Insufficient for all the light and glory that she contained. She was more than beautiful. But the beauty, in the face of all the ugliness that she had experienced, seemed like a miracle.

A woman who had been through the sorts of things that she had would have good reason to want to hide her body. To want to move through life without confidence, for fear of drawing attention to herself again.

But not Sheena.

She put the blame where it was due. On the bastard who tried to hurt her.

She rejected shame. And she rejected the idea that her body was the enemy. It made him feel . . . overawed, really.

Because she was something. She really was something else.

One more time . . .

He didn't know if he could take one more time. He also couldn't refuse her. Couldn't let it go.

He didn't know if he could stand to stop after tonight. No. He couldn't.

He wanted her. For more than just once.

He didn't say that, didn't say anything, as he kissed her neck, down her shoulder, sucking one glorious nipple into his mouth.

He arched his hips up off the chair, and grabbed his wallet from his back pocket. He had a condom in there. Thank God.

Maybe you weren't supposed to thank God for that kind of thing.

He wouldn't know. He was half feral, after all, so how could he possibly have any idea what he was supposed to do in a situation like this.

So he figured a prayer of thanks wasn't too far outside the realm of the acceptable.

He took out a packet and tore it open, then she went to work on his belt, unbuttoning and unzipping his pants, freeing him as she rolled it on his hard length.

He brought her down slowly on top of him, filling her, watching her head fall back as pleasure took her.

And then he couldn't keep his eyes open, because he was so overwhelmed by it. The feel of her, tight and hot, wet and perfect.

She rolled her hips, and started to ride him, her eyes glowing with ferocity as she continued.

He was never one to surrender control, but he did it here and now. With her. With Sheena.

Because this was perfect, and so was she.

Because it was the hottest sex he'd ever had in his life. Except the last time he'd had sex with her.

Everything in him was on fire with molten heat.

Everything in him was ready for release.

But no. Not until she had hers. He put his thumb right at that delicate bud that was the source of her pleasure, and stroked her. She gripped his shoulders, her fingernails digging into his skin, and he could feel her mounting desire. Could feel her internal muscles gripping him hard.

"That's right," he said. "Come for me."

She bit her lip, like she was trying to hold back. Like she was trying to . . .

"Don't be a brat," he said. He reached back and gripped her hair, tugged gently. "You do what you're told."

That did it. It sent her right over, a harsh cry of pleasure, the punctuation mark on that climax.

And then he followed her over. Pounding up inside of her as he chased his own release.

Then she collapsed against his chest, breathing hard.

"How did you do that?" she asked.

"How did I do what?"

"You're not supposed to be able to make me come by being a commanding bastard."

"Some consider it a feature not a bug," he said.

She shifted, and he groaned, because the feel of her naked body pressed against him was just about too much to take.

"Well, it's not my thing," she said.

She rolled her eyes—he had a feeling at herself—and got up from his lap. She was there naked in his living room, which was filled with all this old furniture that had belonged to his great-grandparents. And he had just screwed her brains out on what he was pretty sure had been his great-grandfather's favorite chair.

Talk about improving family legacies.

"Seems like it might be," he said.

"Historically no," she said.

Then her lips curved into a smile. "I don't know how you do it. And I don't really like it. But I like it."

He chuckled. He suddenly came back to awareness enough to realize that he needed to go get rid of the condom.

He stood up, held his jeans in place while he walked into the downstairs bathroom and dealt with practicalities. Sheena followed him.

"Really?" he asked.

"What? I was talking to you."

"Okay. Anyway. You say you don't like that sort of thing."

"Why would I? The whole thing for me . . . with sex . . . has always been about keeping my own control. It's for me. It's not for them. And I like it a certain way, generally. But you don't let me have the control. I both find it very annoying, and very sexy."

"We're even then. Because I find a lot of things about you both annoying and sexy."

"Another way that we're alike."

He huffed out a laugh, and gripped the sink, looking at his reflection, and then past his at hers. Behind him. She was leaning in the doorway, still totally naked.

"Sheena, come on. Who are we kidding? It's not going to just be that one time. Again."

Her eyes went round. "What's the alternative?"

"We do it until we don't want to do it anymore."

And then she laughed. Doubled over and laughed, like he had just said the funniest thing in history. "Right. Because that is a great idea."

"How would you know? Have you ever done this before?"

She shook her head, her glossy dark hair moving over her shoulders in a wave as she leaned back against the doorframe. "No. But you haven't either."

"No. And I've never wanted to. But this . . . It's not burning itself out. So why make a big drama about it. Let's just keep doing it. I don't want to have sex with anyone else. Do you?"

She looked away from him, and for one terrible moment, he thought she was going to say that she did want to have sex with someone else. Or just that perhaps she wasn't quite as be-witched by the whole thing as he was.

That was a punch in the gut. He had spent all these years hooking up and never once feeling compelled to see the woman again, and now that he finally wanted . . . something, maybe she didn't.

Maybe this was where he got what he deserved for being the son of Elias King. For being his right-hand man.

"I don't do relationships," she said. "I don't have the energy for it. I want to open this bar. I want you to do something for *me*. I want to be able to be entirely selfish for once in my life. Can you understand that?"

"I do," he said. "But I have to tell you, the chance for us to have more sex feels pretty selfish to me."

"But I just mean, you know, this isn't . . . This isn't going to be a thing."

"Sure," he said.

"Okay," she said. "Glad we had that talk."

She changed her stance then, leaning against the doorframe with a whole different posture, her eyes roaming over his body. "So let's go again."

"You need to build your strength back up," he said.

Because he didn't think it would hurt her to suffer a little bit. When it came right down to it, she was as desperate for this as he was, or she wouldn't be agreeing. Both of them had a pretty solid fight-or-flight response. And the fight seemed to come out pretty often when they were around each other. Sheena had just been toying with flight.

If they didn't want this to end badly, they simply wouldn't do it. Bottom line. Because it would be easier. It would be easier to stick to their natural modus operandi. That was what it came down to. So she was desperate.

"I'm fine," she said, narrowing her eyes.

"Maybe you should drink some orange juice. Get your vitamin C up."

"Maybe I should come over there and get *your* vitamin C up." She lifted her brows. "How about that?"

"Was that a double entendre? Because it was a weird one."

"You liked it," she said.

He did. Because he liked every damned thing about her, as it happened.

Irritating. But true.

She came up behind him, and wrapped her arms around his waist, pressing her breasts to his back.

He straightened, and closed his eyes, then put his hand down over hers. They stood like that for a moment, and he didn't know what the hell was happening. What the hell had just changed?

"Take me upstairs."

"Yes, ma'am," he responded.

All his heavy talk about how he didn't follow orders had met a bitter end. Because the way that she was touching him, the way that she was looking at him, would have any man desperate.

He let her lead him upstairs, to his bed. And then it was Sheena's turn to take damned good care of him.

Chapter Fourteen

WHEN SHEENA WOKE up in the morning, there was a large, masculine arm draped over her waist.

Holy shit. Had she actually . . . ?

She rolled over onto her back and looked up at the ceiling. It was the same white shiplap ceiling that she had been looking at for the last several days, but this was not the same bedroom.

She looked over at Denver. And her heart did something heretofore unknown. It froze for a moment, then felt like it expanded, before thumping hard against her sternum.

"Oh no," she whispered.

She had fallen asleep with him.

He had taken her hand and led her upstairs, and had thoroughly wrecked her resistance last night in his bed and she had . . . fallen asleep with him. She had never done that before.

She had never stayed the whole night with a lover.

That was . . . It was getting clingy. *Desperate.*

Relationship.

She had been very clear that wasn't what this was.

"Good morning," he said, still not opening his eyes.

"You weren't asleep?"

"Afraid not," he said. There was a slight smile on his lips, but he still didn't open his eyes.

"Well, what do you think of all this?"

He turned his head then, and his eyes fluttered open slowly. The light hit them, all blue and brilliant, and her breath caught.

Damn him for being so pretty.

"You're beautiful," he said.

He said that with ease. She had heard it a lot of times, but there was something about the way he said it that did something to her. To her stomach, to her throat. To her heart. It was genuinely annoying. It really was. Why did he have to affect her so deeply?

It was the sex. Because while she had good luck getting herself to climax in her previous encounters, that's what it was.

It was her knowing exactly how to use a man's body to her advantage.

But that wasn't what it was like with Denver.

He took charge. He said things and did things she wouldn't have even known to fantasize about. He was showing her things about herself, and it was annoying. Because she didn't especially want some guy to teach her about herself.

"I wasn't going to stay the night," she said.

"Well, let's look at this reasonably. You have been staying here for the last few days. Your car is still over by the event space."

She clapped her hand over her mouth. "Why does everybody think it's there?"

"Oh, everybody knows you're sick. You haven't been down to work."

Well, she supposed that was a relief. Nobody thought that she was mooching off of Denver. That would be annoying.

Or trading anything for sex. That would also annoy her.

She didn't care if people knew her and Denver . . .

That stopped her short. She wouldn't have cared if people knew that she and Denver had slept together, and considering the power of the town's rumor mill, many people probably did know, because it wasn't like they were subtle when they headed out of the bar.

She didn't know for sure, though, because this illness had put her out of commission in a very weird way.

But yeah. People knowing that she and Denver King had a one-night stand was a particular thing.

People knowing that she and Denver King were actively sleeping together? No, thank you. That made her want to jump and hiss and spit like a feral cat.

"What's the matter, Sheena?"

"Nothing is the matter, Denver," she said.

"You seem skittish."

"I am never skittish," she sniffed. "It's not in my nature. You're never going to catch me taxidermied and mounted up in some axe throwing bar. Skittish is for rodents. I'm not a rodent."

"You seem a little bit . . ."

"Oh please. Do you traditionally spend the night with your hookups?"

The ensuing silence was strange. She could hear her heart beating in her head. She wanted him to say no. She realized that much to her chagrin. She wanted to be special.

And what the hell was that?

"Of course I don't," he said. "But I'm not worried about it. Because I already said that I wanted to keep doing this with you. And I think practicality dictates sometimes it's going to make sense to spend the night."

"All right. Fair. How many nights a week are we talking?"

"For spending the night? Or for sex?"

"Either. Both. Pick a boundary."

"Do you need boundaries?"

She tried to imagine this just free-floating. Having no rules. Then just coming together and tearing each other's clothes off whenever they felt like it. Yeah. Okay. There was something kind of intoxicating about that, but mostly she felt like she was free-falling through space trying desperately to find something to grab onto other than Denver's broad shoulders, because she had already left marks there last night, and she didn't need to go grabbing hold of them again.

"Three days a week," she said.

He groaned. "Only three days?"

He looked boyish then, and Denver King was not *boyish*.

But she was also not fluttery, and something in her stomach *fluttered* just then.

"You are ridiculous," she said. "All right, fine. How about we just see how it goes?"

Yes, she was screaming internally. But the truth was, she wanted him even now. Right this second.

And it was a good thing she did, because he kissed her and rolled her onto her back and pleasured her for a good thirty minutes before they went downstairs for coffee and to get ready to go to work.

She had to go back and get her car, so that meant her first stop was the event space. When they arrived, there was a full crew of Kings already on hand.

"Sheena," said Bix. "You're better!"

"Yeah," she said, trying not to project *I just spent the morning doing unspeakable things to your brother-in-law* right out at the cheerful other woman.

"Denver said that you were really sick."

"Yeah," she said. "I was."

"Sorry about that," said Bix. "Being sick is the worst. Though, it's a lot better when you have somebody take care of you. Back when I was living the van life if I got a cold I would just pull over somewhere and hope that nobody disturbed me while I convalesced in a sleeping bag."

Bix was one of the few people that Sheena had ever met who'd had it harder than she did.

Bix's father had been a moonshiner, and Bix had ended up striking out on her own, trying to put some distance between herself and her father's criminal empire. She could hard relate.

But Bix didn't have siblings who looked out for her, and she had lived a transient existence for a while, stealing what she could to survive. Sheena was glad for Bix. That she had somebody like Daughtry in her life.

After all that.

But the way she said that hit a little too close to the bone. Because she and Denver were not Bix and Daughtry. They weren't going to be. That was just a fact.

She was in no danger of forgetting that. Not when they had agreed to a kind of no-rules situation, but one that had very clear parameters.

And she didn't need that. She didn't. That aching sort of feeling, where she had wished for somebody to take care of her, was the closest she'd ever gotten in her life to feeling . . . Whatever. It didn't matter. She didn't even want what Bix and Daughtry had. She could be happy for somebody else without wishing she had the identical outcome. Could recognize it was good for somebody else without thinking that it was necessary for herself.

So she did her best to banish her internal lecturing, and the slight pang of wistfulness in her stomach, because neither were very helpful.

"Yeah, it was definitely better to have Denver take care of me than to be convalescing at home by myself," she said.

Because not saying something would be churlish. And look more than a little bit suspicious if not outright ungrateful.

"Denver is good like that," said Justice. "He was basically the only good parental figure we had."

"In fairness," said Landry. "Maybe our mom was okay when she was around. It's just none of us can really remember."

"She was fine," said Denver.

And she realized she had never heard Denver say anything about his mother. Not even once.

Fair enough, she didn't talk about her own. Because the memories were scant and just disappointing. Her sisters were her half sisters anyway. That was why there was such a big gap between them.

For a while it had just been her and her father.

And . . .

"I better get out to the bar," she said. "We have a lot of work to do if we're going to have it ready for Christmas."

"I'll walk you to your car," said Denver.

She bit back a terse comment about how that was completely unacceptable, because she wasn't actually trying to alert anybody to the fact that there was something going on with them.

And resisting something that simple, that chivalrous, was definitely going to have the *lady is protesting too much* vibes.

"I'm going to have to go home tonight," she said.

They had washed and cleaned the one outfit she had with her, so she had been fine today, but she was itching to get back to her things, her face cream. Her makeup. A different pair of panties.

"Sure," he said.

She couldn't read his emotions there. Maybe he was glad to

have a break from her. Maybe he was disappointed because he wasn't going to get laid.

Though, she felt like she could certainly squeeze in some sex before she went home.

She thought about the logistics of that for far too long during the workday. The wiring was in, and new plumbing had been done. They were closing up the walls, and Sheetrock was going up. Sadly for Denver, much of the molding was not salvageable.

But she had chosen some wallpaper that was done up in an old-fashioned style, to mimic what had been there before.

The structure of the place was good, and all the wood floors needed refinishing.

Making the bathrooms modern was one of the bigger projects, but that was well underway.

The crew had put in the axe throwing lanes during her convalescence. And she had to resist the urge to test them out. Resistance that didn't last when the crew left.

She went and stood at the end of the throwing lane, picked up one of the axes and drew her arms back over her head, letting it fly. It went true and struck the heart of the target.

"Yes," she said. "I've still got it."

"Damn," came the all-too-familiar voice behind her. "That's incredible."

"My throw? You've seen me do it before."

She didn't even turn. Because she knew it was him. No question about it.

"This place," he said. "It still looks like the old gaming hall, but it looks like an axe throwing bar too. Pretty damned impressive."

"Well, since I had a surplus of sick days, I can't really take credit for it."

"I did some work over here while you were down and out."

She lifted a brow. "Really?"

"Yes," he said. "It needed the manpower."

"So you aren't really all that surprised to see it like this?"

"I am," he said. "Some of this is new since I was last here a couple of days ago. They're really working fast."

"I didn't sleep with Manny, you know." She didn't know why that mattered. Except that he was helping her, and they were sleeping together, and she just didn't want it to seem like she went out of her way to have sex with men so that they would do favors for her. She didn't keep contact with the men she had sex with so that was impossible.

"I know you didn't," he said. "Not that it matters."

"How come you know that I didn't."

"Because you said you didn't."

"You don't really know me, or if I'm a liar."

"I know you're not a liar," he said.

"He used to get picked on at school. He was a quiet kid. He was just trying to go to school, get an education. And people called him all kinds of racist shit. It made me mad. I punched somebody one day. I got punched back. After that, we were friends. And nobody messed with him again. Not that he couldn't have defended himself, it's just that he . . . he was afraid to. Afraid of what would happen to him. To his family."

"That makes sense," he said. "That he looks out for you now too."

"He always did. He's a good guy. And believe me, there were a lot of guys who were not good. I was a really lonely girl, and I was always the kind of pretty that attracted . . . whatever attention I wanted. So you know. I took that attention. It made me feel good. Why not? The men could be judgmental about it, even though they were also there. Somehow I was a slut, but they never were."

"Yeah. Well. That's very boring and predictable, isn't it?"

"In my experience, people tend to be boring and predict-able. Manny is a notable exception to that. And that's why he's been in my life all this time."

"You're not predictable," Denver said. "Or boring."

"I don't know. I'm feeling like challenging you to an axe throwing competition. Which in the grand scheme of our rela-tionship actually feels a bit predictable."

Something to shift the conversation away from getting too deep.

Except she looked at him, and saw that he had a deeply contemplative look on his face that suggested she was not going to get her way on that score. "All right," he said. "Let's throw."

He went to the end of the lane, and cocked back his weapon, before sending it flying. He was much improved from when he had thrown with her the first time off the edge of that embank-ment. Though, in fairness, a flat throwing lane that was actually made for this was much easier.

She watched, hungrily, as he easily lifted the axe back out of the target. Why was everything he did so damned sexy?

Rhetorical. He *was* sexy. So, what other option was there?

"Why doesn't it surprise me that you defend everybody?" he asked.

"Why doesn't it surprise me that you wiped everybody's fevered brow?"

"I guess we are who we are," he said.

She chuckled. "Neither of us are really as badass as we pre-tend to be, are we?"

"Speak for yourself," he said. "I think I'm pretty badass."

"I've never heard any of you talk about your mom," she said. "In fact, I've never even heard anyone in town talk about your mom."

Denver paused, and let the axe fly. "That's because there's not much to say. I meant what I said earlier. She was kind of a nonentity in our lives. Our dad was in control of everything. Every narrative that ran through the house, that belonged to him. And there was a point where she just couldn't deal with it. And I think the prospect of being in a custodial disagreement with a full-on narcissist who had quite a bit of money and power just didn't appeal to her. So she decided to leave us."

"That's . . . It's awful," she said.

"You know, I didn't really notice a difference when she was gone. Because she let Dad do whatever he wanted. She didn't protect us. She didn't sweep in and take care of us when he failed to do so. Dad was the present parent in our lives. That's what's so hard about the whole thing. Honestly. I bought into his lies completely and totally. Because he was the one that was there for me. He was the one who taught me how to ride a horse. How to shoot a gun. He was the one who was proud of me. Who spent time with me. And yeah, there was a lot of stuff that wasn't ideal. Sometimes you could go away from talking to him and feel all kinds of bad about yourself, because at the end of the day my dad was a master manipulator. But as a kid, you don't see any of that. All you see is the parent that shows up for you. The one who teaches you to do things. Even as far as dinner went . . . my dad was the grill master. Where do you think I learned it?"

"Denver . . . I'm sorry."

"I know I keep saying that to you, and I keep telling you to just accept it. Why is it so annoying when you do it to me?"

"I don't know. Maybe because it's always annoying when somebody tries to apply sympathy to a wound you just want to be left alone." She threw the axe, and it went wide. She winced. "I don't really remember my mom either, she left when I was so young. I understand what you're saying."

"Your sisters are a lot younger than you."

"They have a different mother."

"Did she live with you?"

"Yeah, she was my stepmom for a while."

"What did you think of her?"

She frowned. She didn't think about Tonya very often. "I don't know. It was clear that I wasn't supposed to think about her as a mom. She made that really clear. She wanted me to help out, with the babies and such. With the house. But she made me call her by her first name. She wasn't bad, don't get me wrong, I actually like her in a lot of ways. But she wasn't a mom. You know? And she wasn't really a mom to the kid she gave birth to either. She had Abby and Whitney and Sarah in short succession, and it was like she could never quite find her footing with it. She and my dad broke up, and I think she thought that she would go get a job somewhere else, and that would be fine with the girls because he already had me when they met. But of course, her visits became fewer and further between . . ."

"When your dad died she didn't come back."

"No. At that point she wasn't visiting anymore. She wasn't keeping in touch. At that point, we were all on our own. I started to hate her then. But I never did before. She was a tough woman, and in that way, she was a decent influence on me. But the leaving . . . I can't forgive her for that. Except I used to worry that she was going to take the girls away from me. Because the only thing that scared me more than having to raise them by myself, was having to live without them."

Which sometimes felt like what she was doing now.

Navigating this world that had centered around those girls without them there every day.

"It's just not even surprising," he said. "That's just how it is. For both of us."

"Yeah. Our lives are littered with disappointing adults. And when I was a kid it made a lot less sense. I thought adults were supposed to have it all together. I think I held a lot of resentment in my chest over that for a number of years. But I don't now. I mean, not about some things. Because I'm the same age as they were when they were navigating all this stuff, and I don't feel like I know it all. Or even half."

"You also would never leave innocent girls to fend for themselves. I know that, because you didn't."

"Neither did you," she said.

"I guess not."

She beat him soundly at axe throwing, and they both walked out of the gaming hall.

"Where's your truck?"

"I walked over."

"Well. You want me to give you a ride back to the house?"

"I was fixing to come home with you," he said.

"You . . . you were?"

"Yes. I was."

"Yes," he said, wrapping his arm around her waist and pulling her in for a kiss. Until that moment she hadn't realized just how starving she was for that. She wanted to strip all his clothes off then, but he slowed it down, made it just about their mouths meeting, his hand gliding over her cheek, his tongue sliding against hers.

She shivered.

"Denver," she whispered.

It was like he had bewitched her. Like he had turned her into something she had never been before.

A creature made entirely of need and flame.

One who was ready to melt at any given opportunity.

When they finally parted, she was breathing hard. And in no fit position to argue with him.

"Okay. Get in the car then."

"Sure," he said, chuckling.

"How old were you when your mom left?" he asked.

"I'm not entirely sure. Maybe around two? Something like that. I genuinely don't remember her. And honestly, you can't miss what you never knew."

"I feel the same. I mean, I was a lot older when our mom left. Eleven? Maybe? But she was kind of a ghost in the house. I guess, on some level I can feel some sympathy for her. Sympathy for what she must've been going through, because I know that our dad was a twisted son of a bitch. He was probably gaslighting her, and making her feel like she was a bad mother, I don't know. He probably strong-armed himself into the position of being world's best dad, right? Because he was basically building a small army of his own sons. He never had much use for Arizona."

"Poor Arizona," said Sheena. "Good thing she's a badass bitch."

"She is that," he said. "And I wish I would've seen that when I was younger. There were a lot of dynamics. And I was pretty blind to them. But he was good at appealing to each of our egos. Making us all feel special or not special, depending on what suited him at a given time."

"Your dad could have been a great cult leader."

"In a way he was. He had all those men willing to blindly follow him. To risk themselves to enrich him. I mean yeah, he was paying them, but he was definitely keeping most of it. I don't know how the hell he managed that. He's a scary bastard."

Denver really wasn't like him. Whatever he thought. There was less smooth cult leader to Denver, and more rough edges.

He was honest, and strong.

The fact that he felt guilt about different things that had happened when he was in Las Vegas was exhibit A that he wasn't anything like his dad.

She didn't think Elias King had ever felt a drop of guilt even once in his whole life.

She told Denver so.

"I don't know that that's true," he said.

"You don't know that your dad never felt guilt?"

"I don't know if that makes me decent that I do. It's almost worse in some ways. I know that there's something wrong with it, but I did it anyway. Because I was just so tired."

"It's okay to be tired."

"Yeah."

He said that. Yeah. Easy agreements when he wanted out of conversations. She was learning something about him. Which made her feel slightly unnerved.

Made her feel off-center. But hey, they were doing this thing. She supposed that conversation was inevitable. But that was the whole working-together thing. It made it difficult to keep this compartmentalized to just sex.

Finally, they got to her place. And this time, it wasn't quite so dark, and he examined the shingles on the side of the house. "This place needs a little work."

"Yes," she said slowly. "You're not wrong. But I've been waiting and putting my resources into other things."

"I get that. But at some point, you should put some resources into this place, because it's yours. You deserve to live somewhere nice."

"Rude. Also, I intend to move, remember?"

"Right. After the bar is self-sustaining."

"Exactly. After that, I'm going to leave this place."

"And what place are you going to go to?"

She went past him, and into the house. "I don't know. I was thinking . . . a city, maybe. I could go to Colorado. It seems like they would like an axe throwing bar. Or maybe I'll go to Europe. Maybe I can wow them with my very American concept of a quaint bar activity. Just somewhere else. Somewhere I'd get to be different. I can't do that here. Do you ever feel like that? Like you're just so entrenched in all the expectations here that you can't . . ."

"Yeah, I guess so. But then, I took that show on the road. And you know how I feel about that."

"Right. Well. I haven't had a chance to do that. So."

"You really might go to Europe?"

"No. Chances are I'll end up somewhere near one of my sisters. Especially if Abby ends up marrying Alejandro. Because they might have babies. And it might be fun to be an aunt." A smile slid from her face. "Of course, that's diametrically opposed to my bid for freedom."

"Loving people is inconvenient," he said.

He knew. He knew exactly how it was.

She really didn't have to tell him.

"Yes, it is. There are things that I want, and they're kind of opposed to the other things I want. Because I fantasize about cutting all ties sometimes, but you know, my sisters aren't here and . . . and I kind of hate it." She laughed. "I wanted to be no strings attached, footloose and fancy free, but the problem is you never are. When you love people you never are. They're gone, they're not my responsibility, but I worry about them obsessively." She frowned. "We really are parents without any of the glory."

"I don't know that there's ever any glory in parenting. But it's a good point. My siblings are all still there, and I'm grate-ful for it, but they've moved on in a way, and even Penny is off and married. I'm happy for her. I'm happy for everybody. But they went to this place that I can't . . . I can't follow them to it. And that's good. It's fine. I don't want them to be like me. Not exactly. I get what you mean, though. It's the exact thing that you wanted, but it leaves you lonely in a very specific way."

"Yes. That's exactly what it is. It's everything I wanted, and somehow . . . it didn't fix anything. Because I still think about them most days before I ever consider doing something for myself."

He was something she was doing for herself. If she could really put it that way. It made it sound a little bit base. Though there was definitely something base to this thing between them. And that was part of the fun of it.

She had never really gotten to explore the full extent of an attraction like this before.

Of course, she had never been tempted to. That was the thing. In the past, attraction like this had been extinguished quickly. Well, in truth, she had never experienced attraction like this.

Especially not combined with any sort of . . . camaraderie.

The terrible thing was, it wasn't unpleasant.

Devastated to report it was in fact enjoyable.

"We should have gone grocery shopping," he said, suddenly looking distressed. "You haven't been home in almost a week."

"I definitely have stuff in the freezer," she said, not really worried about anything except her half-and-half. If she couldn't have coffee the way she liked it in the morning, that would feel like an indignity.

She'd been through enough.

"What kind of stuff?"

"I'll feed you," she said.

He didn't have a car; after all, his intent was clearly to stay the night. Apparently, that was a thing they did now. She opened up the freezer and dug through it, producing a couple of frozen potpies. "These take about an hour, but it's definitely worth it."

She started to open up the boxes, hit the preheat button on her oven and put two different pies on a couple of cookie sheets. He had learned to barbecue for his siblings. Her cooking had always been a little bit more rudimentary.

Of course, her siblings had been younger.

Right then, she wished she had been a little bit more of a domestic goddess.

But she had just been in survival mode.

She tried. She made boxed birthday cakes when the time came, and she cut rounds off of cookie dough logs to make sugar cookies at Christmas.

When the kids were in school, she had always tramped up into the woods behind the house and cut down the most Charlie Brown–ass Christmas tree that she could find. They had a little box of decorations. Things that the girls had made at school, some scraggly tinsel that she wrapped around flattened cereal boxes to keep it from getting tangled.

She hadn't bothered to get anything out yet this year.

Denver didn't have decorations in his house either, though.

"You must have done a lot of work to this place over the last few years," he said.

She turned around to see him sitting on the couch in the little living room area. The house was tiny. The kitchen and living room were one. There were two bedrooms. Two bathrooms. And one of the bedrooms was combined with the laundry room.

But she had done her best to keep it clean. To keep it nice for her sisters.

She had done her best.

She really had.

"Glad you approve," she said. Because apparently she was going to be prickly with him for whatever reason. Just because. He was being nice.

But she was . . . uncomfortable. With the closeness that it created.

Real or imagined, it was intense.

"Do you not have men over very often?"

"Try never. I never need men to know where I live."

She wondered if, like her, when she had asked if his hookups normally spent the night, he was looking for evidence that he was different.

That was . . . silly, maybe. Pointless for both of them.

And still, she couldn't quite banish the shimmer of pleasure that created inside of her.

"It's a safety issue," she said. "And anyway, you already know where I live. You spent years skulking around these parts."

"I was never skulking."

"You were skulking a little bit."

"Maybe that's how disaffected men in their early twenties who don't actually understand emotions deal with worry."

She huffed a laugh. "Well, maybe this is how disaffected young women in their late twenties deal with the fact that they're actually pretty pleased that the man they considered to be . . . a friend . . . is a little bit jealous in a fun way."

"A friend," he said, grinning.

"Don't let it go to your head," she said, looking at him in a narrow fashion.

"Do you like Christmas?"

It was a strange question, she knew. It was just, it was strange that he was throwing himself into this whole thing, working as hard as he was to host this big Christmas tradition. For some reason, she felt compelled to try to understand more about it.

"Why?"

"You know, the whole thing that you're doing."

"Right. I would say that has less to do with Christmas, and more to do with the fact that I want to prove something about where I stand with the collective."

"They respect you," she said.

She watched his face, and she could see that he had never really considered that.

"I guess so," he said. "Which is nice. Especially after . . ."

"From what I've heard about everyone on that ranch, they don't have any right to judge you for your daddy's behavior. Did any of them have a good dad?"

He shook his head. "No. And when it comes to fathers, I think the McClouds might win for the worst one. Personally. But I think my dad caused the most problems in a far-reaching way." He cleared his throat. "For years there were rumors that Gus McCloud killed his dad."

"Oh, I know," Sheena said. "Gus is . . . a legend about town. And with women. I mean, he was before he married Alaina."

He looked at her out of the corner of his eye, and she felt pleased that he was jealous again.

"Not a legend I experienced, Denver. You are my only Four Corners conquest."

"Good."

"I told you, you're not my type."

Tension stretched between them, and she thought it might be pushing it for them to have a quickie before the potpie was done. But then he was crossing the space and kissing her, and that was more comfortable than all this conversation anyway.

When she got the potpies out of the oven, she was still naked. And she brought them into her bedroom.

He was sprawled out on the bed, naked as the day he was born, though larger and more muscular, she imagined.

They opened up bottles of beer, and dug into the pie. It was a strange, hedonistic thing. She never ate in bed. Not even now that she lived by herself.

She had been trying to set a good example for her sisters when she was raising them. Had been trying her very best to give them normalcy.

Something they could carry forward into their real lives.

"So," she said, taking another big bite of the potpie. "You never told me if you like Christmas or not."

"I don't know," he said. "I never really thought much about it. We would have it off and on through the years when my dad was feeling generous, or feeling like punishing us, depending on whatever was happening. That's how he was. So, I think there was a time when I saw it as something kind of sharp and dangerous. If we liked it too much then we were in danger of losing it on one of his whims. You know?"

She nodded slowly. "Yeah."

"What about you?"

She froze. She hadn't really counted on him turning the question back around on her. And it pushed against the door that she liked to keep locked in her mind.

One that she didn't like dealing with.

She didn't like remembering it in the privacy of her own head, let alone talking about it with somebody else. So she just never did. Historically.

But then, she didn't have men spend the night historically. She didn't eat potpie in bed, historically.

Especially not after having ridiculously hot sex on her couch in her living room.

So there wasn't much going on right now that had historic precedents.

"I did," she said. "When I was little. Back when . . . I don't know, when he tried. A little bit. I think some of it was when Tonya lived with us. It's vague."

It wasn't vague. But she was intentionally making sure that it stayed vague in her mind's eye.

She was intentionally making certain that she didn't let the memories become too sharp or too clear.

Because there were just things better left unremembered.

At least, that was how it usually felt to her.

And right now was no exception.

It wasn't about keeping something from him. It was about not letting the memory turn into a knife that could cut her clean.

"And afterward?"

"Well, I had to keep doing Christmas for the girls, you know?"

He nodded. "Yeah. I know. Kind of. My siblings were older, when my dad left. I mean, Daughtry was grown. So we were kind of past that point. No tooth fairy or Easter Bunny or anything like that."

"Oh, I was all of those things," she said. "I had a lot of fun with that. I even did Elf on the Shelf."

He looked at her like she had grown a second head.

"You did?"

"Yes," she said. "I did. It was fun. It gave them something to do and it . . . I don't know. It's something I kind of wish would've been done for me. I wanted them to have some magic in their childhood. God knows I didn't have any."

She gritted her teeth, because the back ones itched, and she wasn't quite sure why.

"You were good, Sheena. For them."

"Yeah. And I had to cajole them into coming back for Christmas this year."

"That's what kids do. They grow up and leave the nest. I mean, I've heard. We've all stuck close to home. I guess maybe I'm not trying to restore the magic of childhood for my family. But the magic of our land. Four Corners. King's Crest. I love it. I always have. Even when my dad corrupted it, I never blamed the ranch. I knew that it was special. I wanted to rescue the ranch from him too."

"You did," she said.

They finished eating their potpie, and drinking their beer.

She set everything on the nightstand, and didn't bother with cleaning up. Then they fell straight into each other's arms. And when she went to sleep, it was on purpose. When she woke, she didn't panic.

Because Denver was there, and it didn't even feel wrong.

Chapter Fifteen

THE NEXT MORNING, Denver got up bright and early, and hunted through Sheena's fridge. Thankfully, he found bacon and eggs.

He knew how to cook breakfast, not because he did it to impress women—that would have required him spending the night with one ever—but because he knew how to feed his hungry siblings.

He scrambled up some eggs, fried bacon in a skillet, and when Sheena emerged, wearing a giant sweatshirt that was an insult to her incredible body, she looked intrigued.

"You cooked for me?"

That cautious pleasure in her eyes would fuel him for the rest of his natural life.

"I just spent a week cooking for you," he pointed out.

"At *your* house," she said.

"I was hungry. My appetite waits for no sleeping beauty."

"Why are you single?"

He lifted his brows. "Childhood trauma?"

She laughed, a hard crack that hit him square in the chest. "Okay. Right."

He didn't feel all that single right now, though. Because single implied that he didn't have an obligation to her. While it didn't feel like an obligation as such, he knew that he wasn't going to sleep with anyone else. Not right now. And he would get feral if she touched somebody else.

So it was definitely not *nothing*. It was closer to something like an attachment, even.

"We have to get fueled up for work today," he said.

"*Joy*. And I actually mean that. My week of laying around was not the greatest."

"You don't like sitting still?"

"No. Too much time with the inner demons," she said, tapping on her temple.

"I hear that."

He fixed a plate for her, and she sat down with a steaming mug of coffee. He followed suit, sitting across from her at the small square dining table in the kitchen area.

"What's on the docket for the day?" he asked.

"Fixtures in the bathrooms," she said. "The counter is going in on the bar. The wallpaper should be going up . . . And shelving. Which means I get to put our favorite dead animals in their rightful place."

"I don't want to miss that," he said.

"I'll be sure to reserve some of the corpse-decor decisions for when you're around."

"Thank you, Sheena. I really appreciate the kindness."

She wrinkled her nose, and he could tell that she was trying to stop herself from smiling. Like she was making an effort to not be amused by him.

Fair enough.

"Pack an overnight bag," he said casually as he shoved his last bite of eggs into his mouth and got up from the table.

"I'm sorry, what?"

"Pack an overnight bag. For my place."

"I thought we discussed three days a week."

"We did. And I dismissed it. So, I'm not sure why this is surprising to you."

"Denver King," she said, standing up from the table and going into her room. "You are pushing it," she shouted.

He grinned, and poured himself another cup of coffee. When she returned, she had a bag slung over her shoulder because she had packed an overnight bag.

"You're into me," he said, moving over to her and grabbing the handle on the bag, meaning to take it from her. But she didn't release her hold. So he ended up pulling her to him, and kissing her on the mouth.

"I'm into your dick," she said.

Then she let go of the bag, and turned away from him. He had to pause and take a breath, because the impact of her had him off balance.

He followed her out of the house and to her car and put the overnight bag in the back, and got into the passenger seat.

"You are so secure in your masculinity. Riding bitch in my Camry."

He leaned back in the seat. "What do I have to be insecure about?"

That earned him a little choked sound.

Good.

They drove to the ranch in relative silence, and when they got there she pulled him right up to the event space and he leaned in and kissed her. He didn't know what the hell he was doing. Except if he lived a different life, and he was a different man he would have kissed his woman in broad daylight in front of everyone any day of the week.

She shot him the evil eye when they parted. "Fresh."

"Proud to stake a claim."

"OMG, you are so possessive!"

He looked at her, hard. At the flush in her cheeks and the glitter in her green eyes. "And you hate that?"

"No, I don't hate it, you irritating boll weevil."

And there was no real heat in that at all.

"Good. Because I don't know what the hell it is, but there's no use fighting it."

She rolled her eyes. "Now, Denver, I always think a fight might be worth it. I love a fight."

"I'll be happy to oblige later. Naked."

"Deal. Get out of the car and go work."

He did, and when he got out, he saw Landry standing in the doorway. He tipped his hat to his brother and smiled, refusing to look caught or shamefaced or whatever he expected.

He heard the sound of Sheena's tires on the gravel as she drove away and that left just him and Landry.

"You failed to mention *that* little development yesterday."

Immediately, he regretted all of his choices. Well, not all of them. But putting himself in a position where his family would see him and Sheena kissing. He regretted that. Because he didn't want to try and articulate what it was. He was having a difficult enough time with that in his own damned head. It worked, as long as they didn't go trying to spool it out and explain it. Which meant he didn't especially want to do it now.

"What's there to say? I'm sleeping with her?"

Which sounded like not enough. But what else was there?

"Is that all? Because I've sure as hell never seen you kiss a woman on your hallowed land."

He started to say that hell yes, he was just sleeping with her. Because what the hell else would it be? But it wouldn't come out. It damned well refused. Because how could he ever say it was just sex? He had told her things he had never told anybody else. Including his brother.

"I don't know," he said, finally. "She's working here, we have a partnership. I can't say it's *simple*. It's a stupid idea from that perspective, actually."

"Well. I guess I'm kind of glad to hear that you're making a stupid decision."

"Thanks," he said, moving past him and into the event space. Where unfortunately Justice, Daughtry and Arizona also were.

"Good morning," he said.

"What's this?" Arizona asked. "My oldest brother is being an idiot?"

"Just the same kind of idiot we all tend to be," he grumbled.

"What?" Arizona asked. "Does that mean that you . . . ?"

His sister looked way too hopeful. He had to squash that and fast.

"I did not mean feelings. I meant sexual idiocy. Which seems to run in this family."

"Speak for yourself," Arizona said. "I'm one and done."

"I'm *almost* one and done," Landry said.

"I'm not," said Justice.

Daughtry looked ruefully back at Justice. "Same."

Justice cleared his throat. "I mean I'm done *now*. It's just there was a lot more than one. Like a lot more."

"I got it," said Denver. "Thank you, though. Super interested in your body count."

"Are you sleeping with Sheena?" Arizona asked.

"How did you guess?" he asked, monotone.

"Oh my gosh. I knew it. That's amazing. You two would have really hot babies."

"That's the weirdest thing you've ever said to me," said Denver.

Arizona shrugged. "I'm just saying. You are both genetically blessed people."

Well, he knew that Sheena was. And while he couldn't speak to his own genetic blessings as far as the physical went, he could say they had a hell of a lot of chemistry. But he wasn't going to say that, not to his sister.

"Well, we are not going to have babies. Thanks."

"Birth control is not one hundred percent effective, Denver," she said looking at him pointedly. "I seem to recall you having a conversation with me about that when I was a teenager."

"Nobody had that conversation with me," said Landry. "And I can tell you, I probably needed it."

"Be real," said Justice, looking at Landry. "Were you and Fia actually using birth control?"

"Not consistently," said Landry.

"Okay. Now that we've all had *that* conversation," said Denver, "can you all get out of my life?"

"We're just shocked that you have a life," said Arizona.

"What do you mean? I have *lived* plenty, children. What do you think the money came from? I was out winning at poker games. Do you think they had those at a petting zoo?"

"No," said Justice. "Don't get it twisted. We don't think that you're a monk. We just think that you don't have much of a personal life. Those are two different things."

It irritated him because his brother was right. And he knew exactly what he meant by that. He didn't normally let anything personal get tangled up around him. Not anything that didn't have to do with the family.

He didn't even have a personal life that was separate from the ranch. He had compartments. And nothing got too close to his actual heart.

Which was necessary. Most of the time. Not that Sheena was . . . It was complicated. He had friends. It was like that. Except a little bit more. A little bit deeper.

"I like her," he said. And that earned him a whole lot of keen smiles. "So that means you have to be nice to her. And not annoying."

"Dinner at your place tonight?" Daughtry asked.

"No," he said.

"I think so," said Arizona.

"You guys," he said. "Please let me get laid in peace."

"You do too much in peace," said Arizona. "Somebody should ruffle your feathers a little bit."

"Consider them ruffled," he growled.

"We are absolutely coming for dinner tonight," Arizona said.

He knew at that point there was no arguing with them. He did text Sheena to let her know. Both that everyone knew, and that they would be at dinner tonight. And so would she.

She sent him a middle finger emoji. *You can't make me come to dinner.*

I can.

He sent her some ways he might find to force the issue that were downright indecent.

But she didn't argue with him anymore.

He didn't go check on the work that day; he went straight back to the farmhouse, to get it ready for Sheena to be there.

And he ignored his sister's amused expression when she came in and he was sweeping the kitchen.

Then they set about to getting dinner on. And he heard a knock on the door.

"Do you want me to get it?" Arizona asked.

"No," he mouthed, before going straight to the door and opening it. "Hi," he said when he saw Sheena. "They're feral."

"You started this," she said. "I don't have any sympathy for you. In fact, I might join them in giving you a hard time."

She stepped into the house. "Hey! I'm fucking your brother."

That earned her a round of applause. Both from his siblings, and from their respective spouses.

"You're all dead to me," he said.

"You weren't discreet," Sheena said. "Don't write checks your ass can't cash, King. I had nothing to do with this."

"I *like* you," said Arizona.

"I also like her," said Bix.

"Of course you do," Denver growled. "Because she's as uncivilized as you two."

Bix went over and gave Sheena a high five.

It wasn't long after that that they were all seated around the crowded table, and he couldn't deny how well Sheena fit in.

She wasn't thrown off by his family's rough manners. In fact, she encouraged them. And clearly enjoyed them.

He would almost suspect that his family liked her better than they liked him.

Which didn't annoy him. Not really.

Sheena was likable.

"We're making cookies tomorrow," Fia said, from down at the other end of the table. "You should come with, Sheena."

He watched her face.

"Oh. I don't . . . I don't need to do that."

"But we'd love to have you," said Rue. "It's a lot of fun."

"It is," Fia insisted. "We're also going to be getting some baking done for the big Christmas party. Things we can freeze."

"I don't . . . I don't really know how to bake," Sheena said.

"That's okay," said Fia. "We have more accomplished bakers than you can shake a stick at. And we are very good teachers."

"Go on," he said. "You'll like it. And if you don't, you can hold it against me. Because I encouraged you to go."

"You really do know how to get to a girl," said Sheena.

She was met with further cajoling by the other women and finally, she relented.

"If they can spare me at the bar," she said.

"They can spare you," said Denver.

It was late when everybody left, and Sheena waited until after that to go and get her bag and bring it into the house.

"I know they all know," she said. "But I thought rolling in with an overnight bag was pushing things a little bit."

"I thought that you liked to push things."

"I do," she said.

There was something she wasn't saying.

"What?"

"I like your family. I don't care that they know. I've never been embarrassed about sex. You know, having assholes hanging around who tried to push themselves on me, it . . . it could've gone one of two ways. But I am really stubborn. And I refused to let it make me ashamed. Of my body, of liking men. Any of that. I don't really do embarrassment when it comes to sexuality. Not my thing. So that isn't my problem. And I guess . . . it didn't occur to me that we should keep this a secret. Because like I said . . . I've never been shy about sex. But part of me doesn't want to share this with anybody."

She hadn't told her sisters then. It was strange; he had kissed her in public, and it must have meant that part of him wanted someone to know. Maybe to make it a little harder for her to run away. He wasn't entirely sure.

But he could also understand what she was saying. This was new. That it was different. And maybe it wasn't even anything. Because his feelings on love and all of that hadn't changed. But he liked his life better with her in it than he liked it without her. So. There was that.

"I don't want to sneak around," he said. "And . . . I'm okay with them knowing."

"Great," she said. "I'm working on being okay with it."

"I'm glad," he said.

"Let's be done talking now," she said, heading toward the stairs.

"Fine by me," he said, taking off his shirt as they went.

Whatever it was. It worked for him. Worked for them.

And that was good enough for now.

Chapter Sixteen

SHEENA PUT A sweater on and put her hair in braids. She looked *nearly* tame. Seasonal, perhaps. Festive, even. Which seemed like it should be the goal for baking Christmas cookies.

Denver had already gone out to work. They'd had breakfast together, and then she had settled in to wait for Bix to come and pick her up.

She was still feeling weird about . . . Well. Everything. Being sort of folded into the family last night. Seated around the dinner table like she was one of them.

It had been a big group thing a lot like the town hall meeting. But it was different. Because Denver didn't seem so separate there. Not with his siblings. She got to see him being part of something. It had been . . . nice.

She pushed at the warm feeling in her chest, because she was certain that it was dangerous. She shook her head.

It's not dangerous. He's just a guy.

This was all circumstantial. They were working together, so it made sense for them to spend the night together, and to see each other basically every day. It was all in aid of sex. But they had conversation because it was polite. She even made basic conversation with her one-night stands.

So there. That was all.

She poured herself some coffee in one of Denver's thermoses, and then went to the front door to watch for Bix's truck.

It didn't take long for her to pull up. Bix was small and blonde, with a pixie like face and the demeanor of a particularly tetchy ferret.

She was a very funny match with the straitlaced Daughtry. Who was definitely the most straightlaced of the King brothers.

She and Denver were so much alike.

Without really trying to, she went through the pairings.

Arizona was edgy next to her husband, Micah, who seemed steady and laid-back.

Justice was wild, while Rue seemed exceptionally organized, a soothing influence. Fia and Landry were a little harder to gauge. They had the new baby to look after. They also had a teenager, and they gave off serious parental vibes.

Still, it seemed like the couples did best when they were opposites. Not that she and Denver were a couple.

She opened up the front door, then closed it behind her, moving quickly down the steps, and she got into Bix's truck.

"Good morning," she said.

"Good morning," Bix replied. "Ready to bake?"

"Not really. I don't know what I'm doing."

"I don't either," said Bix. "But it's nice that they include me. I'm not that helpful. But it's . . . it's crazy to be part of the family. I mean, I have a family, obviously. I didn't pop up out of the hole in the ground. Even if it feels like it sometimes. But, you know. It's just . . . I don't know. It's nice."

"I have a family," she said. "My sisters. I raised them."

"Like Denver."

"Kind of," she said.

"With the Kings . . . just relax and let them do their thing," said Bix. "I find it's futile to resist them. They all think they are so tough and bad. But honestly, they're the nicest people that I've ever met. Anywhere."

For some reason, that actually scared her little bit. Because if the Kings were the nicest people that Bix had ever met, and Sheena was planning on leaving, it just made her plans feel kind of small and sad. She didn't like that.

"Come on, they have to be a little bit annoying."

"It's a lot," said Bix. "Especially when you're like me and you're basically used to living by yourself. I've had to acclimate to having people around. *Person* around, even."

She was used to having people around. She wasn't like Bix. It was just . . . she was used to it in a different capacity. She occupied a really specific space in her sisters' lives.

The same way that Denver did.

He took care of her effortlessly, because he was treating her the way he always treated people.

What have you done to take care of him?

Well. That seemed a lot like reciprocity. And she wasn't necessarily in the market to go thinking like that, considering that she wasn't trying to do a relationship. She really wasn't.

But it made her think. About what he was used to. About what he had gotten in his life and not before.

And if there was anything she could do . . .

She cleared her throat and looked out the window. The whole area that they lived in was beautiful. Small towns nestled in mountainous pockets, all the way out to the ocean a couple of hours away.

But there was something particularly beautiful about Four Corners Ranch.

It was eighty thousand acres of ranchland. A fact that for some reason was buried in the back of her brain.

Hell. There were information plaques about it in town. Seeing as it was the biggest ranching spread in the state of Oregon.

Though, she always felt like it shouldn't be, on a technicality, since they worked the land together, but it was technically four separate parcels.

Not that she had a horse in the race of who had the biggest ranch in the state. But maybe it was just an attempt for her brain to minimize the King family, and everything they had.

She had been to Sullivan's Point for the town hall meeting, and had seen the gorgeous, brightly painted farmhouse, with the chandelier hanging from the weeping willow. But she had never been inside.

"It's a lot," Bix said, by way of warning as they walked up the front steps.

She was about to ask what Bix meant by that, but then the door opened, and they were greeted by four redheads.

Fia, Quinn, Rory and Alaina. "Welcome," Fia said, essentially dragging her inside.

And that was where she got a good look at exactly what Bix meant.

The kitchen cabinets were painted a cheerful yellow, the dining table a brilliant turquoise.

The whole place had been attacked by color. It was definitely not what you would expect in a traditional farmhouse, but it was brilliantly quirky.

Sheena couldn't say she was usually fond of quirk.

But it was impossible to resist the Sullivan sisters.

There were mixing bowls in all shapes, sizes and colors set out on the table, along with large glass jars of milk, bowls of eggs that still had dirt on them from the chicken coop. Thick slabs of butter that had definitely been hand churned, and not purchased at the store. A watering can full of raspberries, and a bucket full of blackberries.

"From the greenhouse," Fia said, gesturing to the fruit. "We try to keep things going year-round. And we've got a system that allows us to do that. I just prefer to have everything fresh. It isn't that we couldn't freeze them—I just don't like to."

"Fia is type A about berries," Alaina said.

"Yes," said Fia. "I am."

Fia's red hair was up in a bun, and she was wearing a polka-dotted apron, a burp rag draped over her shoulder and a wrap with her little boy snug inside on her front. She looked cheerful, even as she was wrangling a baby, and Sheena did not think she would have such a good attitude if she was trying to work and hold an infant.

Not that she ever would. She flashed back to last night with Denver. No. They were very good with condoms. Probably because he carried similar paranoia. Also, she was on the pill. She had never believed in taking chances. Neither with disease nor pregnancy. So condoms and birth control pills were always the order of the day.

She didn't want a baby.

She ignored the strange, wistful stab in her chest. It only got worse as she looked around the kitchen. At all of the beautiful things.

At this moment. That's what it was. An intense, colorful explosion of home. Togetherness.

Lila, Fia's redheaded teenage daughter, was helping with the proceedings too. As were Rue and Arizona. Along with Violet and Evelyn Garrett, who Sheena had never met before.

While Fia got the recipes and ingredients put in order so that they could establish a good workflow—her words—Evelyn introduced herself and treated Sheena to the most insane story she'd ever heard.

Everyone in town knew that Sawyer Garrett had ordered a bride on the Internet. Or rather, had placed an ad online looking for a wife after he had ended up an unexpected single dad. But actually hearing the story directly from Evelyn was something else.

"This was such a culture shock," she said. "I lived in the city for most of my adult life."

"Which city?" Sheena asked.

"Sheena," said Evelyn. "There is only one city."

Behind her, Violet, Evelyn's sister-in-law, was rolling her eyes and making faces.

Evelyn turned around. "Yes, Violet?"

"Nothing. But I think you overestimate the geographic reach of New York. We just don't think about it as much as you think we do."

Evelyn laughed. "Yes. I have picked up on that since moving out west."

Now that she had said it, Sheena could hear the New York accent in the other woman's syllables.

Then it seemed like it was storytime for everybody, which Sheena was fascinated by. The ways in which these women had found love, and found themselves here, was fascinating. Violet had moved from Copper Ridge after meeting Wolf Garrett when he came to stay at the bed-and-breakfast that she managed. They'd had instant chemistry, and it had produced an unplanned pregnancy.

Sheena gave another quick round of mental thanks to the birth control gods.

The Sullivan sisters, of course, had been born and raised here, but Alaina had ended up married to Gus McCloud, and now did most of her work over there.

Quinn and Rory had married off the ranch. Quinn had married a rancher at a neighboring property, while Rory had married hometown legend and military veteran Gideon Payne.

Arizona had found love when she'd reconnected with a man from her past.

Sheena had already heard the story of how Bix had ended up trying to make moonshine on the King's land when she had been found by Daughtry the cop, but she happily listened to it again as they started to put cookie dough together. Which then led in to Rue's story. She and Justice had been best friends for years, and it took her getting left at the altar by another man for them both to finally realize they were meant to be together—not just as friends.

Then they got into the story of Fia and Landry.

"It's a ballad," Bix said cheerfully.

"It is not," said Fia.

"Yes, it is," said Lila.

And it was fourteen-year-old Lila who started the story. In the middle, Sheena thought.

With her adopted parents dying, and Landry coming to find her.

She noticed that Fia's eyes were full of tears.

"Landry and I were way too much alike," Fia said. "Angry, passionate and using each other to escape." She tossed Lila an apologetic look. "We were in love. It was just we were fifteen. When it all started. When I got pregnant with Lila, I was sixteen. And I knew that this was no place for a baby."

Something twisted in Sheena's gut. Because if she'd gotten pregnant at sixteen, it would've been an absolute nightmare. There would've been no way she could bring a child into that house. With the kind of men who'd been around. She didn't have to know Fia's entire situation or story to see the very real desperation and sadness in her face.

To understand it and empathize with it on a level that was physically painful.

"We didn't tell anybody. I went away, and I gave her up for adoption." She stroked her baby's head. "He was so angry at me. And we could never reconcile how differently we felt about it. But then . . . then Lila came back into our lives. And it forced us to deal with each other. It forced us to say all the things that needed to be said. We never stopped loving each other. Just like we never stopped loving Lila."

Everybody was sniffling by the end of that story.

"Sorry," Fia said. "I know."

It was a story filled with sadness. Loss, but ultimately hope. And it made Sheena's whole head itch.

Because it spoke of something that she herself couldn't find in her to believe in normally. It was all a little bit too magical. All a little bit too neat.

Except of course it wasn't neat. Because Lila had lost the parents who had raised her from the time she was a baby, and Landry and Fia had lost years together.

She'd always had a feeling that love, at its ultimate core, was a selfish thing.

But the way that Fia talked about it, about her feelings for Landry, and most of all about her love for Lila, turned something upside down inside of her. And she wished desperately that she could put it right.

Because what Fia was talking about wasn't weak. Not in the least. It wasn't selfish. It wasn't anything like what she would have said.

She had just been thinking she didn't fully get their connection, or understand it. But it was so much deeper, more intense, than she had imagined, watching them as a married couple. Watching them parent.

They had been to hell together. And more importantly, they'd come back from it.

That was rare.

For some reason, Sheena had to believe that.

That mostly, you just had to sit in hell and make the most of it. Mostly, you didn't get to just . . . make everything okay.

"So you haven't made cookies before," Bix said, changing the subject.

"No, Bix. Thanks for giving me up. I thought you were also the baking novice."

"Yes," Bix said. "But I have done this before. So it gives me a slight edge over you, and I'm enjoying that. Since mostly, I'm as untamed as a bobcat."

"She is," said Alaina.

"I am very good at baking premade cookie dough."

She didn't think she was imagining that just saying premade cookie dough made Fia and Violet shudder.

"It's easy," said Fia. "All you have to do is follow the instructions."

"I don't like being told what to do," Sheena said. "Not even by a cookbook."

"Well, luckily for you, it's not a cookbook. They are recipe cards written by my great-great-grandmother, and they are imbued with authority."

She was irritated, because her own self was arguing with her about how much she had been enjoying authority lately.

This was not an invitation to think about Denver and sex.

Even worse, though, it brought her back to thinking about reciprocity.

"Can I take some of these cookies with me?" she asked, as she did her best to measure and dump ingredients into the bowl. It wasn't hard. She just felt . . . weird about it. About this whole thing. About being folded into this hearth-and-home thing. She was used to living with all women. That wasn't it. She was used to unquestionably being the caregiver, and there was so much caregiver energy in here right now, it was a lot.

Women who were soft, and capable, who were willing to teach her. To give something to her.

Pieces of their own wisdom. Pieces of their hearts.

It was a strange and powerful experience, and it made her think back to the days when sometimes women had been burned as witches.

Maybe because the sharing of feminine knowledge seemed a lot like witchcraft.

How to put simple ingredients together to make extraordinarily complex things.

How to survive the heartbreak of having to give up the child you loved but were ready for. And how to open your heart again when love stood there and knocked.

How to leave everything behind and change your whole world with nothing but the hope of love as your guide.

The power of forgiveness. Of sacrifice. Of change.

Of standing firm, when it was needed.

Yes. It was a whole lot like witchcraft.

And Sheena felt alive with it.

Marked by it.

Changed by it, just a little bit. Though, probably when she left this room, heavy with friendship and the smell of baked goods, she would just go back to being herself.

Because short of seeing her father's lifeless body on the ground, very few singular experiences had changed her.

"You can take cookies to Denver," Fia said, smiling.

"Who said I was doing that?"

Her instant response was to be combative. Rather than honest. She winced. "I mean, I do want to take them to Denver. He took care of me last week when I was sick. Which was maybe the nicest thing anyone has ever done for me." She was lying. It was absolutely the nicest thing anyone had ever done for her, except all the other nice things that Denver had done for her over the years.

It's out of guilt.

What did that matter? It had made a difference.

She didn't know if she had ever made a difference to him.

No. She hadn't. She had come here to pay him back. Monetarily.

And now suddenly she was realizing that Denver had transferred that caregiving to her, but she hadn't done any of that for him. He had even cooked bacon and eggs for her in her house.

"What is his favorite food?"

All the women looked at each other. "I don't know," Fia said.

"He usually kind of leads the charge on the cooking," Bix said. "But I assume that barbecue is his favorite, because that's what he always makes."

"He likes fruit dessert a lot," Rue said. And of course, of all the women there, she had known Denver the longest. She had been Justice's best friend since they were children. "I remember one time he picked up an apple cake from the farm store, and he basically hoarded all of it for himself."

"Oh. Do you . . . ?"

But Fia was already moving, grabbing a recipe card out of the front of the little box that seemed to contain all of them. "This is the recipe," she said. "Washington apple cake. It's packed full of them. We have a big bed of apples down in the root cellar."

"I'll go with her," said Bix.

"We're making cookies," she said.

"Well, now we're going to make an apple cake too," said Bix, dragging her out of the kitchen.

She followed her around the side of the house, and to the root cellar doors.

Bix opened them up, and the two of them went down the stairs into the cool darkness.

"This is crazy," she said, looking at the floor-to-ceiling jars of jam, the bins of carrots, potatoes, apples.

"Fia is like the world's tastiest hoarder," Bix said. "I love it."

Sheena picked up the big tub of apples, and the two of them went back up into the kitchen. Where they began the process of peeling and chopping countless apples, since Fia decided that they would also make these cakes for the Christmas party, and freeze them. Denver's cake would be done in the traditional way, and they decided to add some cranberries to the ones for the Christmas party, for color and cheer.

Sheena just followed directions, since she had no idea how to modify a recipe on the fly. She could barely follow one.

But by the time they were finished, she had produced a reasonable, and only slightly lopsided apple cake.

And that was when she got another idea.

"Bix," she said. "You seem like the person to ask about this. I think I need a Christmas tree."

"I am definitely the person to ask about that. Because I have a pickup truck and a general disregard for laws."

"If we cut it on private land, it's not illegal, is it?" she asked, even though she didn't actually care because she was certain she had cut many illegal Christmas trees in her time.

"Don't know, don't care," Bix said cheerfully.

And Sheena knew for a fact she had asked the right person.

Which was how she and Bix found themselves hauling a massive tree into the back of her truck, sweating and swearing. And then hauling it up the front steps of the farmhouse, and bringing it in.

"I think you're supposed to leave these outside for a day or so to get all of the creepy crawlies off of it," Bix said.

"I don't have that kind of time," said Sheena. "Anyway, I never did that."

Of course the trees that she got were always small and sparse. Partly because she felt sorry for the trees. They didn't have a lot going for them. Not good health or aesthetics, and it wasn't like anyone else was going to choose them to be a Christmas tree. But also because they were light and easy for her to handle on her own.

She had never wanted to ask her sisters to help; she had always wanted the Christmas stuff to appear as if by magic.

But today, she had Bix to help with magic.

"It did just occur to me, though, that I'm going have to go home to get some of my Christmas things."

"Do you want help?"

"No," she said. "You can go and keep a lookout on the work they're doing. Text me updates."

Bix grinned. "I can do that."

She drove out to her house, then, and rifled through all her Christmas stuff. Then, because she was feeling . . . cheerful? Maybe that's what this was—she grabbed her Elf on the Shelf.

She didn't have near enough ornaments for Denver's tree, and she stopped by John's store on her way back, and purchased two large plastic containers of shatterproof ornaments that had probably been sitting there for ten years.

She got the tree put in the stand, and began decorating.

By the time she was done, it was an adequate attempt at a winter wonderland. And she had apple cake on the table.

Because Denver had done so much for her.

She just wanted to make him feel even half as good.

Chapter Seventeen

BIX HAD BEEN weirdly chatty at the end of the work shift today, and Denver didn't have the patience to go and check on the bar when all was said and done. He knew Sheena wasn't there anyway, since she had been out doing the baking for most of the day, and after that had apparently gone to run errands. Bix had been vague on what.

When he went into the house, though, it all became clear. There was a Christmas tree in the living room.

All lit up and bright. The tinsel on it was ragged, and didn't match; the ornaments were just as eclectic, but it made him smile. Created a deep tug of nostalgia in his chest that he hadn't realized lived there.

There were other twinkling lights around the room, a tiny red truck with a little Christmas tree in the back, sitting on the doily on that little side table by his great-great-grandfather's favorite chair that he had banged Sheena in. He would always think of it that way now.

He didn't see any sign of Sheena, though. He walked into the kitchen, and saw an apple cake on the table.

That dessert was his favorite thing that the Sullivans made, and they did not do it often enough. And there it was, right in the center of the table, like she knew.

Like she *knew* him.

He went back out into the living room, and turned toward the stairs, where he stopped. There was a condom on the bottom step, in its wrapper. Another one three steps up, and another.

Desire tightened his stomach.

If she wanted to leave a trail of protection to lead him to her that was fine with him. Though, he was thinking he was going to use every single one of these tonight.

Another one, then another. All the way down the hall to his bedroom.

He pushed the door open, already anticipating the sight that would greet him.

Maybe she would be lying on the bed, totally naked. That gorgeous tattoo on display, her legs . . .

"What the fuck."

Because lying on the bed, surrounded by condoms, posed in a very suggestive position, was an elf, *not* currently on the shelf.

And that was when he heard riotous laughter coming from the bathroom.

He turned and opened the door, and found Sheena, standing there in nothing but a black lace bra and panties. "I was hoping for a threesome tonight," she said.

"Absolutely not," he said.

"Come on," she said. "It's funny."

"It's disturbing as hell."

"He's watching you, Denver. Making sure that you're being a good boy."

"I am not a boy," he growled. "And I think we both know that I have been very bad."

"Works for me," she said.

He dragged her out of the bathroom, and grabbed hold of the elf. Which he threw into the bathroom, and shut the door. "I don't want it in here."

"It's a Christmas tradition," she said.

"Not in my house."

"Come on," she said. "It is the season of—"

He cut her off with a kiss, and she started to laugh as he parted her lips and slid his tongue against hers. The last laugh turned into a groan.

He couldn't say that he had ever made a woman laugh during sex before.

Then she looked up at him, her green eyes mischievous, and it was his turn to laugh.

And he knew for a fact he had never laughed when he was this hard, this turned on.

"Thank you," he said. "For the cake."

"You're welcome," she said. "I made it myself. Is it poison? You'll find out later."

"Brat," he said, lifting her up and throwing her down on the bed. Because he knew exactly how she liked to be touched. Exactly how she liked to be handled.

And that meant he could push boundaries with her in fun and interesting ways.

He grabbed a handful of the condoms on the bed. "You're ambitious, Sheena. I like it. But you should know better than to challenge me."

"You have work tomorrow," she pointed out. "I don't think there's that kind of time."

He groaned. "Wouldn't it be nice if there was, though? Nothing but days to do this?"

He had certainly never expressed that sentiment once in his life.

"I like that fantasy," she said.

He growled, and took her bra off. It had been stunning, seeing her breasts for the first time. Seeing that tattoo. He saw her naked casually quite a bit now. But it hadn't lessened the impact of her. Her beauty. Her body.

And the way it made him feel.

He took his time pleasuring her. Kissing her over every inch of her body. Making her cry out. Bringing her to the peak, over and over again before letting himself inside of her. And when he did, he went deep. He lifted her thigh up over his hip and thrust, slow and measured, trying to draw it out. Trying to satisfy and torment them both.

She shuddered, shook beneath him.

The feel of her fingernails on his shoulders was as familiar now as the sight of the mountain range out his bedroom window. The scent of hay on the air.

A part of who he was. A piece of the life he lived.

The feel of her, tight and hot around him, was the same. Something he'd gone a long time without, but now couldn't imagine ever losing.

When she arched beneath him and cried out his name, he gave himself permission to let go.

He buried his face in her neck and said her name, over and over again.

And then he held her.

Secure in the knowledge that tonight she would sleep in his bed, and they would wake up together.

"Do you ever do a quickie?" she asked, huffing as she lay there.

"I feel like the time we were attempting to beat the potpies we went pretty quick."

"You know what I mean. You destroy me every time."

"Good," he said. Because she destroyed him.

And he was never quite sure what to do about it.

He got off the bed and went into the bathroom, then jumped, because he had forgotten he had thrown the damned elf in there. "You're going to torment me with that every day, aren't you?"

"That is my plan," she said.

"Great."

"I do what I can."

He discarded the condom, and washed his hands. "Yeah. Thanks for the cake. It's my favorite."

He remembered then, a defiant thought he'd had only a couple of weeks ago. That she didn't know him. Didn't know his favorite food.

"My favorite dessert," he said. "My favorite food is brisket."

She smiled. "I actually probably could've guessed that."

"What's yours?"

"Brownies. And . . ." She wrinkled her nose. "I like noodles in any form. Italian, Asian. Noodles. When I worked in Maple-ton and I had to grab myself dinner I would always get Thai or Italian. And I really don't care what the sauce is, or what all is in it, I just love it."

"I'll take you out," he said.

It came out very intense, and he hadn't meant to.

"Okay," she said, looking away from him.

She got up off the bed, and walked toward the bathroom, past him. And even though he wasn't looking at her, he could feel her freeze.

He turned and looked into the bathroom, and saw her, standing there at the sink, staring.

She was looking at her toothbrush, which had been sitting there since she had come to stay two nights ago.

"My toothbrush is in your bathroom," she said.

"Yeah," he said. "It makes sense."

He felt something like panic tighten his stomach, except Denver King didn't panic, so that definitely wasn't what was happening.

"That's . . . I'm sorry," she said. "That's a little bit too much for me."

"You . . . you baked me a cake. You tried to molest me with your elf. And the *toothbrush* is too much for you?"

"This wasn't supposed to be a toothbrush-on-the-bathroom-counter thing."

"Why not?"

And right then, he felt resolved. Right then, he realized what all this was. It was a relationship. That he wanted it.

"Let's try it," he said.

"I . . . I don't see any possible good way that it could go."

"Was today good?"

He ignored the disquiet inside himself. All the things that were inclined to agree with her. That were oriented toward running, rather than staying.

"Yes," she said. "Today was good. But you know that can't go on like this forever. Things don't just stay the same. They get . . . they get tense. And angry. And difficult."

"How do you know that?"

"Because I know that. Because I know that's how life is. It doesn't get steadily better. Any more than it stays in a sweet spot. It's always changing on you. And it's kind of a bitch."

"All right. You have a point. And that's definitely been true in my own life. Though, overall it's better now that it was."

"Yes. Because we both worked hard to set clear boundaries and live our life according to certain rules."

"But today was good," he said.

She nodded. "Yes, Denver. Today was good."

"So let's do this until it's not good anymore. Haven't we had enough bad days? Why don't we . . . why don't we try it? So that we can have more of this."

He believed himself. It was a really good sales pitch. He thought he sounded totally reasonable. They were both naked, and he could see she wasn't immune to that. He could see that she was distracted by it. He considered that a point in his favor.

"Okay," she said. "Okay. We'll . . . we'll give it a try. For now. While I'm here. Because you know I'm not staying. And chances are, it's going to go south on us before I leave. You realize that, right?"

"I mean I have some real concerns that that elf is going to kill me in my sleep," he said.

"Entirely possible, because I actually don't know how the elf feels about men. He's been perfectly benign for me and my sisters."

"Sheena," he said. "We had so much shit piled on us. You know that. You really know that. And now we have this good thing. I like you."

"I like you too," she said, wrinkling her nose. "It sounds so middle school."

"This is not middle school," he said, moving to her and putting his arm around her waist. "We don't have to know what the future is."

Except, she was right about one thing. He knew that there would be an end. Because . . . that really was how things went.

Life moved in waves and phases.

And he didn't want to marry her. Didn't want to have kids. So it could only ever be . . . this. But it was such a damned good thing.

He was willing to take the consequence for however sharp it would be at the end.

He didn't say that, though, because he didn't think it was a particularly compelling sales pitch.

"Yeah. Okay. Let's see what this is like, I guess."

"How often am I going to have to talk you down?"

"Probably every day," she said, turning to face him, forcing a smile. "I'm skittish."

"You said you weren't skittish," he said.

"I also said that I didn't do relationships. But here we are."

"Yeah," he said, bringing her in close and kissing the top of her head. "Here we are."

Chapter Eighteen

THEY WERE IN a race against the clock to get everything finished in time for the Christmas party. The bar was almost done, and the biggest thing happening at the moment was training employees. Sheena had done a little bit of that in bartending, but it was another thing entirely to be training people for what, at this point, was a theoretical business. She knew what she wanted to accomplish. She knew what she wanted the business to look like, but she had never run it practically. A sign hung up in town produced results, and she had five people apply almost immediately. She hired them all. They were varying degrees of competent, but she needed all hands on deck, and needed to get them trained as quickly as possible.

So while there was still construction and rearranging happening around her, barstools being installed and tables going in, she was going over the finer points of how the business ran.

Two of the people who applied had some great axe throwing skills, while the others needed to be trained so that they could help give instruction. But after about a week everything was dialed in, and the furniture was in place.

After everyone left, Sheena looked around inside.

The floor was polished. The stools around the bar were rustic but new looking. They had the capacity to serve beer on tap, which they would do with the Four Corners beer.

The door opened, and her heart lifted when she saw that it was Denver.

"The place looks amazing," he said.

"It does," she said.

It still had the look of an old saloon, while also managing to look like something new and exciting. A place where people would want to hang out.

It was different than Smokey's. So hopefully nobody would get bent out of shape about any potential competition.

In her mind, they weren't competing.

She was just offering something new.

In some ways, making herself part of the community. It was such a small place that any new business could really change the landscape of Pyrite Falls. She swallowed, her throat suddenly feeling achy.

"We need to talk about food. I was thinking maybe we could put together really simple weekly menus. With like three items on it. Make picnic boxes, almost. Ribs, brisket sandwich, a chicken breast and drumstick. Then we can have some macaroni salad and potato salad."

"Sounds good," he said."

"Since we don't have a big on-site kitchen here."

"No. This way they can all be refrigerated here and reheated here."

"I don't want to be too big of a burden."

"With the amount of traffic you expect, I should be able to devote a day a week to it. It's not a big deal."

Except it felt like a big deal.

"It is a very big deal, though," she said. "Because it helps me a whole lot."

"I am also making money from this venture. Having food here is only going to be beneficial for me too."

"I guess," she said.

Except she wanted it to be because she was special. Because that was the sort of insidious little thing that built inside of her over these past few weeks.

During this . . . this relationship thing.

"My sisters get in tomorrow," she said.

"Yeah," he said.

"I think Abigail and Alejandro are staying in a vacation rental thing above the bar? But Whitney and Sarah are staying with me. So . . . I'm going to have to be home."

He nodded. "Yeah. I get that."

"What?" She looked at him. Because he had said it was fine, but there was something else that she could see there.

"It's just that you could all stay with me. I have plenty of room. Whitney and Sarah wouldn't even have to bunk up."

No. That felt . . . that felt way too far.

"No. The girls are expecting to stay home. And . . ."

"And are you planning on pretending that we aren't together?"

She frowned. "You want me to introduce you as my boyfriend?"

The word was just so bland in context with Denver.

Even though she supposed he was her boyfriend. More or less. That made her want to hide.

Boyfriend. Talk about sounding middle school.

"I don't think you have to call me that for them to get it," he said.

Except there was nothing to get. They were a thing. It was established at King's Crest. His siblings knew. But no, she hadn't talked to her sisters about it. She had avoided having them on any video calls so that they couldn't see she wasn't staying at home. So that they wouldn't know she was slowly pack-ratting all of her things to Denver's place.

Getting deeper and deeper enmeshed in this thing. Which was scary if she really paused to think about it, but wonderful if she didn't.

"I don't have to be around if you don't want," he said.

And he really did mean that. She could see it. He wasn't being passive-aggressive or anything like that.

He was . . . he was being honest. Because he actually cared about whether or not she was comfortable. Damn him for being so perfect.

"Why don't we go together?" she said. "To pick them up from the airport. And we won't label it or say anything, but I'll sleep at my place."

"Okay," he said.

"Are you laughing at me?"

"I am a little bit."

"They're going to ask me about you. It isn't like I'm going to deny you three times before the rooster crows."

"That's a little sacrilegious."

"Well. It's me we're talking about here. That shouldn't shock you."

He sighed. "Okay. I guess we'll do this thing, then."

Family Christmas. He didn't have to say it. That was what they were doing. A family Christmas thing. Because her sisters were going to come to the Four Corners event, and he was going to help pick him up from the airport. And it felt very real all of a sudden.

She didn't stay that night. They had dinner together, and she made the case that she needed to go home and get things set up. Which was true. She did need to do that.

She sighed when she arrived at her dark, empty house. Her stomach felt tight.

There had been a time when this place had felt like her sanctuary. A place away from the bar, from all of the rowdy, demanding men who thought that she owed them a debt just because her body was shaped in a way they liked.

Yeah. There had been a time when it felt like a sanctuary. And right now it felt lonely.

She flicked the lights on, trying to make herself feel like it was more full than it was.

It didn't really matter, because tomorrow her sisters would be here.

They would be driving a few hours to pick them up, and bringing them back here.

And the house wouldn't be empty. It would be full in a familiar way again, and she wouldn't feel quite so out of sorts.

She slept fitfully too. Like the empty bed was unusual, when for almost her entire life an empty bed had been normal. And it was only these past weeks, so there was really no reason . . .

There was just no reason.

The next morning when she woke up, she had two texts from Denver, and that made her smile.

She called him rather than texting back.

"Hello."

His voice was still rough with sleep.

She imagined him lying in bed, naked, looking all disheveled. Though, he better look a little less disheveled than normal. Since she hadn't been there to ravish him.

"Hi," she said. "To answer your question, I think we should leave in about two hours."

"Sounds good. I'll get up and take a shower."

"Now I really do wish I was there."

She knew that he would think she meant because she wanted to get in the shower with him. And that was . . . true. For sure.

But there was more to it than that. And increasingly, there was a lot more to it.

She just felt a little bit less of everything when he wasn't with her.

The thought was both destabilizing and unwelcome.

Because Sheena Patrick had worked hard to never feel like less just because somebody wasn't around. Because that was the inevitability of life. People left.

It was just how things worked.

Her mother had left. Her father had died.

Her sisters had grown up and gone away.

It was the way things were. And there was no use getting maudlin about it.

There was no use being wistful.

And there was definitely no use tying herself and her feelings of well-being to another person.

"I'll meet you down there," she said.

They were going to take his truck because it had a big back seat, and enough room in the bed to throw all of their bags in. Alejandro and Abigail had insisted on renting a car, so that she could show him around a little bit. Which was good. Because it would've required them to bring two vehicles to fit everybody in that case. Well. Unless Denver didn't come. And honestly. That just didn't seem like what she wanted. Not anymore.

He came and picked her up not long after, and they fought over the radio the whole way to Medford.

There was no real waiting at the airport. There was only one baggage carousel, and one terminal.

When her sisters came out of the glass revolving door, she ran to them and hugged them.

They had all managed to get flights that connected in Portland, and had taken the same one to Medford.

"Flying north just to get south," Abigail grumbled, but smiled all the same.

And right then, her sisters realized. That there was somebody else there.

"Abigail, Whitney, Sarah. Alejandro. We haven't met. I'm Sheena. This is Denver." She did the world's most awkward combined introduction of all time.

"Denver King," Abigail said.

"Guilty," said Denver.

And she knew he meant that in the literal sense.

Abigail looked from Sheena to Denver. "Nice to meet you," she said.

Sarah and Whitney nodded in agreement.

"I think you have to go over there to get your rental car," she said, gesturing to the counter that was just a few paces from where they were. "I got it," Alejandro said, walking over to the counter while they continued to stand by the baggage carousel.

"I'm glad you guys came," she said. "Really. Christmas wouldn't have been the same without you."

"You should see the bar that your sister just got put together," Denver said.

If she wasn't mistaken, there was pride in his voice. She just stood there and stared at him.

"Is it cool?" Sarah asked.

"So cool," said Denver. "In fact, tomorrow night you all should come out to King's Crest for dinner, have some barbecue, and throw some axes. Sheena can give you a demonstration."

"We didn't discuss that," said Sheena.

"I know," he said, looking unrepentant.

Without thinking she pushed against his shoulder.

And that earned her three very interested looks from her sisters.

Alejandro and Abigail got their car, they loaded up all the bags in both vehicles and they made a caravan headed back toward Pyrite Falls.

Whitney and Sarah peppered Denver with questions about how Four Corners Ranch worked, and he was more than happy to give them all the information they wanted.

"We have to stop for something," Denver said, swinging off the freeway so that they could stop at a Target. Inside, he picked up a fake tree, and a whole bunch of Christmas decorations.

"What are you doing?"

"All of your decorations are in use," he said. "And you need something. Since you all are staying at your place."

He was revenge Christmas decorating on her. All that reciprocity again. And it made her chest warm.

"I think you need an elf," he said, stopping in one of the aisles.

That brought out horrified sounds from her sisters.

"What?" Sheena asked. "You all like the elf."

"*You* like the elf," said Whitney.

"She does," Denver said. "A lot."

She grumbled the whole way through the aisle, and he put a Santa hat on her head because he thought it was funny to see her in one when she was so grumpy. Then he bought the hat, and she ended up wearing it all the way back to the house.

They had bought the ingredients to make cider, and Sarah put it on, along with some Christmas music while they set about to decorating the small house.

Alejandro was interested in everything. Asking Abigail how it had changed since she had been a kid, getting context for all the stories that she had undoubtedly told him about her life.

"He seems nice," Denver said, coming to stand alongside Sheena.

"He does," said Sheena. "I really hope he is. Because I don't want to go to prison. But I'm not *afraid* to."

"I do like that about you."

"Thank you."

"You should have more confidence in yourself, though," he said. "I don't think you'd get caught."

She laughed. She went into the bedroom, and took the presents for her sisters that she had wrapped a couple of weeks ago out of the top of the closet. Then once the tree was decorated, she put them underneath.

Denver looked at the presents speculatively, but didn't say anything.

"Sorry," she said. "Didn't get you anything."

"You got me enough," he said. So only she could hear.

He looked around the room when it was all done, then at her. "I should head back to the ranch. I'll see you all over there at some point tomorrow."

"Yeah," she said.

He didn't kiss her goodbye. And she was a little bit disappointed, even though she recognized that he was doing his best to maintain boundaries, which she would have said that she wanted.

"Well," Abigail said. "You're going to have to tell us all about that."

She sighed. "He's my boyfriend."

Her sisters' shrieks nearly broke her eardrums. She looked at Alejandro, who was clearly confused.

"Sheena doesn't do relationships," Abigail said. "And also, he's this guy that our dad used to run around with. Because his dad was the boss, and also a criminal. He's less of a criminal, and actually, he did a lot when we were growing up to try to help us. In fact, he paid for us to go to college."

"I'm going to need a longer, more detailed version of that later," Alejandro said.

"Don't worry," Abigail said. "I'll be sure to draw you a diagram."

"Your boyfriend," Whitney said, her eyes big. "Are you going to *marry* him?"

"Gross," said Sheena, ignoring the kick in her stomach. "I'm not going to marry him. I just thought it was a nicer way of saying that I'm sleeping with him. I have to protect your delicate sensibilities and whatever."

"You *like* him," Sarah said.

"Yes. I *like him*. But . . . that's all. It's a casual thing. It's a . . . Just a thing that will be a thing for as long as it's a thing."

"Sure," Sarah said.

"We believe you," Whitney said cheerfully.

"Hey," Abigail said. "I was actually wondering if you still had our yearbooks."

"Yes," said Sheena."

"Still in the bedroom?"

"Yeah, up in the top of the closet."

"Okay. I just wanted to find something."

The three sisters went out of the room, leaving her with Alejandro.

"So. You and my sister," she said.

He nodded. "Yeah."

"I heard you want her to meet your parents."

He nodded. "Yeah. I . . . While she's not in here. I wanted to ask you . . . I want to ask her to marry me. But I wanted to ask you first."

Sheena felt like she had been punched in the stomach.

"You want to propose?"

"Yeah."

"And you wanted to ask me?"

"Abigail has told me all about her childhood. It's really clear to me that you're the only actual parent that she had."

She was touched. She was honored. And she was also angry. Her stomach tense, her whole body hollowed out. Because her dad should've cared about this. Should have cared enough to live.

He should have been a better dad. So that he could be here for this. Because Abigail was amazing. She had graduated from high school, and she had fallen in love. And she was going to live in the ass crack of central California forever.

Which was fine. *It was just fine.*

And she was healed, which was great. She wasn't limping around like Sheena, insisting that she was never going to have a permanent relationship. Because that's how healed she was, and that was fantastic.

"If my sister wants to marry you," she said, "then I want her to marry you. You have my permission to grand gesture propose. It has to be awesome. And the ring has to be great."

"I promise."

A few minutes later, the girls came back in, holding yearbooks, and wearing . . . "Are those your prom dresses?"

"Yes," they said.

She turned to Alejandro. "Are you sure about this?" she asked quietly, so that Abigail, Whitney and Sarah wouldn't hear over the sound of their giggling.

"I've never been more sure about anything in my life." And he wasn't looking at Sheena. He only had eyes for Abigail.

Sheena found herself jealous in that moment. Of her own sister. What a stupid . . . what a stupid thing.

But it would be amazing. If somebody would look at her that way.

You don't want him to.

Yeah. That was what she told herself. And she was pretty good at sticking to her guns. So she wasn't going to change her mind. She wasn't.

He didn't drive home. He drove to Gold Valley. A Hail Mary pass, because it was going to be pretty late by the time he rolled in. And right when he got to the main street of town, he saw the shop owner reach out and start to turn her sign. He got out of his truck in a hurry, and walked toward the door.

She stopped.

And then she decided not to turn the sign.

He walked in ready to apologize, but she smiled. "You have perfect timing," she said.

She was a pretty woman, with sort of a bohemian style, her long blond hair loose. She was wearing a white dress in spite of the chilly weather.

"It seems like you were just about close," he said.

"Yes. But I'm always happy to stay open for somebody looking for something last-minute."

"I need . . . something . . . something . . ." How did he encapsulate Sheena?

"Are you looking for a ring?"

The question caught him off guard. And there was something in his chest that seemed to bump up against his heart. "No. Not a ring. A necklace. Or a bracelet. A necklace." Yes. He wanted to see her in a necklace. "She's . . ." Beautiful. Strong. Unique. A badass. "Got green eyes."

"Okay," the woman said. "I'm Sammy, by the way. Sammy Daniels. The designs are mine, and I make them mostly with local gemstones. So you can find some things here that are pretty unique. It sounds like she's unique."

"You got that from green eyes?"

She shook her head. "No. From the look on your face."

That nearly knocked him on his ass.

"So the necklace has to be really special," he said. "Because she is an . . ."

She pulled a piece out from behind the counter. "This one is new. The chain is made to look like a vine. And there's this purple stone in the center that represents a flower."

"It's like vinca," he said, rubbing his thumb over the gemstone.

"Kind of," she said. "Though, a lot of people consider that a weed, so I wouldn't have used that comparison myself. At least, not as a sales pitch."

He shook his head. "No. It's not a weed. It survives."

"Do you want me to pull out some more pieces?"

He shook his head. "No. This is perfect. Can you gift wrap it?"

"Yes."

He stood and waited while she did that. Sheena had bought presents for everybody else, and there was no gift for her under the tree. He couldn't have that. Couldn't stand it.

She needed to have a gift.

Only Whitney and Sarah were staying through Christmas, so he knew that they would be opening presents early. He just needed her to have this before the Christmas party. Before the grand opening of everything.

She handed him the box, wrapped neatly in silver paper, with a purple bow around the outside.

"Perfect," he said. "This is absolutely perfect."

He walked out of the store, and the flashing neon sign of the tavern down the way caught his eye.

It reminded him, just suddenly, of Vegas.

That almost made him laugh. One neon sign on a tiny main street in a small town was hardly like Las Vegas.

But that one flash of memory. That one, clear reminder set his brain along the path that it always went when he thought of his past.

And everything was blurry. Because it had always been blurry there. Booze and anything else he could find to numb himself.

He could so easily see himself at that table. Chattering. The way that he did, to put everybody off.

Mundane trivia. Pretending that he was interested in what they had to say.

Yeah. He was just as good at bullshit as his dad.

Made everybody think he was their friend before he took all their money and ran.

He tightened his hand around the necklace.

Sheena needed a Christmas present. So he had gotten her a Christmas present. That was all this was.

And they were . . .

It was Christmas, and her sisters were here. He wasn't going to get tripped up in his own head.

He got into his truck, and drove away from the store, the necklace sitting in the center of the seat.

And for the whole drive, he just did his best to think about nothing.

Chapter Nineteen

IT WAS JUST two days until the grand opening, and Sheena was excited, and a little bit of a wreck, and apparently hosting her sisters for a sort of pre–grand opening thing tonight at the axe throwing bar.

Denver had promised to handle all of the logistics.

And when she drove her sisters to the location, she could see that he had been serious about that.

There were four trucks in the driveway, and she could see people moving around inside.

The Kings and their various spouses. Plus Denver.

"This is the place," she said.

"This is incredible," said Whitney.

"Thank you," she said.

They walked inside, and there were big foil pans filled with meat and sides laid out along the bar. Bix was behind the counter, drawing beer.

"As the brewmaster, I am here to make pairing recommendations with whatever meat people want. I figure people should get good and drunk before they start throwing axes," she said.

Everybody seemed happy with that.

They piled up plates of food, and her sisters were introduced to everybody.

This was like . . . It must be what it was like when people had big families.

But they aren't your family.

She had to remember that.

They ate, and talked, and then some competitive games started in earnest. All of the throwing lanes were full of different pairings of people, and Sheena gave a quick group instruction, which had everybody crying with laughter because of all of the inherent double entendre in said instructions.

She opted to compete with her sisters, and of course destroyed them soundly.

She looked around the room. This was what she had worked so hard for. This was . . . this was it. Her baby. Her ticket out of here.

Except . . . it was beginning to feel like home. They really were all beginning to feel like family. And it was beginning to feel like less and less of a goal to get the hell out of Dodge.

That thought made her feel tender, a little bit bruised.

"Hey," said Denver. "I . . . Can I talk to you for a second?"

"Sure," she said, her heart going tight. For some reason, she was suddenly overcome by dread. By the possibility of what he might have to say to her.

What if . . . ?

What if. Today was a good day.

He wouldn't do anything while your sisters were here.

That was true. If she knew anything about him, it was that.

So he took her outside, and she let him.

She remembered that day when she had walked back here and he had come upon her in the forest.

The impact of him.

"I got something for you. And I was going to wait until it was a gift exchange, or whatever. But now . . . I don't want to wait."

Her heart skipped. This was not what she had been expecting. "You got me a present?"

After she had been such a jerk to him yesterday teasing him about how she had bought him one.

"Yeah," he said. "I did."

"You didn't have to do that."

"I know."

He reached into his coat pocket, and took out a flat, silver package.

"What is this?"

"You're gonna have to open it."

So out there, in the dark, she did. She tore open the silver paper, and then found a white box inside. She opened that, and found a velvet black box.

For a second, she felt disoriented. She thought of Alejandro talking about getting her sister a ring. But this was too big to be a ring box. And why her brain should go that direction at all . . .

No. It just shouldn't. Because she knew. That wasn't what this was.

"Open it," he said.

Because of course he was completely unaware that for a second she had stopped breathing.

She opened the box slowly, and inside was the most beautiful, perfect necklace. It looked like her tattoo. If he had designed something for her on purpose it couldn't have been any better.

"How did you . . . ?"

"I drove to Gold Valley last night. It's not like I preplanned this. So don't go thinking that it's . . . You know, that I'm that nice or anything like that. It's just . . . I didn't like that you didn't have a present so I went and found you one. And she just happened to have this."

She shouldn't be upset that he was downplaying it. He was trying to be humble, or something. But it sounded almost like he regretted giving her jewelry. Like he knew that it could be taken the wrong way.

"It's really pretty."

"Let me . . ." He reached out and grabbed hold of the necklace, taking it out of the box, the chain looking so delicate in his hands.

"Turn around," he said.

She swept her hair to the side and turned, and he draped the necklace over her head, before clasping it behind her. The gem fell with a heavy weight against her collarbone.

And his hands felt warm on her neck.

She closed her eyes. And waited for him to move closer. But instead he took a step back.

A wave of disappointment crashed through her, and she couldn't even quite say why.

"Thank you," she said. "It really is beautiful."

"I thought you could wear it to the grand opening."

"I'm going to owe you a lot more money back. This must've been expensive."

The look on his face was unreadable, but it wasn't happy.

But he was the one that had pulled away from her. He was the one who had given her a necklace and then wanted to downplay it. He was the one who was being weird, not her. And she had said that because she thought that was the direction he was moving. And she didn't want . . .

"I'm kidding," she said.

"Good," he said. "It was a gift not a payment."

"Great. Thank you. I love it." She knew she sounded mad

about it, but there was really nothing she could do about it right at that second.

She felt vaguely mad. Which was odd, because she didn't think a person should feel vaguely mad while they were receiving the most gorgeous jewelry they had ever seen in their lives.

"We better get back."

"Great," she said.

They went back inside, and she did her best to paste a smile on her face.

Because she didn't understand what the hell that was. Or why it was making her feel so imbalanced. She didn't . . . she didn't need this. It was stupid.

They were supposed to be having fun. Having sex. Being . . . this thing that they were. This friendship, or whatever it had turned into.

Where he gave her jewelry, and she thought about him all the time. And she hated being at her house when he wasn't there because it reminded her of what life had been like before Denver. Not before he was leaving money in her mailbox, but before he was holding her at night in bed.

She . . .

She refused to think it all the way through. She just did.

She went over to the bar and leaned in. "Have another drink?"

"Holy shit." Bix's eyes went round. "That's a gorgeous necklace."

"Thank you," she said.

Bix narrowed her eyes. "Are you okay?"

"I'm fine. I'm . . ."

"You don't have to explain. You're with a King. I get it."

"Daughtry and Denver are *not* the same."

"They're a little the same," Bix said. "Daughtry's exterior is his bulletproof vest and badge. Mr. Do Everything by the Book. That's his shield. Denver's is different. But there is one.

And I think underneath that they have quite a bit in common. Which means . . . they are occasional pains in the ass."

She laughed. "Yes. That's exactly it."

Except she had a terrible feeling that right now the problem was her. Her feelings. And the fact that she didn't quite have a handle on them the way she wished she did.

She also didn't think it was fair for Bix to try and draw comparisons between her experiences with Daughtry, and Sheena's experiences with Denver, because she and Denver were not headed in the same direction as Bix and Daughtry.

Bix and Daughtry were married. They were forever. They were in love.

She and Denver were sleeping together. And were occasionally mad at each other. And sometimes not mad at each other.

So whatever that was.

She had her drink, and pushed through the rest of the evening. Everybody having fun until it was so late they were all exhausted.

She still felt uneasy. And she couldn't say exactly why. It was whatever this thing was with Denver. The necklace that was sitting heavily on her neck.

"I can give them a ride back," Alejandro offered when everyone was ready to go.

She wasn't quite ready to leave. And she couldn't say how her sister's almost fiancé had guessed that. Only that he had, and that made her like him even more.

Because he paid attention. And he would pay attention to her sister.

"Thank you."

Everybody piled out of the bar, and left her there alone.

She had told Denver that she would wait for him to put the animals up, but she was feeling kind of angry and spiteful.

She went into the employees-only room, where the animals were kept.

Then she took them, along with a stepladder, out into the main part of the bar. She brought it up underneath one of the long shelves that ran along the wall that wasn't completely covered by throwing lanes.

She put up the woodchuck, and looked at it.

"You're perfect," she said.

She heard the door open, and footsteps behind her.

She sighed. "Yes?"

"You *really* are mad at me," he said. "Putting those up without me."

"Do you blame me?"

"No," he said. "I acted like a dick. I'm sorry."

"Okay. Well. This was fun."

He frowned. "It's not over," he said.

"Do you get to unilaterally decide that?"

"No. I just mean . . . We've had plenty of fights."

"Sure. Fights. This was different. You gave me a present, and then you were weird and standoffish about it."

"I'm sorry. I don't . . . I don't really know how to do things like this. I wanted to get you a present. I didn't like that you didn't have something under a tree. Then I thought maybe it was too much. Then for some reason I was standing out on the street in Gold Valley thinking about Las Vegas."

"What?"

"I don't know. The point is, I don't actually know how to behave. And that's my fault, and I'm sorry. I was worried that it was maybe too heavy of a gesture."

"Do you feel like it was?"

"Not really. I went to get you something that seemed right. And the necklace was there. It was perfect for you. From what I know about you. It spoke to your strength and the tattoo when . . . I don't know how to do any kind of feeling."

"I didn't ask you to."

He looked at her for a long moment.

"No. You didn't."

"For what it's worth, it's a beautiful necklace."

"Thank you. Can I try again?"

She could just get mad. She could throw the woodchuck at him. She could tell him that he had behaved badly and she didn't want to let him walk it back, because it wasn't fair.

But then he might leave. She didn't actually want that.

"Go ahead. Try again."

He moved toward her, reached behind the back of her neck and took the necklace off of her.

"Denver . . ."

He looked at her, his gaze serious. "Sheena, yesterday I saw another example of you taking care of everybody else, and nobody taking care of you in quite that same way. And I couldn't bear it. I wanted to do something to make sure that you had as good as you gave. I went and I found this. I think it's perfect for you. Because it's like you. It's an eternal vine and flower. Like your ink. Like you are. So I wanted you to have it. And I can't say that it's a promise or that it means anything. Because you know this whole thing is . . . uncharted territory. But I can say that whatever becomes of us, this is the truth of you. And it's how I see you. If nothing else, I want you to know that. That I see you."

She found it hard to breathe. Because that was the nicest thing that anybody had ever said to her. She wasn't sure it was entirely true. She had always hoped that she was that unkillable flower. But tonight she had felt easily crushed.

A consequence, she thought, of cultivating this life where the presence of a man mattered so much. And it did. It mattered so much.

And this . . . this gift from him, it wasn't a promise. It was more of that honesty that scraped against her skin like a blade.

But she couldn't fault him for that.

Well. She could. But it would be foolish.

He hadn't lied to her. Not at any point.

But then, deception was never really her trigger. It was not being loved enough.

"Turn around," he said.

She did, slowly. Just like outside. But this time, he was the one that swept her hair to the side. This time, he moved the necklace around slowly, the feel of the metal on her skin almost erotic as he slowly did the clasp.

She turned around, and his eyes were hot on hers. Right then, she felt equal parts despair and need.

Would it always be like this with him? Would it always be bliss, followed by complicated sex that left them raw enough to add some edge to that happiness? And then fights, with moments of making love to erase all of the anger. To make it sweet.

It was exhausting.

There were so many feelings between them all the time, and neither of them had the vocabulary to figure out what they were. Speak them out loud and turn them into some form of sense. It was always tearing off clothes and short, ragged breaths.

It was always kisses that said more than words, and climaxes that brought about the kind of oblivion that felt comforting in a familiar sort of way.

Because this had become familiar. Because they had let it become their language.

And she couldn't put a stop to that now.

Because right now, she wanted him. Right now, she wanted to affirm whatever this was.

Right now, she wanted to get back to who they were, and what they knew.

He kissed her. Hard and deep, and she surrendered. Because

she needed to. Because she needed to speak this language. The one they both knew fluently. She needed to feel like she understood him again. More than anything.

It felt risky to do it right here in the bar, but it also felt right. What they hadn't done at Smokey's, even though they had both wanted it.

He started to pull at her clothes, and she helped him discard them, flinging them down to the floor, not caring where they landed.

She tore his T-shirt up over his head and paused to admire all the glory that was Denver King.

Broad shoulders that had carried the burden of everyone and everything for years. Broad shoulders that bore the weight of the sins of his father, and continued to do so, no matter how much he tried to atone.

She didn't bear the burden of her father's sins. She bore the weight of his apathy.

And it was heavy.

She couldn't even imagine how heavy it was for Denver. But she didn't know how to help him carry it. There was an attempt. She tried to do things to care for him, just like he tried to do it for her, but they were both so imperfect. Misshapen little puzzle pieces trying to find a way to fill space that they hadn't been made for. Or maybe they had been at one time, but they had been so mangled by their experiences that it was all impossible now.

She couldn't say for sure.

But she knew that she loved kissing him. She knew that she loved the feel of his muscles beneath her fingertips. She knew that she loved that salty taste of his skin.

So she licked her way down his chest, down his abs, so that she was kneeling in front of him, working his belt, undoing his jeans.

He groaned as she freed him, running her tongue from base to tip. Before taking him all the way.

He was definitely the biggest man she'd ever been with, but she was highly motivated, and she had a certain set of skills.

She wrapped her hand around the base, took him all the way, impossibly, before letting him slide out slowly.

Over and over again, until he was shaking.

Maybe there couldn't be anything else. Maybe there wasn't any more in either of them.

Maybe this was as deep as it got. Absolutely no pun intended.

But it felt like something. That she was the only woman to ever have him for this length of time. That she was the only woman who had ever gotten to know every little thing he liked.

She knew that when he was thrusting deep inside of her if she licked his neck, he would shudder. Shake. That it would take him closer to the edge. She knew that he'd just about lost it entirely when she swallowed his cock down her throat. She knew that he liked it when she made eye contact with him while she did it. So she looked up at him now, and watched him grit his teeth, the tendons in his neck standing out with effort as he tried to keep control.

She didn't want his control.

She wanted his surrender.

But he was so careful to never give it. Not until he was good and ready.

That was the problem. They were so very much the same. And everything was a power struggle.

Because between them, what else could it be?

They had both spent their lives relying on their strength.

Giving it up wasn't something they could fathom.

But maybe that was the key. Maybe that was what she had to do. Maybe that was what had to change. She could keep on fighting him. Keep going toe to toe. Keep on meeting him for every challenge.

But what if she simply . . . didn't?

When she gave herself to him instead?

What would that change?

Her heart was thundering fast, and she licked him one last time before standing up slowly.

Then she wrapped her arms around his neck and kissed him. Deep.

Soft.

Not as a challenge. Not as a gauntlet being thrown down. But connection. Their mouths meeting, and to the best of her ability, her soul attempting to touch his.

He lifted her up onto the bar top, and brought her to the edge of it. "Sheena," he growled against her lips.

"I don't have a condom."

Her heart clenched. "I'm on the pill."

That was trust. It was letting go of a lifetime of being shielded. She had never let a man . . . Ever. Hadn't even wanted to. The very idea totally freaked her out. No barrier. Taking part of him like that.

But not Denver. No. She wanted him. She wanted this.

"Are you sure?" he asked.

"I'm sure," she whispered. "I'm totally sure."

He pressed the head of his arousal to the slick entrance of her body, and began to move forward, inch by excruciating inch. He didn't claim her in one thrust as he often did. It was like he was savoring it. The feeling of taking her like this.

She let her head fall back, but only for a moment, because then she couldn't bear to not be looking at him.

He was too beautiful.

Inside of her like this, lost in his own pleasure. In his own need too.

Denver.

She just wanted him so badly. All the time.

There was no end to it.

It was something. Something more even than this. Something deeper.

Those feelings she didn't have words for.

A grounding, dark need that rolled through her like thunder. All the way down to her soul.

To the most vulnerable, needy part of her.

A place she had tried to shut off a long time ago.

Because life was relentless and loss—in all of its forms—was just too painful sometimes.

Because the trail was too sharp, and if you were soft, then it cut too deep.

But this . . . This was deep. This was real.

And she wanted more. More.

She wrapped her legs around his back, urged him on. Whispered in his ear, she wasn't even sure what. Because she didn't even know what she was feeling. All of the words in her mind were nothing more than endless impressions of need.

Nothing more than everything.

That was all.

And right then, his thrusts began to get harder, faster. He looked into her eyes, and she felt it. Just as she felt him. Sliding deep, touching those hidden parts of her. And she was very, very scared in that moment that she had completely unmade herself. That she had gone to that stubborn plant and compromised the roots in some way. Began feeding them with the vitamins that it was now dependent on. So that what was once wild had now been domesticated. Because what would she do without him? Without what he gave her?

When she had never had it, she didn't know. And what you didn't know couldn't break you.

You couldn't miss it.

You couldn't want it.

Couldn't need it.

But those thoughts were lost, and a storm of need surged as he began to fray around the edges, as his control began to break.

She flexed her hips forward, trying to take him deeper.

He growled. She could feel him, different than all the other times before. And maybe it really physically felt different. Or maybe it was just trust.

Maybe it was just that next step.

But she couldn't fear it. Not right then.

He cupped her face, and kissed her, while he held her tight with one arm around her waist, continuing to take her deep and hard.

And as she felt his control slip away, she let go of hers.

Their climax hit at the same moment, her internal muscles pulsing tight around him, as he spilled himself into her.

There were no words for it. Well. There were. Profanity. But that was about it.

"Come home with me," he said.

"Okay."

She didn't have any resistance left inside of her. And even if she did, she didn't want it.

She just wanted him.

She held him for a long time after. Or maybe he held her. And then finally, they got dressed, and went back to his place. She tried to ignore the feeling of home she felt when they walked inside.

And if she slept better in his bed than she had in her own last night, she tried her best not to think about that either.

Chapter Twenty

HE WAS BARBECUING like it was the most important barbecue of his life. And hell, it basically was.

His contribution to Four Corners was coming to a head right now.

The inauguration of the event center, the responsibility of hosting a Christmas event. Of introducing the community to the work he'd done.

He hadn't really thought about it, but there was no better way really, to say that the Kings were different now than they had been than by throwing a Christmas party.

His ancestors were probably rolling in their graves. He damned well hoped they were.

If not burning in hell.

He was open to either.

He had all the smokers occupied, and all the grills going hot. He knew that everything in the event space was set up perfectly, because he had been up at four o'clock this morning making sure it was all ready to go. Every table and tablecloth in place. Every corner festooned with a garland. He had never cared about garlands in his life, and now he cared about them a lot. To a comedic amount, some might say.

He was just checking the chickens when he heard the sound of tires coming up his driveway, parking in front of the house.

Sheena.

She had left this morning, telling him that she had to go and get something fancy to wear for tonight, which had set his imagination on fire.

Last night had been . . .

Just thinking about taking her bare like that left him aching.

They had gone back to his place, and slept. Like they were trying to outrun that fight.

Like the intimacy from their coming together had exhausted them.

Enough that even this morning, they hadn't come together again.

Which was unusual.

But maybe she was back now. He couldn't really leave the meat. He was considering how to make a compromise on that when Sawyer Garrett and Gus McCloud came into view.

"What the hell are you doing here?" he asked.

"Good to see you too," said Sawyer.

"It's just unexpected," he said.

"We thought we would come by and see if you needed any help," said Gus.

He frowned. "Is that code for saying you don't trust a King to handle this?"

It was Gus's turn to frown. "No. And if I did, it would be a bit rich. Considering."

"You're a little bit of a folk hero, Gus."

"All I'm saying is, if we don't let failure stay in the past none of us are going to fare very well."

"Well. Why are you here?"

"To help," said Sawyer. "You've always contributed food to everything. Consistently. You're a difficult bastard to know, Denver King, but I have always known that you were decent. Even if you are an asshole."

Denver snorted. "You have not always known I was decent."

"Much the same as I haven't always known that I was decent," said Gus.

He snorted again. "Listen. I appreciate the help but . . ." He looked at the sheer volume of food he was cooking. "If you want to grab some tongs, you're welcome to."

"Absolutely," said Gus.

"Sure thing," Sawyer said.

They stood there, manning the grills, not really making much conversation.

It was strange, to think that they had grown up together. They had gone to the same one-room schoolhouse. They had formed this collective together. And yet, they didn't exchange a whole lot of words.

"How are . . . things?" Sawyer asked.

"Are we doing small talk?" Denver asked.

"Some people like it," Sawyer said. "There must be a reason."

"Not one that I can think of."

"Well, then maybe you want to talk about something a little bit more serious," said Gus. "Like the fact that I think you want to let us invest a little bit more in these new ventures of yours."

"I don't understand why you want to do that," Denver said.

"Because," Gus responded, "you're trying to figure out a way to be an island even in this collective, and it's unnecessary. Nobody needed you to do that. Nobody asked you to do it."

"I'm aware of that," he said, his teeth gritted. "But it's my choice."

"You can't do this forever," Gus said. "Believe me. There's a certain point where you can't keep trying to atone for the sins of somebody who isn't here anymore. You know, there was a day when I realized my dad didn't think about me anymore. And I thought about him a lot. It's difficult not to. Every time I look in the mirror I remember what he did to me." Denver looked Gus full in the face, at all the burn scars that marred his skin. "But he left here. He left here, and he's off doing whatever the hell he wants. Albeit with fewer resources than he would like. But he doesn't think about me. And I was still letting him have an iron grip on my life. That's not justice."

"I'm not really concerned with justice for myself," Denver said.

He kept his eyes on the chicken in front of him.

"Well, maybe you should be. Because we are all fine." That came from Sawyer.

He looked over at him. "There's still a lot to do . . ."

"No, there isn't," said Sawyer. "Look around you. Everything that our parents did to hurt this place, to hurt us, we've all put a stop to it. We've all built something new. This is a new generation. A generation like this ranch has never seen before. We work together more than we ever have. We are more successful than we've ever been. There was a time when I believed that marriages here were cursed. Truly. I hadn't ever seen a different outcome. You know my own father was useless with relationships. He chased off every woman who tried to love him."

"There's no need to even bring up my dad," said Gus.

"The Sullivans imploded," Sawyer said. "Albeit in a less spectacular way than the rest of our families. And then . . . you all didn't fare any better, did you?"

"No," he said.

"But it's changed now. And you've been part of that. And still . . . you hold yourself separate."

"My dad is a little more complicated," Denver said. "He would've been a damned fine cult leader. But I don't say that as a means of absolving myself. We all participated in his criminal empire. With the exception of Arizona. Because he never even pretended to be nice to her. But his sons? In one way or another, we believed in him. It isn't just my dad's sins that I'm trying to atone for. It's my own. And if I have to keep giving more than I get, I'm okay with that."

"You don't, though," said Gus.

But he did. He couldn't articulate why; it was just that he did. It was extremely important. And he didn't need Gus McCloud to understand him. Didn't need Sawyer Garrett to think he was right. He just needed that to be the case. Because he couldn't rest.

He couldn't . . .

This thing that they were talking about, this utopian time they were talking about, he couldn't afford that. Couldn't risk it.

"Yeah. I get it," Gus said. "You were part of the bad that your father did. But you've also been part of all the good that we've done here. When he went away, you banded together with us, you put your own hard-earned money into this place. In all honesty, Denver, if you hadn't invested your money when you did, we never could've gotten this place off the ground. We were in a hole that was too deep. You were a big part of saving this ranch. I hate to break it to you, buddy. But you're one of the good guys."

"You say that like being a good guy is a destination."

"Oh no. I don't think it's a destination. But I think it's something available to anybody that wants to be that. Because that's not what men like your dad or my dad want. They want their own happiness above anyone and everyone else's. Does that sound like you?"

He thought of himself. When he was free. In Las Vegas. When he didn't have anything or anyone else to consider.

He thought of himself with Sheena. The way that he had pushed through the emotional discomfort she had about their relationship, so that he could have her with him like he wanted.

"More than I would like."

"Well. That's not what I see," Sawyer said.

"Thanks, Sawyer," said Denver. "That's what I was waiting for. Your stamp of approval on my life. It's really too bad that you are already married. Because I might propose."

"You really are an asshole, King," said Sawyer. "But it doesn't mean you aren't a good guy."

"Whatever makes you feel better."

He really did think that was part of the problem. They wanted to put him in a box that made them comfortable. They had all arrived at a specific place. All of them. Every single member of the four families was romantically paired off. Happy. That really hadn't happened, ever, in the whole history of the ranch.

In the grand scheme of things, him not being paired off was just . . . fine.

It didn't do anything to take away from the fact that this really was the happiest time the ranch had ever experienced. So that was all fine and good.

But it was like they all wanted things tied up neatly with a bow. They wanted too much.

And he had to stay on guard. He knew that.

"At the very least, why don't you start coming out to some of the poker games we have at McCloud's Landing."

Denver laughed. He couldn't help it. "You do not want me at your poker games."

"Sure, we do."

"You don't want me there, trust me. I am not a hobbyist poker player."

"I know you won a lot of money on the professional circuit . . ."

"Do you also know that I'm a card counter?"

He was satisfied with the shocked expression that earned him.

"Isn't that against the rules?" Sawyer asked.

"It's frowned on."

"Okay, maybe come and teach us that trick," Gus said.

"No. I don't give away trade secrets. Anyway. You either have it or you don't."

"How about this," Gus said. "Don't be so much of a stranger."

As they were readying the food, and preparing it to be transported over to the event space, he pondered those words. He wasn't sure he had any idea how to accomplish that.

Half the time, he was pretty sure he was a stranger to his own self.

He didn't even know how to decode himself, let alone make himself more accessible to anyone else.

Except Sheena.

Sort of.

He thought of how he'd been with the necklace.

He had been such a jerk. But he felt torn up in a strange way after he had bought that thing, and something in his chest had felt uncomfortably large when he'd given it to her. And he didn't know what else to do but try to play it down.

But when he hurt her like that, he just wanted to fix it. And when she had acted like that meant it was the end of them, he couldn't bear it.

He still couldn't say why.

Because he was the one who had told her they could just do this while it was good. While it wasn't hard.

They drove over to the event space, and when he got there, the first thing he saw was her. Standing right outside the door, wearing a tight, purple dress that went just to her knees, a slit up the side revealing a shapely thigh and just a little bit of her tattoo. Her hair was up, which was unusual for her, and the necklace glinted against her skin.

For a moment he was at a loss for words. For a moment he was at a loss for everything. So he turned his attention resolutely away from her and focused solely on the party. On getting all the pieces locked together.

He couldn't afford the distraction of her. Not right this second.

Because he could just keep doing this. If he could get to a certain point. Then maybe eventually . . .

He looked around the room. It was great. It was perfect.

The chandelier at the center glittered, red ribbon cascaded around the room, pine boughs decorated everything. There were white Christmas lights hung in glorious curtains down the barn walls.

This place had been a ruin a year ago.

And now . . . it was this.

And just in an hour almost everybody at Pyrite Falls would be here.

And it still wasn't enough. It just wasn't enough.

He had to keep going. He had to keep moving. Maybe he should consider playing a few more poker games. Earning more money.

Doing something. He just had to keep doing something.

The back of his neck itched, and he turned around. Sheena was staring at him, from across the room.

He gritted his teeth, and made his way over to her. "Don't you need to go to the bar?"

"I have the staff getting things ready there."

"And you just trust them?"

"That's the point of hiring staff, Denver."

A totally foreign concept to him, because he liked to have his hand in everything. Though he supposed that was why she had said it that way.

"I particularly like the card table over there. I assume poker playing will occur?"

"That was actually the McClouds' idea. I don't play casual poker."

She laughed. "Would you play with me?"

"It's not fair," he said. "Because I would win."

For a moment, everything around them got fuzzy. And the only thing he could really pay attention to was her. And he couldn't afford that. Because he needed to pay attention to this. To the party.

"I'm going to be really busy tonight."

"I know," she said. "And I am going to go to the bar. But I just want to stay and . . ."

"And what?"

"Watch you. You work so hard for this. I know it matters to you."

She knew that it mattered to him. "Why do you think it matters to me?"

"You want everybody to see you. How much you care. That you are a good man."

That he was a good man.

The trouble was, he didn't especially believe that he was.

But the place began to fill up, and he had to admit there was something a lot like satisfaction sitting in his chest alongside a burning need that felt a lot like being pushed. Pushed forward. Pushed to do more. To do better.

Some of the ranch hands, who had a band that played at the town hall meetings, had offered to come and play Christmas music, and they had all dressed in their nicest clothes. Black suit jackets and boleros. Black cowboy hats. The fiddles almost sounded like violins as the haunting country Christmas arrangements filled the room. And Sheena made her way over to him. "Dance with me, cowboy."

He was powerless to resist. Even if he wanted to. Just looking at her changed things. Took that weight off of his chest. Shifted something in his soul. He took her in his arms and they went out to the dance floor. It was like they were the center. Of all of it. Everything. Even if he was more outlaw than knight in shining armor, and she was more warrior than princess. Right then, it felt like maybe they could be something more. Something different.

He hadn't done much in the way of slow dancing that extended beyond holding a woman against his body just so they could feel each other, a promise for the evening of debauchery that was to come. But with her, he tried. And what surprised him most was how it felt like flying. She smiled up at him, the look on her face holding the kind of joy he'd never seen anywhere. Much less looking right out at him.

People were enjoying the food. Enjoying the music. Enjoying the games.

"Go to the bar," he whispered into her ear.

"We can't do that," she said. "You have to stay here, don't you?"

"We can dip out for a minute."

He took her hand and the two of them walked out of the building, down the path, which they had lit up for tonight's event. People were meandering between venues, holding hands, laughing.

Right there in the middle of the winter darkness, the gaming hall/axe throwing bar was lit up bright. He could see that there was a crowd of people inside. That her staff was moving around efficiently, with big smiles on their faces.

It was . . . more. Better than he had imagined.

A rousing success on a level he hadn't allowed himself to dream of.

They walked inside, and there were games being played, the sounds of axes hitting targets. People were sitting around the bar eating and drinking, dressed all in their finery. He could see that the Wild West of the place appealed to the crowd that had come out.

This idea that he and Sheena had collaborated on was . . . better than he could've possibly imagined.

People were taking selfies right in front of the shelves that had the taxidermy rodents.

"I love that that's a hit," Sheena said, her eyes on exactly the same part of the room that his were. It didn't even surprise him at this point.

That she was looking at the same thing he was. Right when he did.

A couple he didn't recognize, who introduced themselves and said they came from out of town, asked if the bar was theirs.

"It's hers," he said.

"Well, that isn't entirely true," she said, putting her hand on his forearm. "It was my business proposition, but Denver's land. Plus, using this building and making it like a saloon was his idea."

The woman took notes, and said that she ran a social media account for things to do in the area, and she would be looking to feature that. Sheena gave details on pricing and on how to call to get a lane reserved.

After that, everybody in the bar realized that Sheena was the owner. And she was fielding enthusiastic comments about how fun it was.

It was almost impossible to get away.

When they did leave, and they got back to the event space, Arizona was beaming. "Denver, you won't believe this. We booked up for the whole rest of the year. Weddings, mostly. But quinceañera, and an eighteenth-birthday party, a couple of gold and anniversaries. This space is literally full up. Every weekend."

"What?"

"I'm not even kidding. There's nothing around here for hours that can compete with it. I've been sitting here literally putting things into the calendar and taking deposits."

"I . . ."

Of all the things he had imagined, he definitely had never thought that tonight they would get so many requests for reservations that they were completely full.

It was a great idea; he knew that. He'd known that there would be a demand for it, but he had no idea that it would be so intense, or on that scale.

"You really did it," she said.

Sheena took his hand and squeezed it. "Look at you," she said. "You saved King's Crest."

Not that there had been any danger of it failing. Not before this, anyway.

"It's not going to be famous for Dad anymore. It's going to be famous because of this. This is what people are going to think of. The beef, the beer, the bar. Look at what you did," Arizona said.

It was such a strange feeling, the accomplishment that bloomed in his chest. And he couldn't say that he liked it all that much. It was uncomfortable. And more than that, it was a temptation. A temptation unlike anything he'd experienced before.

Then Daughtry, straitlaced and absolutely the last person on earth to call attention to himself, went up to the stage and interrupted the band. Denver stopped. He watched his brother snag a microphone, and looked out at the crowd. "If anybody has enjoyed themselves tonight, then they owe a big thanks to my brother Denver. Denver made this possible. Not only was it his idea, but he pushed to get this done for the past year. To bring about change to Pyrite Falls, while keeping the integrity of this place intact. This isn't a development like you would get from some fat cat who came in from the city. This is the kind of development you get from somebody who feels a real responsibility for the place, and the people who live here. Not only has he given us all some cool things to do, but he has also figured out ways to get more people visiting town. And that's better for all of us."

There was a huge round of applause, and Denver could barely hear it over his heart beating in his head.

They were all acting like he was some kind of hero.

He had never been.

He was . . . he was still the guy that had ridden with his father back in the day. Still the guy who had come to their house to collect debts. Underneath it all, that's who he was. And he couldn't forget that. They shouldn't either.

People were clapping, and Daughtry was gesturing for him to come up to the stage. Sheena squeezed his hand.

He looked at her, like he was hoping she would throw him a lifeline. "Go on."

He did, but he didn't want to. He got up to the stage and grabbed the microphone. "I don't deserve the glory for this," he said. "It's . . . it's my family. It's the collective. It's this community. That's what I've been trying to contribute to for all these years. What I've been hoping to help heal. And that's all I have to say about that. Everybody here deserves the applause."

He got down from the stage, and was met with more applause, which he chose to believe was for the rest of them. That it was his turn to be in the position Sheena had been back in the bar.

And through it all, she stood by his side.

The party went until late.

It was nearly midnight when the doors to the barn opened, and he saw fat snowflakes falling from the sky.

Even though it let a rush of cold air in, they let those doors stay propped open, so that people could look out at the snow from inside the glowing barn.

Right then, with the snow falling in the background, Abigail's boyfriend got to his knee and pulled out a ring.

She put her hand over her mouth and nodded enthusiastically, even before he asked the question.

He looked at Sheena, who had her hand pressed firmly to her own chest.

"Did you know he was going to do that?" he asked.

"Yeah," she said softly. "I'm so . . . I'm so happy for them." Her eyes glistened, her words wistful.

He didn't know why it made him feel like he'd been stabbed in the chest. To see those two young people he didn't even know well get engaged.

"He put a hold on this place. For next year," Arizona said.

He hadn't even realized that his sister was standing there. Sheena smiled broadly. "He did? That is so . . . amazing. She found such a good man."

There was clapping and cheering when he slid the ring on her finger, and Arizona snapped a picture of them kissing in the barn door. "Definitely going to send that to them."

Sheena and Denver lingered until everybody had gone. Until the room was empty of people. All that was left were the tables. The echo of that Christmas music, long gone quiet.

Sheena walked over to the bar and grabbed a bottle of wine. She poured a glass for herself, and then another, carrying it over to where he stood. "How about we play a game?"

"What game?"

"Five-card stud. I've heard all about your poker skills, King. So let's play."

He stood there, feeling like he was having an out-of-body experience. Here he was in this place that a year ago had been an old, dilapidated barn, staring at this woman who he hadn't known a year ago at all, but who now felt integral to every breath he took during the day. Holding a glass of wine. Being extended an invitation to play poker.

It was Vegas. But it wasn't.

Sex. Alcohol. Gambling.

But made new. In a different place. In a different context.

It was almost unbelievable how different those same things could be here. With her.

"I'm going to win," he said, shaking his head, trying to dispel that strange out-of-body feeling as he walked over to the game table.

"That's fine," she said cheerfully. "Although, you don't know everything about me."

"Are you a secret card sharp?"

"It's not a secret. I have won many poker games."

"Probably not as many as me." He picked up the stack of cards on the table and gave them a quick, competent trick shuffle before starting to deal.

"Show-off," she said.

"Yes, I am."

He forgot to count cards. He forgot to do anything but stare at her.

They sat there, getting nothing and everything as they played. Hand after hand, letting it get later and later.

Like neither of them wanted the night to end. He looked across the table at her, at that purple gem she was wearing.

If he were to buy her a ring, he would get one that matched it.

He looked down at his hand of cards. And for a moment, he was frozen.

It was too easy to imagine them here, standing in the doorway, with him proposing and that whole audience of people standing there cheering them on.

He looked up at her, and the first thing he wanted to do was apologize. Because he didn't know how the hell he had let things get to this point.

But the look on her face stopped him.

"I love my father," she said.

"What?"

"I'm sorry. That must seem so desperately random to you. Watching my sister get engaged, I just . . . I had this feeling of relief. I escaped. All the things I've been running from. I don't have to keep running. My sisters are okay. They were even before Abigail and Alejandro got engaged, but that just clicked something into place for me. I've still been living like the past can hurt me. And the truth is, of course the past can hurt you. If you don't learn from it. I thought a lot about the kinds of things I do and am historically. But what it comes right down to is that if you don't learn from history you are doomed to repeat it. I learned a lot. And I need to trust that. I don't think I'm doomed to repeat a damned thing."

He didn't say anything. He just kept looking at her. Held captive by every word that was coming out of her mouth.

"I don't even like thinking about all the ways my dad was good. Because it hurts too much. After he let his friend . . . After he failed to protect me in that way, I just made a wall around my heart. When none of his good intentions mattered. Because everything he said didn't mean anything if he didn't protect his own daughters in the end. But the truth is, my Christmas decorations came from my dad. He used to buy us little presents. Little dollar store dolls every year. There was always an orange in our stockings. He used to read to us the night before Christmas." She laughed. "And then he got drunk and passed out, and he was often hung over on Christmas morning. He would make strong coffee, and he didn't really see the use for breakfast. But he always did something for Christmas dinner. Usually a ham and some store-bought mashed potatoes. There was a time in my life when I believed in him. I knew that he wasn't always doing the right things. I knew that he took drugs. That he drank too much. I also knew that he didn't want us to be hurt by that. At least, that's what he said." Her eyes glittered with tears. "I decided it was a lie. All of it. Because it was easier to believe that than it was to just believe that . . . that love failed. That it was weak. I just turned him into a villain, because that was so much easier."

Her words made it feel like his chest was being wrenched apart. And part of him, a strange, small part of him, envied her in the strangest way.

Because nothing his dad ever did or said was genuine. At least, not so he could trust it. He had believed his dad too. But it had all been manipulation.

Maybe her father had believed at one time that he would stop what he was doing.

"When he died I was numb," she said. "I miss him, Denver."

Her eyes were bright, glistening, and a tear slid down her cheek. Dropped down onto the table. It didn't make a sound, yet somehow, left an impact in his chest that was something like an explosion. "I miss him, and I . . . I didn't realize it until now."

Without thinking, he moved across the table, took her hand and stood her up. Then he pulled her into his arms. "I'm sorry," he said.

She cried. Against his shoulder, holding on to him. The Denver that everyone here tonight thought he was would know the right thing to say. The right thing to do. The right thing to feel. He didn't think her father deserved these tears. And that was the problem. He wasn't that Denver. He was an angry, vindictive man, selfish to his core. Because his gut instinct was to tell her that her father deserved to be writhing in the grave. For all that he failed to do for her. That all his efforts hadn't been enough. And a bargain Barbie doll didn't make up for the ways that he'd left them. But that wasn't what she needed.

He knew enough to know that. "Let's go home," she whispered.

He wrapped his arm around her and they walked out of the barn together. He drove them back to the house. Her car was still at the event space, but they would get it tomorrow.

Then he took her hand and led her upstairs. And when they got into bed together, he pulled her close to him. He didn't kiss her. Didn't touch her. He only held her.

Until her breathing was deep and even.

Until he was starting to fall asleep.

For the first time, they didn't lose themselves in the storm.

They just rested.

Chapter Twenty-One

WHEN SHE WOKE up it was still dark outside. Crazy, because she and Denver had probably been up until two in the morning. And then . . .

He was still asleep, his arm wrapped around her. They hadn't had sex last night.

She lay there next to him, just listening to his deep, even breathing.

They hadn't fallen into bed and made love and fallen asleep because an orgasm was the best sleeping pill available.

They had gotten into bed to be together. Hold each other. They had slept together because it was better than sleeping apart.

She had opened up a vein last night. And he had just listened.

She got out of bed, and he didn't stir. She made her way over to the window and looked out. The moon was full, the sky clear, and she could see it reflecting on the bright snow all over the ground. She had never let herself think of all those good memories. She had never let herself go there, because it was just too painful.

Because she had decided a long time ago that love was a weakness. Both in her and in her dad. She had done her best to get rid of that weakness.

She wasn't weak for loving her dad.

The thought was enough to make her dizzy as she stared down at that snow-covered ground.

Feelings didn't make you weak.

Maybe that was the only reason her dad had ever been strong in any capacity with them.

She had been so disappointed with his shortcomings that she had erased everything that he ever did. Everything he had ever tried to do. He hadn't done Christmas just for himself. He did it for them.

He hadn't kept his girls and tried to raise them after his wife had left because he didn't care. His caring had been imperfect. Because he had been very flawed. He had failed them.

In so many ways.

He had never pretended to be reformed. None of that had been pretending.

Not the perfect or the imperfect.

It wasn't that the weakness was real but the strength wasn't.

And perhaps, the love he had for his kids was the strongest thing he possessed.

She wasn't going to go twisting and turning to make him a hero. But he was maybe a little more than she had ever believed.

Because maybe love was a little more than she had let herself believe.

It was what had kept her going after he died.

The love for her sisters.

The love that had been stored in that house up until that point. A tear slid down her cheek, and another.

She looked back at Denver, and her heart nearly shattered. She loved him.

That was what she'd been trying to avoid this whole time. Like it was a plague. Because it could make her weak. That was what she had believed. She had seen all the ways that love had made her feel weak and broken in the past, and that was the narrative she had given herself about it, because it was just easier.

It was never the love that hurt. Not really. It was all the things around it.

That day her father had died, she had looked at Denver King, and she had seen something. Deep down in her soul, she had known something.

She was glad she hadn't figured out what it was then.

She had needed to wait.

To struggle, to succeed, to fail. To get her sisters raised and out into the world. She had needed to build herself up, and find all the ways that she could be strong alone.

It had brought her to this point. To this point where she could finally remember all of the things about her childhood. Where she could accept its complexity. The good and the bad.

Yes. All those years had been important. But they had brought her here. To his bedroom, to his bed.

She had told herself that her dream was to leave. To get far away from here. She was glad that she hadn't done that yet. Because there had been healing to do that could only have happened in this place.

She had felt like Four Corners might be magic when Denver had brought her here for the first time.

Maybe that was the poetry in all of this.

Her father had allowed his life to be torn apart by Elias King.

And Denver King was the piece that built her life into the strongest it had ever been.

She was tired. But she knew she wasn't going to sleep for the rest of the night.

When Denver woke up, there was a mug of coffee sitting on the nightstand.

He sat up, and realized he was alone in bed. "Sheena?"

He looked around the room, then heard footsteps coming down the hall. She appeared in the doorway, holding her own mug. "Good morning."

"Morning."

"It's about time you woke up," she said.

"Were you waiting for me?"

She smiled. A strange smile that he couldn't read. "Yes. I think I was."

"Last night was amazing," he said.

"We didn't even have sex," she said.

He frowned. "I know. That's not what I meant."

"Yeah. I know. I was actually thinking about how amazing it was that even without sex it was . . ."

"Are you okay?"

"I need to tell you something," she said.

"Yeah, sure."

"I realized something last night. I realized a lot of things last night. But the most important one is that I know what this is."

"What's that?" he asked before he could think about whether or not he really wanted to know. He asked before he really sat there and looked at her eyes. Before he had a chance to be afraid of what she might say next.

"This is one of those forever kind of things. It was from the beginning. We didn't want to put a name on it, didn't want to put a label on it because we both knew that. We both knew that we were dealing with something a whole lot bigger than we had ever dealt with before, and I know that's why I completely freaked out. Because it was never just sex, was it?"

"No," he said. His chest felt sore. She was right, though. It had never been just sex. It was impossible to believe that. A lot of women had come and gone from his life, fleeting, and not remembered. There had always been more to their connection.

"I love you," she said.

The first words that came to his mind, to his lips, that he held back and refused to speak were *I will fail you.*

He knew that. Felt it out of the depths of his soul. But he couldn't say anything. Not right then. Not in that moment. Because he was just staring at her. This beautiful, strong woman who had come into his world and changed it in so many ways, culminating in last night when . . .

It was like everybody thought he should just be done now. Like he was accomplished. Like he had finished everything. Like he should just tell Sheena that he loved her too, and they could get married, and they could play house. They could have a couple of kids, and . . .

And he would rest. And what would happen then?

Would he want to get away from it all sometimes? Would he drink a little bit too much? Would he twist himself all up in knots and convince himself that he deserved a break?

Would he be that version of himself that wanted to indulge every selfish whim?

Because that was the only thing he could imagine across the finish line.

"Sheena . . . I told you already. I can't."

"Yes. And I told you that I couldn't. I really believed it. Denver, I thought that love was weak. I thought it made you weak. I thought it was something that weak people used to try and erase all of the terrible things that they did. Like my dad could say that he loved me, and it would erase the fact that he went on a two-day bender and left us by ourselves. Like it would erase the fact that he failed to listen to me, to protect me. That is not what it is. Love is that heaviness. It's that thing that you and I took on when we were far too young. That thing that drove us to raise our siblings, even though it was hard. For us, love was never weak. For us, it was our strength. It's why we're here. It's why I took your money and I sent my sisters to college, and I didn't go. It's why I waited and waited to even try to fulfill my own dreams. It's why you have done nothing but work tirelessly to atone for what your father did."

He shook his head. "That's guilt for me. I don't need to speak for you, Sheena, and I don't want to. But I've always known that love was strong. It was strong enough to exploit the weaknesses inside myself, and if I don't stay on top of those weaknesses, then I don't know when they're going to come out again. Because my father took them and he used them. But he could never have done that if I didn't love him. Yeah, I always knew that love was strong. That love and loyalty when twisted could topple an entire community. I lived it."

"So what does that mean? What does that look like for you? What would your life be?"

"If I just stick to my responsibilities. If I never let myself get complacent. If I . . ."

"What are you afraid of?"

"Being him," he said. "Hurting somebody the way that he hurt people."

"It can't be true," she said.

"No. I already told you . . ."

"That's a story you tell yourself, Denver. That you might hurt people because he liked to gamble? The difference between you and your father . . . There are so many differences between you and your father. But let's take the gambling. The drinking. The sex. You did that away from home. You did it in casinos. Where everybody there was on equal footing. And in fact, it was entirely possible that you came from less. Less power, less money. You drank where it was appropriate to drink. You had sex with women who wanted you. Who didn't owe you money or any of the other suspect reasons your father was able to get women into bed with him? The venue, the circumstances, that matters. You can't erase them."

Her words destabilized him. Shifted the ground beneath his feet. And he wasn't even standing. He was still lying in bed, that cup of coffee getting colder and colder on the nightstand.

"You look at life as what you want to," he said. "But I have to look at it the way that it makes sense to me. For me. And this . . . this is not what I want."

"You don't want this?"

There was a look in her eye that was deadly.

"No," he said. "I just wanted a casual . . ."

"You're a liar," she said, and then she dropped her cup of coffee directly onto the ground, spilling it, cracking the mug. "You talked me into this. You told me to see where it goes. You told me that it would be worth it. And now . . . now you're sitting there calling me a coward with your whole chest?"

He sat up. "Sheena . . ."

"I told you that I loved you," she said. He got out of bed, and moved to stand near her. But her eyes were a blaze of fury. "How dare you? How dare you ask me to be brave. At every turn, you asked me to be brave, but you can't do it. You were in control of all of this. You were happy to have me with you, in your life, in your bed, until I challenged all those lies you tell yourself."

He sighed then. What he had done to her. This was the pain he had never wanted to cause, and he had done it.

And what future would she have if she stayed with him? What could he offer? There was nothing. Nothing better that he could do. Nothing better than he could be.

He had to hurt her now. He had to. To save her from more pain later, and she would be glad of it. Because she would leave here; she would leave him. Things would be better for her. They could only be better.

"This isn't what you want," he said. "You said yourself. Maybe you'll go to a city, maybe you'll go to Europe. But not here, Sheena. You were never supposed to stay here."

"You don't get to tell me what I want," she said. "You . . . I always thought that you stayed away from me because you were afraid that you would scare me. I think I scared you. You kept your distance because you don't know how to do anything else. It's the closeness that scares you. You want to write checks, and you want to do things, because otherwise you're going to have to stop, and you're going to have to actually get to know the people in your life and let them know you. You didn't go away to Las Vegas because you wanted oblivion, you went there because you wanted anonymity. You compartmentalize all these pieces of yourself so that nobody ever knows you. But what I don't understand is why. You don't want people to think that you're good. You don't ever want this work to be finished. You act like a man running scared, Denver King. You seem like this big, tough guy with this bulletproof exterior for all the world to see, but it isn't true. Go to your town hall meetings that you have every month, and you don't even know the people there."

He felt like he was being run straight through with the sword. For all that she had just said that he was bulletproof, he felt like he didn't have any defenses against her words.

Because they were true. Each and every one of them. By design, he kept everybody at a distance. By design, he had constructed a life where he didn't even know his own self all that well.

What are you afraid of?

Those blazing green eyes called him a coward.

And he had never seen himself as a coward. A lot of things, but not that. She didn't know anything. Not really. And he felt himself starting to get angry. Because he couldn't look back and see a father who loved him. He could only look back and see himself being exploited. He couldn't look back and find redemptive qualities in his childhood.

So good for her, good for her for finding a bright spot, and a way to categorize love that didn't make it awful. He didn't have that.

"I do what I have to do," he said. "You only know this version of me, so don't act like you can see for certain what I would be if I wasn't this. Don't act like you know things. Deep truths about me that not even I know. You know what I've shown you."

"Devastated to report," she said. "Everything you do suggests that you're a good man."

"Sheena . . ."

"If it isn't your actions, then what is it? What is it that makes you good? What is it that makes you bad?"

"Everybody can fail. Everyone can be corrected. You have to guard against it. You have to make the choice. Every day. And every damned day, I wake up, and I know that my job here on this ranch isn't done."

"That's what you're really afraid of, isn't it? That someday the work will be done. And then who will you be? If you're not everybody's savior, then what are you?"

"The work will never be done, so it doesn't matter. Things don't need to be like this between us. It doesn't need to be . . ."

"Yes, it does," she said. "Because you . . . you make me hope. You made me want something more than I ever thought I could have. You made me believe that there was something better out there, and now you're just taking it away? I want you to sit with that. I don't want you to be able to lie to yourself. I don't want you to be able to say that the life you're leading now prevents you from creating victims, because that's what you did. Except I'm not going to sit down to be victimized. Every choice you make has a consequence, Denver. Keeping yourself at a distance doesn't prevent people from being hurt by you."

"Listen." He reached out to grab her arm, and she jerked away from him.

"Don't touch me. Not ever again. You know what, I'm glad that I realized what I did. I made myself vulnerable to you, but it wasn't a weakness. It was a strength. You're exactly what happens when somebody allows fear to control their life. That's what you're doing. You're living in fear. I'm not. I am stronger than that. And you can go to hell."

She turned around and slammed the door behind her, and he heard heavy footsteps on the stairs.

Go to hell.

Denver King had always known that it was a lofty goal for a man like him to avoid hellfire altogether.

But he had never imagined that for him, true hell could be found right there on earth.

Sheena felt like her heart was breaking apart. Each and every breath saw shards falling away, embedding themselves in the walls of her chest. She had thought that she'd been through enough. Really. She had.

Worst of all, she had gotten to a place where she trusted that Denver wouldn't hurt her.

After being so wary. After being so cautious. She had . . .

She stormed out the front door of his house, tears blinding her vision. She reached into her purse and grabbed her keys. And without thinking she put the keys between her fingers and punched at his truck, leaving behind a satisfying dent, and then she walked along the length of it, dragging the keys around the side. If she was a Carrie Underwood song, so be it. That had always suited her better than one of those devastated love songs where the protagonist was lying on the ground. If she had a knife on her, she would've slashed the tires.

Instead she took her necklace off, and dropped it into the dirt, next to the truck.

The white lines on his paint job didn't do anything to make her feel better. Didn't do anything to make her feel like she wasn't dying. And no amount of infusing all of this pain with rage would make the hurting stop.

This wasn't fair. She had never thought that she was going to be the girl with a happy ending, until the last few weeks. Then she had started to believe it. She had started to believe that she deserved it. She had started to believe . . .

She hated this. She might even hate him as much as she loved him.

She didn't know how to cope with this. Because she had never . . .

She walked, tears blinding her eyes as she tried to make it to her car.

She heard tires on the road, and tried to wipe her tears away.

The truck stopped. It was Bix.

She wiped her running nose.

"Oh dear," said Bix.

"I'm fine," she said. "I'm just headed to my car."

"It's never a good day when a woman who is involved with one of the King men is weeping walking down the road early in the morning."

"You make it sound like that's a common occurrence."

"Well, it's not entirely outside my experience."

"I just keyed his truck," she said.

Bix's eyebrows lifted. "Nice. I threw a rock at Daughtry."

Sheena frowned. "You . . . threw a rock at him?"

"Right in between the shoulder blades. He deserved it."

She thought of Denver. Of that tortured look on his face. Well, he was the one torturing them. He didn't have the right to look all upset.

"I'm sure that he did," she said.

"Let me give you a ride," Bix said.

"I probably need to let off a little steam," said Sheena.

"Come on," said Bix. "Get in the truck."

She relented, because she figured the woman who had thrown a rock at one of the King brothers was probably the best audience for the story.

Except, she found she didn't really have the words to tell it.

And it was difficult to even think about it, since it meant being vulnerable, and admitting that she had told the man she was in love with him, only to be told her face that he . . .

But wasn't that what part of this was about? She had actually changed. These last few weeks had changed her, and just because in the end he hadn't been able to make as big of a change as she had, didn't mean she had to discard all the good things.

"I told him that I loved him. And he told me he didn't love me."

"I'm surprised you didn't key his nuts," said Bix. "I would've been tempted to."

"Well. If I had wanted to stand anywhere near him, I might have."

"Wow. I mean, I wish I could say I was surprised. But that's sort of par for the course with the King men."

"But Daughtry married you."

"Yes. He did. But not before breaking my heart. Why do you think I threw a rock at him?"

Bix was pretty bloodthirsty, but Sheena had a feeling that she was also just, and if she threw a rock at somebody, they would have to absolutely deserve it. So it didn't come as any surprise to her that the infraction had been something as serious as breaking her heart.

"I'm just . . . It upsets me, because I never thought that I was worthy of this kind of thing. I never imagined that I was going to fall in love. And I kept telling myself that he and I wouldn't work. Because I looked at you and Daughtry, and you're the opposite of each other."

"No, we aren't," said Bix.

"Yes, you are. He's so straitlaced, and all about the law, and you are . . . You're you."

"And underneath all that, we were two really lonely people who never had anybody to love us like we deserved. I took care of myself, for years. Daughtry pushed away all connection, he just told himself that he had to atone. But underneath all that, we were just so hurt and broken. The only two people who could actually heal each other."

"Oh," she said.

Because that sounded so much like her and Denver. Except Denver didn't want to be healed.

"I'm not an expert on very many things," said Bix. "Unless you want to go fishing. I'm pretty good at that. But what I do know is that wounded animals get mean, and then they run scared. But eventually, if the wound is killing you, you have to get help. I think that his wound is killing him. He pushed you away, which was really dumb of him. Because I've never seen him so happy, and I know I haven't been around all that long, but Daughtry said the same. I think that's what scares him, though. It isn't like we can't relate to that."

She could. It was just that he had convinced her that maybe being happy wasn't something to be scared of.

"Bix, what if he doesn't come around?"

They pulled up to her car then. "Well. If he doesn't come around, the good news is, you had some breakthroughs. So you'll go on, and you'll be fine. Bad news for him, though, because he's going to end up pickled. The last single man on Four Corners Ranch. The savior of everybody else but not himself."

Sheena looked down at her hands. "I would've saved him."

"I know," said Bix. "But he has to want to be saved."

"Right. Well. Thanks, Bix. But I better go home."

"I like you, Sheena," said Bix. "So I hope that you will come back to the ranch. And keep being my friend."

"I will," she said.

She got into her car and started the engine. She didn't even think to turn the heater on as she started to drive toward home. She just shivered.

She had left so many things at Denver's. She had no idea how she was going to come back here. She didn't have any practice with facing down someone who had broken her heart. It was entirely outside her wheelhouse. Because she'd never had her heart broken before.

But Bix was right. Her relationship with Denver had healed some things inside of her. She had that. She was determined that he wasn't going to take away something like that. Not her. She wanted more. She wanted to be better after all of this, not the same.

She certainly wasn't going to walk away from the bar because of him. Or from friends like Bix.

She pulled up to her house, and saw that there were lights on already. She sighed. Well. She was going to have to tell Whitney and Sarah. She didn't want to rain on Abigail's parade. But she and Alejandro were probably still asleep at their vacation rental.

She trudged up the walk, and unlocked the door.

"Hey . . ." Sarah trailed off mid-greeting. "You don't look good."

"I'm not good," said Sheena. "I broke up with Denver." She wrinkled her nose. "Or, he broke up with me. It's hard to say, and I don't have any experience with the sort of thing."

Sarah and Whitney were instantly on the attack.

"I'll gut him," said Sarah.

"I'll put his head on a pike," said Whitney.

"I appreciate it. But I'm . . . Part of me was very healed by this relationship. Though, it was *not* healed me that keyed his truck on my way out. That was trailer park me."

"Well done, trailer park you," said Sarah.

"Well, I'm going to keep aspects of her around. She's useful. She's tough. She knows how to survive." She teared up. "And I know I'm going to need to figure out how to survive this."

Whitney looked devastated. "I've never seen you this sad."

"I've never been this kind of sad before," said Sheena.

She was a survivor. She knew that she would survive this.

The trouble was, for the past few weeks she had seen what it was like to do more than survive. And now that she'd had more, she wanted more.

So the trouble was going to be figuring out what that looked like without Denver in her life.

Right now, she wasn't even sure she wanted to know what that looked like.

Chapter Twenty-Two

"DENVER!"

The pounding on the door mimicked the pounding in his head. He had gotten extremely drunk after Sheena had left, and had fallen asleep on the couch. Now he felt . . . none of the blessed numbness that he felt right after consuming the alcohol. He just felt pain. Everywhere.

"Just a minute," he grumbled, getting up from the couch and opening the door.

To see all of his brothers standing there, looking like the Sons of Thunder.

"What are you doing here?" he asked.

"We heard your dumb ass needed an intervention," said Justice.

"What are you talking about?"

"Have you seen your truck?" Landry asked.

"My truck?"

He stumbled out the front door and went down the steps, and saw a dent at the end of the bed, and then two very obvious key marks trailing down the side of the whole body. "Son of a bitch," he said.

"Yeah, it was a son of a bitch," Landry said. "You. You caused that."

"Sheena keyed my truck?"

"That's the word on the street. By which I mean, that's what Bix told me," said Daughtry.

"What does Bix have to do with this?"

"Bix saw Sheena walking down the driveway this morning crying. And picked her up. We've been waiting for you to come back to the land of the living so that we could tear you a new one."

He snarled, "You have no idea what you're talking about. Relationships end, okay? And ours wasn't even really a relationship. It was . . . it was just a thing. It ran its course. Okay? I'm sorry that she thought it meant more than it actually did." He nearly choked on those words, and he knew they could all see it.

"Wow," said Justice. "I feel like I should step away from you, because you're in danger of being hit by a lightning bolt for telling that kind of lie."

"What are you talking about?"

"You're in love with her, dumbass," said Landry. "And believe me, I am so familiar with all the ways in which you can mess things up even when you're in love with a woman, but you have got to pull yourself together. At least I was sixteen. You're in your thirties."

"It's embarrassing," said Justice.

"Excuse me," he said. "I seem to recall that all you married men did not exactly have an easy path to this."

"No. And in some instances we only made it through because our big brother showed up and told us to pull our heads out of our asses. So that's what we're here to do for you."

It really was like an intervention. He hated it.

"I'm the one that takes care of all of you."

"Yes," said Daughtry. "It's true. You're the one that takes care of all of us, and I think that because we didn't do something to change that sooner we did a big disservice to you."

"What the hell does that mean?"

"It let you keep all your boundaries. And it's not helping you," Justice said.

"We are a family. You don't have to do everything for us, and you don't have to carry everything. It was so clear to everybody that you were basically dying inside last night while you were being praised."

"I . . ."

"Denver, we all love you. We all love you so much. And you don't have to keep doing things to prove that you're worthy of that."

It was the plainest, simplest way to look at his life, he supposed. To see the way he kept on doing things, to see how he was always trying to move to the next thing, and then the next. To keep adding all this work to his tally that showed he was worthy.

And it was . . . He was afraid that it was damned true.

Was he that simple? Was that what he was doing? Was he so self-loathing that he thought he had to give people money and build event spaces and atone forever because if he didn't he wouldn't matter, and they wouldn't care about him?

There was still that fear, that baseline fear that he had clung to, which was that he was protecting everyone else. But Sheena was right. That was thin.

He had gotten close to that realization last night when they had played poker. Alcohol. Sex. Gambling. Him. All those things had gone to Vegas, and he had been ashamed of it then. But with her, there was no shame. He was the same man, but living a different way, and it didn't feel wrong.

It made him think what she had said was right. That what mattered was what you were doing, but more than that, what mattered was why you did the things, where you did the things and who you did them with.

So that poked holes in his theory that he was a ticking time bomb. And it only left that one baseline truth.

That Sheena was right about him, and he was a coward. That his real fear was that if he rested, for even a moment, he would stop mattering. Because his father hadn't loved any of them. He had only seen them as tools to be used. And Denver had never figured out his value beyond that. Even when he had discovered that he was being used badly, even when he had learned to despise his father and what he had done, he had never learned how to separate love from serving that person whose love you wanted.

That's what he was doing, on a grand scale. With the town. With his siblings. With Sheena. Maybe she was right. Maybe he had stayed away from her all those years because part of him sensed this.

Because he would rather leave envelopes of money in the mail than ever connect with her, for real. But it was too late. They'd done it.

And he had lied to her when he'd said he didn't want this. He did. He wanted it more than anything in the whole damned world.

"Tomorrow is Christmas Eve," said Landry. "You need to come up with a grand gesture, or you're going to lose her."

"A grand gesture?"

"Yes. You need to do something. A big something, to fix this."

"But I . . . I'm just now figuring out how to fix myself."

"We can see that," said Justice. "But you're really lucky, because you found a woman who seems to like you just like you are."

"But . . . what if she stops?"

He felt weak asking that question. Foolish.

"Life is a real pain in the ass sometimes," said Daughtry. "And you never know when the bad things are going to come. At a certain point, you have to trust in the love of the people around you. There are no guarantees. But that's true whether you're living life alone or with somebody who loves you. You just kinda have to surrender."

Daughtry, the brother who had worked with his father as much as he had, Daughtry, the one who carried as much guilt as Denver did, believed that. And if Daughtry believed it, then he had to be able to find some kind of way to it.

"I don't know how."

"Go tell her that you love her. It will make sense. Because . . . I had to figure out how to be the man that Bix deserved. Because I knew I couldn't live without her."

That was his real fear. That someday he would have to live without her, so he had gone and made the decision for them, in advance.

He was a fool. Though at least he'd been the same kind of fool for more than thirty years, so he supposed there was a little bit of an excuse there.

He looked back at his mangled truck. Well. Sheena clearly didn't have time for his bullshit.

But that was what he . . . that was what he loved about her. She wasn't afraid of him. Not any part of him. And she . . . she had behaved any kind of way to keep him with her. She had been honest.

Because he could trust her.

And how had he repaid that? With cowardice.

Well. He was done with that.

Even though it made him want to run for the hills. And he would never have admitted that, even to his own self until just now.

But maybe being brave enough to love her wasn't about not being afraid to do it. Maybe being brave enough to love her was about feeling scared to death but doing it anyway.

She had said that love was strength. He had always been afraid of it for that reason.

He had always been scared that it was stronger than he was. And right now, he needed that to be true.

Because this was the weakest thing he had ever done.

He wasn't sure he had found the answer in his own soul.

So he needed love to be the answer.

He looked down, and in the dirt right next to the truck, he saw a glimmer of purple. The necklace.

The vinca. That had to be what Sheena had gotten that symbolized her strength. Her refusal to be destroyed by the things that had happened to her in life. He had not made that same commitment to himself. And he had let it destroy parts of him.

He picked up the necklace, and looked at it. Delicate, but strong. Too precious for the likes of him.

But he wanted it all the same. And her.

He needed it to be strong where he was weak.

He needed Sheena.

He didn't have to know anything else.

Except . . .

"I'm going to need you guys to explain to me what counts as a grand gesture."

Chapter Twenty-Three

IT WAS CHRISTMAS EVE, and she'd got a text from the bar manager that she needed to come down because there was a leak in a pipe. And Sheena was mad, because the only reason that the bar manager would've been contacted instead of her was that Denver didn't want to deal with her, and he was being a little bitch.

On Christmas Eve.

Abigail and Alejandro left, and they had been reluctant to do so. But they had plans to spend Christmas Eve with his parents, and they were engaged now, and Sheena was insistent that they not linger just because she was sad. In fact, she sort of wished Sarah and Whitney had somewhere to be too. Just so she didn't have to perform Christmas when she was this upset.

She walked out of her bedroom into the living room. And saw that the house had been transformed.

"What is this?"

There were decorations everywhere, and there was a plate piled high with cinnamon rolls.

"We decided that we were going to be in charge of Christmas," said Sarah.

"Because you've done it for us for so many years."

"So tonight, we're making duck a l'orange."

"Do you know how to make duck?" she asked.

"No," said Sarah cheerfully. "But like I told Michael Danforth sophomore year, I'm sure we'll figure it out."

"I . . . Never mind. I have to go deal with a ranch emergency." She looked around. "I can't believe you did this for me."

"You've done a lot for us Sheena. And I think we got so busy living our lives that we didn't stop to really look at why we have those lives. It's because of you. And everything that you sacrificed. We love you."

That felt so good to her bruised soul. "Well. At least somebody loves me."

She walked over to her sisters and pulled them in for hugs.

"You should break his windshield when you go over there," Whitney said.

"Maybe I will," said Sheena, smiling.

Her smile faded as soon as she got in her car.

She was . . . Well, that moment had given her a window into what her life was. It was pretty damned good, all things considered.

She felt herself tensing up as she got closer and closer to the ranch. Because it was just so hard right now. She associated it, all of it, with Denver. With how much she loved him. With how hurt she was. She really did kind of want to break his windshield.

No. You are healed.

Trailer park Sheena did not agree.

When she got to the stretch of road that went past the event space, she saw Bix, standing there, waving her arms.

She pulled over, afraid there was some kind of emergency. "What's going on?"

"There's something in the event space that you need to see," said Bix.

"What?"

"Just . . . pull over for a second."

She was too confused to argue. So she put the car in Park, and left it running, getting out and walking toward the event space. "After you," said Bix. "I'll just wait out here."

"What?" But she found herself ushered inside, and then the door was closed firmly behind her.

It took her a moment to realize what she was looking at. The whole thing was filled with Christmas trees, all wrapped in white lights. It was like an enchanted forest inside.

She started to walk slowly through the trees, and then she heard footsteps. Coming toward her.

And then, emerging from that forest, was Denver.

He was wearing a black suit, and a black cowboy hat. He looked so gorgeous it made her heart stop.

"Denver," she said. "What is this?"

"It's a grand gesture. At least, that's what I was told."

"Why?" she asked, her voice a whisper.

"Because my brothers told me that when you mess up on the level that I messed up, the gesture has to be grand."

"Please don't . . . Please don't tease me. Please don't . . ."

"I love you. I'll say that first, and then I have a whole lot else to say, but I just want you to know that I love you."

Her heart was beating so hard it made her dizzy. "I keyed your truck," she said.

"You did," he said. "But I deserved it. And I have insurance. It's fine. I . . . I was scared. You're right. I spent my whole childhood doing things that I knew were wrong, somewhere, deep in my soul, because it was the only way to please my father. And a man my age should be over that. But I never got over it. Because I piled so many other stories on top of it. You were right about that. All those stories kept me from figuring out what I was really afraid of, which was just that if I stopped doing things, if I quit making myself useful, there would be no reason for somebody to love me. I kept people at a distance, the people that I work with here, my own family. I made myself into something unknowable so that I could build a buffer around myself, but you got through it. I didn't want to keep you at a distance, and that was the first time I was ever really compelled to put that emotional safety at risk so that I could be with somebody. But you . . ." He shook his head. "My brother told me that this is about trust. We have both been knocked around so badly by this world. I don't trust the world. But I do trust you, Sheena Patrick. I trust you to be the person that I let all the way close. I trust you to be the one who knows me, even when I don't know myself. Because you did that."

Tears were falling down her cheeks again, she hadn't cried this much in . . . Maybe ever. But this was love. It was the softening of her.

She realized right then that was one of the gifts of loving him. She didn't have to be so relentlessly strong. Because he was there to hold some of it. To hold her.

"I don't want to be the last man standing. Not anymore. I want you. I trust you. I hope that someday you'll trust me."

"I do," she said. "I do because I knew even then it wasn't what you really felt. It wasn't what you really wanted."

"No," he said.

He reached into his pocket, and he pulled out a silver box. It looked so much like the one he had given her that night.

"Oh, Denver, I threw the necklace . . ."

"I know."

She took the silver box, and she opened it up. There were two boxes inside. A flat, black velvet box, just like the one the necklace had been in. When she opened it, the necklace was there.

"I found it," he said.

She nodded, a lump in her throat. And then she let herself look at the other box. Small, black velvet just like the other one.

"Denver," she said.

He picked the box up, and he opened it for her. And inside was a ring. The band was like a twining vine, the stone in the center purple.

"You are the most extraordinary woman I've ever known," he said. "More than that, you're the most extraordinary person I've ever known. I never wanted to get married, I never wanted to have kids. I want to marry you. I want to have kids with you. After raising my siblings I never wanted that. Not until you. I could never see a future like that. And now that I love you, it's the only future that I want."

Everything in her broke open. All of the desires, the hopes, the dreams that she had ever held back.

They could have babies. They could be married.

They could have forever.

"I love that you're strong. But with me you won't always have to be."

She threw her arms around his neck. "Yes," she said. "Denver, let's get a dog."

"A dog?"

"Yes. A dog. I loved my dog, and then I lost him and I didn't want to ever lose anything I loved again but that's not me anymore. I want more. I want everything. You and babies and . . ."

"Yes, Sheena, all of that. And a dog."

He pulled away from her and got down on one knee, then he took the ring out and slipped it onto her finger.

It was the most beautiful, lovely, normal thing that had ever happened to her. The kind of thing she had thought she would never be allowed to have.

But here she was. Having it with him.

Because of him.

The first time she thought he was beautiful, her world was falling apart.

But really, and in the strangest way, that moment she'd seen him was the beginning of her world being put back together.

Leading to this moment, and all the days after.

And one thing Sheena knew for sure . . .

She knew what happiness felt like now.

Epilogue

FOUR CORNERS RANCH was founded on an ideal that was never fully realized until Sawyer Garrett, Gus McCloud, Fia King, and Denver and Daughtry King got together to try and repair the legacy that their parents had so badly damaged.

When they set out to fix the ranch, they didn't realize that they would also begin the process of healing the wounds that the past had inflicted on all of them.

Denver King might have been the last man standing, but he more than made up for it with how he loved his wife.

Hell, they all did.

Town hall meetings looked a lot different a decade after Denver and Sheena said *I do*.

For one thing, there were so many children.

Sawyer and Evelyn had three, Wolf and Violet two of their own, Elsie and Hunter with four. Gus and Alaina had a passel of redheaded girls, and one son who looked up to his father like he was the best man on earth. And for sure, he was one of them.

Brody McCloud and his wife, Elizabeth, had raised Elizabeth's son Benny together, along with four other children—all girls. Lachlan and Charity had all boys, which feminine Charity often laughed about. Elsie bought her mugs and T-shirts that said Boy Mom, which she pretended to hate, but used.

Quinn and Levi and Rory and Gideon each had two, a boy and a girl, also redheads. Landry and Fia had two children still at home, with Lila having gone off to school, and moving away to another small town to open up a veterinary clinic.

She had just gotten engaged. To a cowboy.

Landry just about burst with pride whenever he talked about her.

Daughtry and Bix had feral twin girls who took after their mother, and Daughtry often said he wouldn't have it any other way. Rue and Justice had three kids, two boys and a girl, all with their father's mischievous grin. Arizona and Micah had Micah's son, plus one.

And as for Denver and Sheena, who felt like they'd already each raised a family . . .

They'd ended up with five.

Five kids to fill the farmhouse with the kind of joy it had never seen before. Five kids—who did a decent job completely ruining his great-great-grandfather's favorite chair. Which was fine. It needed to go. Hell, everything needed to go, and they had finally modernized it after those kids had spent their early years destroying it.

They had Christmas. Boy, did they have Christmas. Like King's Crest had never seen.

With all of the siblings and cousins and spouses. They had to have their celebrations in the event space. They outgrew that farmhouse.

But it was safe to say that the whole lot of them had outgrown all the pain that had been left behind.

They had made something new.

Together.

They still had the town hall meetings at Sullivan's Point, though they had to keep the doors open, because the crowd of people overflowed out into the yard.

Sheena was trying to get the kids to sit still, and Denver was giving up with the two youngest, scooping them up onto his lap, when Sawyer Garrett walked up to the front of the room.

"Okay," he said. "We got a few things on the agenda today. So we best get down to business."

One thing was certain.

Four Corners would go on.

★ ★ ★ ★ ★